MORE THAN A MONSTER

A GRENDEL PRESS ANTHOLOGY

RACHAEL SWANSON

GRENDEL PRESS

ISBN: 978-1-960534-05-7 (Paperback)

Cover & Typesetting by Susan Russell
Story art by Dany Rivera
Edited by Rachael Swanson
Proofread by Kasey Kubica

Contributors:
"**Woodwose**" by Jennifer Povey
"**The Last Days of Monster Park**" by Bert S.G.
"**Mouths to Feed**" by T.M Morgan
"**The Sacrifices for Our Children**" by Zachary Rosenberg
"**His Little Helpers**" by Alex Wolfgang
"**Ladies First**" by David Rider
"**Quarry**" by Liam Hogan
"**A Sliver in the Vein**" by J. Syringa
"**Starved**" by Rachel Nussbaum
"**SWIPE**" by CM Toolson
"**Shiny Objects**" by Valerie B. Williams
"**Morning Fire**" by Mike Deady
"**De Casibus**" by J. Rocky Colavito
"**Larin**" by Rachel Ashcraft
"**Take My Hand**" by Christie Hansen
"**Vesper's Garden**" by Ville Meriläinen

LARIN

BY RACHEL ASHCRAFT

Draconium Lindus: thought extinct – An unusual example is found in the half-tryth, **Old Tales of the North**, author unknown. The tale in question addresses a peculiar case of a Lindwurm or dragon born of a human queen cursed due to her greed. Even more peculiar, this wurm was the twin of a human boy.

—Excerpt from "Wurms of the World" by Redvin Halknor

Like my mother, I want. I came from the womb snapping. When I slithered between my mother's legs and caught the midwife's questing hands in my teeth, the blood came from the burst skin and into my mouth like the imported cherries my twin eats with his herbivore mandibles. Like a cow, like a pig. How those teeth pop from skulls when my jaws find them. They are the things I spit out like seeds, often rotten. My teeth do not rot. They are for ripping and rending, and they grow with me, elongating with each passing year.

"Show me your teeth!" my twin, Balth, roars, leaning forward, pulling his lips back. I do not open my mouth like him. My teeth sit interlocked, sharp, each one a knife. I could plaster his hair back against his skull like a sea wind whipping. "Really roar!"

I grin.

He touches the sharpest of my incisors. Blood wells on his finger.

"I won't tell," he says. The sound is there, heavy in my chest.

I crack my jaws and his face alights. I draw my breath in until my lungs are as full as sails, and I let it out then. Balth doesn't cover his ears. Birds shoot from the trees. My muscles tense. I am, after all, the creature, the wurm born of a human mother. We are both hunters. We are both cursed. One isn't born with knives in their jaws, and claws to rend, and scales that cut when touched the wrong way, not to kill.

There is a griffin head on my mother's wall. Its beak is propped open as if in the middle of its death scream. Did its body make the fletches of our mother's arrows? Next to it are a great pair of golden wings and then a smaller pair of moss-green ones as if from a cub. A sad prize from some unknown creature.

I can walk myself up the wall. Rest my head against it. See if there is anything left of the great bird's thoughts. Had it thought itself invincible? Had it had a family? Are all such abominations born of a human mistake? Perhaps it had no such thoughts, as empty as all the other creatures I hunted. They wanted warmth, and a full belly, and to live, live, live in their little, tenuous hearts.

Around my mother, I try to remain small. "My cat," she coos. I practice arching my back. But my claws unfortunately do not retract. There are marks on the stairs from when Balth and I used to race, deep indents from my claws sheering away the stone.

"My great-grandmother killed it," she reveals when she sees me peering upwards. I can hear her heartbeat. It is fast, high, and fearful like the rabbits before I close my jaws around them. I peer at her around my snout, watching her hand move first from her side, where she keeps a dagger, and then to her throat. I nose her hand and she rests it on my head. There are pinprick marks on her skin from when she first touched me. A mother's hand meant to caress wispy threads of hair on a newborn's head, to feel the soft skin. She has never told me this, but I know. I recognize the destruction I can cause embossed on her flesh. Her heart does not stop pounding as her fingers move across my skull.

I have overtaken all of them—the wolf, the fox, the stoat, the badger, even the eagle. We wrestled in midair, her great talons raking down my sides, but in the end, her neck yielded to my teeth. Her marks did not last longer than a fortnight before my flesh healed. Balth is not the same. There is a puncture mark on his left ankle from where one of the barn mongrels grabbed him. He's had it since he was a toddler. If there are others like me, I have never met them. Mother is evasive when I ask her. "You're as human as Balth, as me," she'd said. "You do not need to share a form to be so."

The one scar I do bear, Balth found when we were climbing a tree, my head tilted up toward the sky. He had laid a hand against my throat and all my scales had risen.

"You're missing scales here," he said. I had reached for it with my clawed paw. I caressed the spot, so unlike my natural armor. It felt like Balth's skin. "Maybe it's a birthmark," he'd said, reaching a hand up to catch the first branch. I'd heard twins often had spots in the same place, but when I peered at his neck, as his shirt collar rose and slumped like a ship tossing on waves, he was free of it.

As Balth grows, so do I. He shoots up foot after foot until he towers over our mother. He lies down in the autumn leaves, and I stretch out next to him. At my longest, my length still surpasses his, and I rest my head against the earth. Here I can smell and feel the living beat of everything under the soil. Balth's heartbeat is almost as slow as my own. He may be part wurm, I think. If I am part human, what is stopping him from being something else as well?

"Was our father a wurm?" I touch my neck, where the mark is. Balth does not have any aberrant scales.

I often pick at the spot under my chin. Mother carries a dagger the same length and breadth as the mark. Had she thought to slit my throat when I slithered out? "You almost killed the nursemaid. Not the bite, mere pinpricks," she'd said dismissively, "but the shock. Can you just imagine, giving birth to something like you?" This she tries to say with awe, adoration, but her heart in my presence thrums, and frets, and tells her to run, run, like all my prey. I take a scale between my claws and twist and pull until it comes free with a tearing pain. Blood oozes from the spot, like a chicken plucked. A new scale grows in its place.

Balth brings a princess back after one of his hunting excursions. She is evasive. Her realm is the shadows of the corridors. He tells me her name is Laknya. It means "prudent one."

We are both skilled hunters, but my kills are messier. The tanner manages to be creative with the skins. A puncture mark can be a button for a leather lace. Once he touched my back and I saw him determine what a great breastplate I would make, my natural scales, a suitable armor. I had arched myself, drawn back, and seeming to realize what he had done, he turned back to the pelt that he was curing. One bite and I could end his life. If he ever came at me with his flensing knives, I wouldn't hesitate. I am, after all, a prince. Regicide is a crime punishable by a most painful death, and I would be glad to strike the blow.

I sense Laknya in the shadows of Balth's chamber when I tell him, "I think the tanner thinks to make me into his next pelt."

The tanner cannot be found the next morning. Balth smells like blood, and I know what he's done. He pats my head. Does he see me like a cat too?

On one of my hunts, I find one of my kind. The creature in question is old and dying. I didn't know if we could die. There are pools of blood that I see myself in. It is the same color as mine, red and tinged with gold. Great splinters of tree trunks are strewn about as if this creature had fallen from the sky, thrashing and fighting. I wish for this wurm to be my father, my counselor, anything but what he is now.

"Hallo," I say and move close. The breath from his nostrils smells like salt. "Where are you from," I ask and get close enough to see his great incisors. He could eat me in one gulp. He does not respond but turns his head ponderously in my direction, a mountain moving. He opens his mouth, I think to speak, but only more blood oozes from his throat. His heart is a drum, beating heavily, and my own syncs with it. I want to sleep, go beneath the ground, dirt-settle. I know that he has nothing to tell me. I curl up next to him. *You are not alone,* I think, and I try to mean it for him.

He must have walked with the dead things inscribed in the books Balth and I like to turn through in the library. Illuminated in gold and red—often the red of a spear sticking from their sides—their entrails pouring in pink loops from a wound and their eyes rolled in the back of their heads.

From an early age, I realized what my role was meant to be. I was meant to die like this old one. The hill no longer rumbles with his breath. He is extinguished with not a word for himself. I lie there next to him a while longer, until the vultures begin to circle, until the scavengers come out of their holes, and then I hunt. Their blood is hot, it coats my teeth and rolls in waves down my throat. There is nothing left for the tanner, and there is nothing left of him. But a new one has taken his place. Filled the gap. Humans, I think, are interchangeable. I walk next to the corpse and try to ascertain how he died. There are no outward punctures, nothing breaking his skin. No, the damage has been done within.

The corridors of the castle suddenly seem small and empty. I stalk down to the archers and their museum of corpses. I wind through the armory, past the yard where I hear knights training and sparring. Would my scales deflect their swords? A glancing blow surely, but one meant to go deep, I am not sure.

I find the wurms in the corner, in the dust and shadows, as if pushed there to hide them. They look like they are smiling. Their lips are pulled back and fastened away from their teeth. I coil my back to match their sutured and posed spines. I pull my lips back to expose my fangs. Their eyes are dusty and opaque. They are my size. Half-grown children. Scales have broken away and lie in dust around their paws. I coil under one, press myself against it. It is only skin and sawdust.

That night I eat the armorer. I unlock his door with a claw and slip in. When he sees me in the shadows, he grabs his sword. I am on him before he has the chance to completely unsheathe it, sleep caught in the corners of his eyes as I sink my teeth deeply into his throat. I eat all of him. I think of the wurm in the forest, how he would have been gone in one bite. He takes me more, but in the end, the result is the same.

The next morning, my scales glisten as they never have before. "You look longer... than normal," Balth says. "Stretch out!" He raises his hands as high above him as he can. He is easily seven feet with his arms above his head. When I stand on my hind legs and use his bulk to support my front legs and stretch my neck as far as it can, I shoot past his arms. "You have grown!" He marvels. "So much for being twins," he says with a laugh.

There are whispers of a haunt, a spirit ripping people from their beds. Leaving only blood and their shredded clothes. The armorer has always been peripatetic. His shoes, after all, are gone.

"Went off into the woods, I think."

"That one—always covered in blood."

I listen in the shadows of the yard, curled by the door.

"He'll be back with the head of some great beast. Remember that time he wore it!"

I remember it, the blood coursing down his chest, the head of the bear encasing his own as he lumbered drunkenly around the yard, chasing the apprentices and knights-in-training as they laughed and rained fake blows upon him. The bear in question had been mounted above his bed. Its glass eyes had watched as I ripped out his throat.

The kennel master is harder. He is fast like his hounds and turns and sees me. His recognition, I'm sorry to say, makes me stop. He holds only a cruel whip and flashes it at me. It lands on my snout, tearing my flesh. Blood patters around my feet. The dogs howl as I wrestle him to the ground, bite the hand with the whip until it tears away under my teeth. The rest is simple. Beasts of all kinds die so easily. There is but a beating heart and a thin layer of flesh between life and nothingness.

With each human, I grow another foot.

I quip to the cook that I am not what I eat, but it doesn't even get a chuckle. I eat her next. She is gamey and tough to digest, but I make do.

Balth trains daily and his skin that had once been unmarred is flecked with wounds that scab and scar. Scales do not bloom from him as I had at one time hoped. For a little while, I do not eat from the castle. I let their suspicions dry up.

Balth's betrothed weaves flowers through her hair and spends time at the edge of the forest, with vellum and a paintbrush. I think Laknya must want to see the sea, try to peer across to the place they've whisked her away from, but if she does think of home, I have never seen her betray herself.

How much pressure will it take to snap her bones? I follow her with the intention of finding out. I watch as she unpacks her artist tools. How did she go undetected and slip free of the castle-guard? I can scent that no one has followed her and yet a would-be princess would surely not be allowed without an escort. Drool runs from my jaws.

My mother was careful and my brother more so with his potential pursuits. No, this indicated that she had slipped out free of their notice. Perhaps, she is more interesting than I had first assumed. She unpacks the container with a practiced motion. First setting up the easel, unfolding the legs, the mechanisms twisting as the wood slats click into place. And then she unfolds a set of tri-legs and sets a flat table on top. She runs a finger over her brushes. She takes a brass cup with her to the stream but stops and gazes upward. Her form absolutely still and her heart beats with the forest so that I can no longer distinguish it.

She refocuses on her canvas, shifting from foot to foot. My mouth waters.

"Larin," she speaks. I startle from my crouched pose. My padfall is a stutter much like those two syllables. "Larin," she says again, and this time she looks directly to where I crouch in the dirt. I put my snout out through the branches. She turns her canvas, so she looks at me and I face the slats. "Stay there. I like your snout coming through the foliage. The color of your scales are just the right hue against the leaves. Don't grin," she says. "I want onlookers to not quite know what they're seeing. The eye will make patterns. It will conjure beasts when there are none. And yet here you are. A man in the guise of a wurm."

She uses the length of her brush to measure my form and then she moves back to her canvas and begins to work. She paints with the constraints of the sun. I slip free of my disguise as she works; an unwieldy creature revealed to be incongruous with its surroundings. She beckons me from the bushes. My head towers over her and I stoop to peer at the painting. I find my own eye hidden among the vast swath of green, rendered so lifelike that I feel myself fall once more among the branches. She has imbued gold in the hues.

"You remind me of home."

"Are there many wurms where you come from?"

"There were. You are strange, Larin." The word is accented on her lips and yet is me. I like the syllable elongated this way. It is like being rewritten. "They have all but destroyed your kind. I find them stuffed throughout the castle. Not just wurms, but other creatures, great creatures of lore, of stories, of art, stripped of themselves to become pale replicas rendered by an undivine hand."

I look to her own hand and wonder if she hears my question. She smiles thinly. "I haven't really rendered you. Only the hint of what you are."

My eye peers through the foliage and the closer I look, I see the reflection of the artist caught in my painted eye, change, and shift, and shimmer. It's only the light, I think, catching the gold flecks in the paint, but her form changes from human to wurm and back. The lowering sun catches the scales under her hairline, and they glow gold. When I look again, they are gone. If such a thing can blossom from human skin, what stops me from shedding mine?

I know not whether she is a human or a wurm or something in between, and I can say the same for myself. I have always desired, I think, to be something I'm not. I am so tired, sometimes. And then I think of the rotting corpse of the old one, who fell from the sky. Perhaps, and I'm sure of it, when he was flying, he must have closed his eyes and let his wings rest on the warm trade winds that the ships so love, and he must have forgotten exactly what he was.

For a while, we spend our days like this. Mornings are with Balth and the family around the large, oaken table that has been there through generations of kings and queens. I try to imagine that there are wurms lurking just under their skin, that I cannot be the only aberration. I peer closely at each of them.

My mother raises a wooden spoon to crack the shell of her egg, each turn of her wrist timed like ringing a small bell. Her scales, I think, are green like the dresses she is fond of. They catch the light and glow, and when she is angry, they stand back from her skin like my own.

Balth is a hulking beast with gray and gold scales and his mouth opens to expose fangs twice the size of mine as he tears into his chicken leg, and the grease that drips now around his front teeth is caught easily in the wide expanse of his mouth.

The cook is a flitting thing, a wurm speeding about the room, bringing an armful of platters and cups and cooked, roasted, greasy dishes to satisfy our never-ending wurm hunger. If there is one thing that separates me and Balth it is our motivation to hunt. My jaws clamor for it. My stomach is a gaping hole and to Balth the hunt is a pastime, a way to lessen his boredom. He seeks other places, gone for months, coming back with wagons laden down with pelts from far away—more creatures to adorn our hallways.

I find Laknya's human skin in a pile in her sleeping chambers, a mass of flesh, folded in on itself. She must stretch it around herself like a tunic. Is it so easy to slip free? I hear the muted screams of the men in the armory as she slips from the darkness and into the barrack, taking a man each night, ripping him apart, devouring him, bones and armor and weapons and all. I think she means to wipe out each of them.

Balth and his men find us on the shore. I am curled among the driftwood and stones. She has her paintbrush in hand and has asked me to act natural. I don't spend much time by the shore, but the heat of the stones feels good against my scales and I have curled in on myself, letting my eyes close, letting the sea spray wash over me until I feel myself start to drift. They descend from their ship. They are not wearing their normal chain mail, but an armor that is translucent, catching the sun like fish scales in crystal clear water. I notice the different colors of each of their armor; one green, one blue, yellow with hints of black, a dark almost red-purple, and then as I stretch, the first cry.

"Can never escape these bloody beasts." And one of Balth's men with fresh wounds across his face, raises a spear and hurls it at me. Balth yells for him to stop, lunges for him, but the spear has already left his hand. I dodge but another one thrown from the back burrows into my left shoulder and deep into the stones. There is a feral sound like a wounded beast, and I realize that it is me, like a small, writhing thing caught against an arrow and a tree. There is the sound of swords hitting wood, and Balth's voice above it all.

"You fools, that is my brother. Your prince."

"He looks just like 'em"

"He is not them. He is made of the same blood as me. We are twins. A wound to him is the same as you raising a sword to me. Larin." He calls my name. I have sunk back against the stones that had at first obscured us. I writhe and twist like a worm on a fishhook and blood spills from around the wound. I have felt nothing like it before and then she is bending before me, and for the first time, I see it, just a moment, as her human face elongates, and unhuman jaws sprout from where her small lips used to be. She splinters the spear so that it no longer pins me to the ground.

"Stay still," she whispers, and she is human again. There is a knife in her hand.

Balth approaches us and kneels. "My brother. My man has acted with his own will to ignorantly wound you, blood of my own. He will pay with his life, by my hand. Can you stand?" he asks and bends to inspect the wound. Her mouth is covered in my blood, and she quickly wipes it against her black dress.

"He is a beast deserving of slaughter. You don't see what he is!" the man behind us screams. "At night he comes into the barracks and eats the men. He is cursed and deserving of our spears."

The man chokes as my brother wraps a hand around his throat. He drops to his knees and Balth motions for his sword. There is reticence I see through the burning throb of the spear still embedded in my hide. A sharp-enough point can easily pass through me.

"They are covered in wurms," she whispers against my ear and presses around the wound. "They slaughter us for sport." I see that the hides I had first thought painted in regalia are made of scales.

The sword passes cleanly through the man's neck and his head falls on the stones. Balth stands over him, his chest heaving, his eyes cast in my direction, but I do not think he sees me. I see the pain that lingers there. I see that he believes his men.

The blood blends perfectly with the black velvet of Laknya's dress. It is a practiced motion—something she has done her whole life. She steps forth, her eyes still on their hides. She knows them, I realize. Her skin begins to ripple and change. I reach out with my good arm and snag the velvet of her dress against my claw. I think she will lash out at me instead. For a moment she is in between forms, and then she reverts.

Balth drops his sword and turns to the men. "Who else doubts my brother!" he yells above the waves. There is an uneasy silence. "This is a time to celebrate! Keep unloading." My eyes settle on the blood-stained rocks and the blood still seeping from the headless corpse near my brother's leather shoes.

Balth turns then and approaches us. His hand hovers above my wound, and I wonder if he sees me as one of the speared wurms they hunted. Had he struck the killing blows, a quick sword to the neck? But his hands are tender against my shoulder. "Lucky it wasn't a poison-tipped one, Larin, or you might really be in trouble."

I try to move my claws, but the arm is numb.

"You'll be fine," he says, loops my good leg around his shoulder and lifts. I leave the ground easily under his strength. For the first time, I wonder what it might be like to rip into his throat.

I am dosed and then I am empty. I float, and the spike slides from my shoulder like a sharp knife through meat.

"Do you remember when we used to roar together?" Balth reclines on two chairs he's pushed together next to me. I turn and try to stretch my neck, but my shoulder is immobilized. "Best not to move too much, Larin," he says. "My man rarely misses his mark." He fakes levity. There is still blood splatter on his tunic. I do not think he has ever beheaded someone before, but what he does on his expeditions has always been a mystery to me. I find that I cannot remember him carrying me.

"I remember," I say and shift. He has draped me across his own bed—the cover a great bear's pelt, worn at the edges as if he rubs them in his sleep. Even men like Balth must find comfort somewhere. His marriage to Lakyna is less than a week away. I suspect that he will present her with one of his pelts.

"I haven't heard you roar in a decade; can you still do it? I shouldn't make you. Might jostle your shoulder."

I'm lightheaded and Balth is silhouetted strangely in the light of the setting sun. Glowing, I think. Like he has scales.

"Can you still roar?" I ask. I remember how he would do it until he lost his voice, trying to match the animalistic sound I could create in the back of my throat. I suspect no true human can make such a sound. It's a mark of truly wild things.

"Perhaps we were all wurms in the womb and most of us are fated to be men." He says it low under his breath and he rubs his forehead as if it pains him.

He is shrunken here before me. Small and withered like a skin without the meat. Each breath makes the room shimmer and shift like the great old one breathing its final dying breaths. Saliva coats my teeth, my tongue.

"You're civilized! You're a man!" he says and he wobbles slightly when he jumps to his feet. "You no longer roar, do you, Larin?" There is an empty tankard at his feet, and he kicks it. It rolls under his bed and clanks against others. "Do you know the men howl like wild things when they hunt? They throw their heads back in poor imitation, but it awakens something in them—whatever's underneath this veil of human flesh." He leans in close, and he pulls back his lips to show me his incisors.

They are little nubs. If he filed them, maybe, he could rend his meat the way he wants. I do not say this to him. He is drunk and he leans his head against my side and wraps the bear pelt around himself. I move to allow him to do so and soon he is asleep, curled against my side like a child.

Three more of Balth's men are eaten that night.

I awake to the men at the door. They move quickly, reaching with arms and swords toward us. They rip the still sleeping Balth from the bed and point their spears at me. I shift and wriggle and fall onto the elaborate rug under the bed. I see her in the corner as Balth struggles and fights and demands that they unhand him. This is how they hunt—in a pack. Their scaly armor catching the light of the fire casts, for a moment, the silhouettes of the fallen wurms on the walls. The shadows slip and move, enchanted, like they're living things. I fling one of the men's swords toward Balth. He is bleeding, his fist around the throat of one of his men. His cry is one long scream, and it comes from his chest. I can't call it a roar, but he doesn't sound human. He would like that, I think. I lunge toward them but falter, the bones in my front leg rebelling and depositing me chest first upon the stones.

She's in the corner of my eye and I think they don't see her. They never have. She is invisible in all her forms. All along she has wanted to incite this. I tear at the leg of the man who lunges toward me. His knee splinters under my teeth and he falls screaming to the ground. Their swords beat at my back and I whip and flash and pull them toward me.

The wurms rise around me, their scales burning bright in the light of the fire. Their jaws snapping in the negative space made by the bodies of men converging and falling and tangling themselves around Balth and me. Balth is a master swordsman and even in his drunken state, he hacks and pushes them back—one man against a horde, and I can smell the fear and the adrenaline that I think maybe only animals like me can smell.

How had Laknya appeared to Balth? She is no longer in the corner, but she is there among the armor slipping between the men, ripping out throats, digging claws into soft parts so that they stagger and fall.

I have never seen one like her. Not in the paintings, nor the dead ones in the undercroft. She burns gold and throws back the shadow as if she is something made of the sun. Balth and I are pushed toward the wall. The window is open. They all fall back as she makes herself known. Balth stalls then reaches for her. "Lak—" The sword slips through him as easily as the spear through me and I lunge toward the man, but Laknya has me, her form plowing into my chest, and we fall through the window and into the open sky.

"Balth!" I scream, fighting for purchase on the stones, my claws catching, sliding, but my injured shoulder won't support both mine and Laknya's weight and she is tearing at my side. I still hear them, swords clashing, but there is triumph in their cry now.

"There is nothing for you there!" she screams at me. Blood drenches my side where the wound has reopened.

"Balth!" I shout again. My claws ache against the stones and I feel them begin to slip. And then we're falling. She grips me tighter, spreading the wings that she's kept pressed to her back. The updraft lifts us. I snarl in her grip, trying to pull myself away, flipping over so that she struggles to maintain her altitude and hold onto me. I rake my claws against her belly.

"You'll kill yourself," she says and tightens her grip on me. I'm pleading, my own voice lost in the rushing wind.

"Why did you do it? He's my brother."

"Did they clip your wings?" she asks finally.

I've never had any, I think, and I latch my teeth around her forearm. Her bones are like the toughest steel, but she still screams, thrashes, falls. We tumble together. She pushes at me, howls and curses. The trees rip at us both as we careen downwards, and yet she still manages to catch some draft and propel back up into the sky.

"You're an idiot!" she yells. "They've used you your whole life. They covet your pelt, and your teeth, and your spleen for the supposed magic it contains. They've cut parts away from you to make you docile. You are a wild thing, Larin. Your heart beats with the forest like mine. You don't even know what you are. You've been better than them this whole time and you're blinded. You ate them just like me."

I struggle again like a small forest animal caught in an eagle's talons.

"It doesn't matter if you were born of a curse or born naturally, you are what you are."

I bite down harder until her bones start to splinter, until my teeth start to crack. And then she lets go. The hot air whips past me and I see that she's flown far enough to get us off the coast. My instinct tells me to spread wings I've never had. I almost feel them unfurl from my back. I spin and fall, the wind burning my eyes. And then the water, a shock of blue, holds me.

The island is bones and bones. Wurm skulls and backbones. They are bleached white and left for me. I am in the land of the dead. Soon one of them will embrace me and welcome me. I wrap my damaged body around the closest one. I breathe sand into my nostrils.

"Good. Your spine isn't broken." Laknya stands to the side. Her forearm is raw and bloodied, but her limp is minimal, and she drops a fish still flopping in front of me.

I have no appetite. I think of the sword passing through Balth's chest, and the puncture wounds that lace the fish's body.

"Suit yourself. You want to join them? I'm not going to stop you."

"Did you pull me out?"

"I did. I wanted to leave you to drown."

"Why did you do it?" I ask. I'm not sure what I'm asking her.

"Look around you. Why do you think?"

The bones are not haphazard, and I realize that I'm resting in a graveyard. Some are missing pieces of themselves. Pieces of wings, next to spines, next to skulls. Bleached and white in the sun. Maybe this is how wurms honor their dead. I have only seen my own go up in flames. I try to stand but find that I can't.

"I don't recommend sleeping here. The dead aren't always so still."

She stands close but her eyes gaze above their bones as if it pains her too much to take them in.

"They're your family?" I say finally.

Balth and his men killed them, I think, but don't say. I see that it's the truth. Balth in his golden armor, the same golden sheen as Laknya's.

"Can all wurms change shape?" I ask her.

She says nothing.

"Were you ever human?"

"Never like you," she says.

I had never once thought of myself as human, and yet I realized that all along she had seen me as one of them.

"I saw it first when I painted you. Even as you stood there and thought about eating me, your eyes gave you away. They had lost the forest. I knew then that you had either been human all along or somewhere along the way you became like them."

"I've never been like them," I say and I sound like a petulant child.

"Your little spate of cannibalism opened a door for me. I came with him willingly but only ever with the intention of causing his destruction. How easy to be the princess in distress, part of the wurm's horde, a treasure to covet, to take back into his home, to rescue. And what do I find there? A pet wurm who's dabbling in violence. Even after his men had butchered my family, my brood, razed my island, cut their bodies apart in front of me, peeling their hides from their still warm bodies, what do I find? That he loves a wurm like a human. He loves a wurm like a brother. And yet he is capable of such genocide. Then if that is the case, if all humans share such a trait, then what is keeping them from ripping each other apart? It was simple. They thought it was you, and they thought he was protecting you. That was all it took."

I don't speak. I sink down into the sand. I think I would like to sleep. I think I would like to join the bones that are around me.

She walks the island. I wonder why she doesn't fly. She shifts the bones, lays trinkets and leaves and flowers around their bones, and then she slinks into the forest that makes up the rest of the island.

"Stand up," she says. Her shadow falls over me in the setting sun on the fifth day. "Get up now. I don't want another set of bones to tend to."

I uncurl. My shoulder refuses my weight and the wound is black and festering.

She pulls me into the salt water and I thrash. "So you are alive," she says. She pulls at the wound, opening it, cleaning it, and I limp after her onto the shore. "Follow me. I've been thinking these past few days."

I could leap, rip out her throat, drag her into the sand, and leave her corpse with the rest of her family. Balth has been walking among their bodies at night. A sword in his stomach, wounds bleeding, his eyes dull and empty and seeking for what he's lost. When I reach for him, he vanishes. The same feeling comes over me the night that I ate the armorer. I lunge and she easily pushes me into the sand, holding a claw against my chest, as I writhe and twist against her.

Her teeth are on my throat, closing and tightening. "I can kill you," she says, her words muffled. The beach begins to darken and then at some point she releases her grip.

"Get up. Get up," she says and pulls at me and I think she doesn't realize just how desperate she sounds. In my current state, there is nothing I can do. I open my eyes, turn, and push myself upward.

"Balth was my twin. We are the same."

"Did they cut off Balth's wings too?"

"I never had any."

"What are those scars on your back? The child's wings mounted on the wall? You're just as much a prize as those other wurms turning to dust in the cellar."

"Balth killed the man who wanted to skin me."

"It wasn't Balth."

I stop.

"He tasted sour, if you were wondering. Bad meat." And she spits. "If you can move past it, you can have a good life here."

A good life without Balth, without my mother, without the castle. On this desolate, abandoned island with the only company the murderer of my family.

"You can move past anything," she says.

"Just like you."

She turns then, her incisors sharp and exposed, a growl in the back of her throat.

"I should have let them skin you. They could have worn your scales as they slaughtered each other." She turns then to look out over the sea, surveying her empty kingdom. "They would have killed you one way or another after you started eating them."

Something moves behind us, and I turn to see a face peek from the foliage. "We can hear you," she says. A small wurm slinks from the greenery. "You don't have to be alone anymore," she whispers before the hatchling is close enough to hear. He unfurls his wings and catches the warm zephyr from the lake.

She leads the hatchling back into the woods. I stay on the beach, trying to see if I can make out the castle and my homelands now that the fog has faded, but there is only more water. When the sun sets and there is nothing more to see, only then, do I turn.

About the Author

Rachel is a librarian in the Midwest. When not writing strange tales or traipsing through the woods, she's found with friends or wrangling cats and plants. This is her first published full-length short story. Find her drabbles and poetry at Hungry Shadow Press, Black Hare Press, the Deadly Drunk, Celestite Poetry, and Shacklebound Anthologies: Wyrms and Planetside. Follow her on twitter @RachCraftsTales

ANY
COMICS

WOODWOSE

BY JENNIFER R. POVEY

It was a fine evening in the English Midlands, by the standards of the English Midlands. That is to say, it was neither raining nor imminently threatening to do so, nor was it so cold that one had to worry about black ice on the sidewalk.

Oh, and it wasn't foggy either.

All of this was enough to make it a fine day. Robin Hood was vaguely watching over the square. Nobody ever made statues of Little John.

Just Robin Hood, as if he'd achieved all of his legends on his own; of course, the man probably didn't exist anyway. Robin Goodfellow. A fairy figure, unreal, put together from various stories and legends and wild achievements.

Still, Melville thought, smoothing his fur, it would be *nice* to see a statue of Little John.

Or even Little John portrayed in a movie by the right species rather than some very large human. The woodwoses had more important things to be angry about, sure, but that was what he tended to think about every time he passed the statue.

They'd replaced the arrow, and he wondered what they'd done *this* time to keep it from being stolen, as it was routinely.

He drew no more than the normal number of stares as he walked past the Trip to Jerusalem. He didn't go inside, of course.

First of all, woodwoses weren't welcome in a tourist trap like that. Even nice woodwoses.

Second of all, being as it was a tourist trap, the beer was expensive and the pumps were electric.

No. He was going where he, while not exactly wanted, was at least somewhat accepted. The Bell Inn. Which was possibly older, but it wasn't half cave, and it didn't have that amazing crusades association.

Which meant it actually had locals there, and it might even have a certain handsome, young woodwose he was hoping to court.

Maybe.

There was no guarantee, and he certainly wasn't going to call him first; that was a human thing to do, and while he was a civilized woodwose, there were limits.

Stepping into the pub, he noted one other of his kind present, but it was a greyfur, an elder. Not his, if he was honest, crush.

He lifted a hand to them in any case and made his way to the bar. Human-sized stools were even harder to navigate than human-sized doors, but he was used to it.

After all, everything was human-sized.

"You should be careful," the barkeep said as he poured Melville his pint without asking what he was ordering.

He didn't need to ask, and that was one of the reasons Melville came to the Bell.

A barkeep who knew your usual order was worth his weight in gold.

Well, to a human anyway. To a woodwose, certain more practical materials would be preferred.

"Careful about what?"

"They might not go after somebody like you, but the League is back."

Before work, Melville bathed and groomed himself carefully. It was the natural tendency of woodwose fur to become a matted mess in short order, and amongst other woodwoses, that would be considered perfectly acceptable—even attractive to both males and females.

Humans thought it was filthy. Well, English humans did. African humans held a different opinion.

You did what English humans wanted when you lived in England. You bathed every day and you groomed out your fur until it was silky. You stuffed yourself into clothing on top of it because clothing was their sign of civilization.

It got blasted hot in summer.

Melville stuffed himself into his suit and peered into the mirror. He looked like the picture of a tame woodwose, one nobody had to be afraid of. He forced his feet into shoes and stepped out.

If he could work from home, he would, but his boss wouldn't allow that for anyone, not even the human woman who was painfully shy and got stressed every day.

He might allow it for everyone *except* Melville because everyone knew that woodwoses couldn't be trusted. It was their size, their strength, their wildness.

Their different culture, which the humans had run right over. There had been a time when they could hide in the wilds of Scotland or Wales.

That time was long gone. Now they had been found, scientifically categorized, given a sort of second-and-a-half-class citizenship.

Some woodwoses had fought for certain rights. Melville could even vote, although he was never quite sure that his ballot wasn't somehow marked so it wouldn't be counted.

No woodwose had been elected to Parliament. Legal, yes. Possible, no. There weren't enough of them, and if they banded together, people saw them as a threat.

A woodwose could even take a human mate, not that anyone would. Both species were apes, and some scientists thought they might be able to reproduce.

That supposedly happened in the US with bigfoots every few years. It was never reported by anyone hugely reputable, though.

He walked into the office, went to his desk, sat in the slightly-too-small chair, and checked his email. He was very good at his job, otherwise, he wouldn't *have* his job.

One day he wouldn't have it anyway. They would find some excuse to push him out and replace him with a human.

He tried not to shed all over the chair.

Though, that wasn't something he could change.

He didn't go to the Bell that night. He went straight home. There was an exhaustion flowing over him.

What he wanted to do was run through the woods wearing only what nature gave him. Which was, of course, a perfectly sufficient body covering. Only humans needed clothes because, being tropical apes, they had stopped bothering to grow their own.

Then they expected everyone else to…

He was angry, which wasn't normal for him. He assessed the emotion. Did he want to get rid of it or did he want to build up a nice head of steam so he could let it out without anyone getting hurt? It wasn't good to sit on anger; doing so tended to make it come out destructively.

And an angry woodwose could do a fair amount of damage. His mother had told him never to be angry.

She'd told him many things.

He decided tonight was a night to be angry. He went on the Internet; he had a keyboard designed for his hands. It was expensive, but it was worth it after hunting and pecking on the work keyboard all day.

He'd tried bringing one of his custom keyboards into the office.

He'd never seen it again. Somebody had confiscated it over lunch break and left a note saying that personal devices weren't allowed.

It was a keyboard, not something that could be used to hack into the network. But it was also something that reminded everyone he wasn't human. Something that made it easier for him to be something other than a guy with a bit more fur.

The news gave him a few good things to be angry about. A revival of an ancient sitcom that he knew contained offensive material and knew still would. A kidnapping case that would get a lot of attention because it was a pretty human girl. Some lawyer had managed to kill somebody by driving while tired. An entertainment journalist was complaining about how a game they loved hadn't sold well.

All human faces in these articles, flat and hairless. If it was a woodwose girl who had been kidnapped, it would be relegated somewhere clicks-deep on the site.

If her family were rural woodwoses who tried to keep their own culture, it wouldn't be there at all.

Woodwoses were apes, not humans.

The fact that humans were also apes escaped them.

The last article he read was about the Human League. They hadn't started killing anyone yet.

But they were definitely back.

Melville's boss believed in the traditional five-day workweek with Saturday and Sunday off. Saturday, maybe, you might come in for an emergency.

Sunday, absolutely not. He would rather lose a lot of money than ask anyone to work on a Sunday. He was a devout Christian and assumed everyone else was too.

Melville was *not* a devout Christian, but he wasn't angry about the absolute guarantee of one day off a week no matter what. That was one of the few things he wasn't angry about.

That week, there was nothing pressing enough for anyone to come in on Saturday. He had two whole days where he could do whatever he wanted.

As long as it wasn't what he actually wanted to do. If he really did go run naked through the woods and it got back to his boss, it would be evidence that he was an unstable woodwose after all.

He could lose his job.

Oh, not for that. There were legal protections for off-the-clock behavior. But his boss would find something. It had been made very clear to him.

First that he was a diversity hire, and second that he was a risk and should be very grateful for the chance.

He was quietly looking for another job—not that he thought anything would actually come up. No, he was going to be working there for a long time, or he was going to be working nowhere and putting up with the Job Center making him apply to jobs with obvious bigots.

Sometimes they would grant you an interview just so they could humiliate you to your face.

Next best thing, wear as little as possible and go jogging, *not* running, in the woods. The remnants of the great forest were few and far between, but he knew where they were. He drove, which he didn't do very often.

He drove an American car, which was a little large for British roads since British cars were more than a little small for him.

He found the trail he wanted and set off down it. A couple of women on horseback were coming the other way.

He stepped far enough off the trail to be out of their way, but not so far he'd partially vanish into the trees. He'd learned *that* lesson.

Horses were not overly smart creatures, and if they couldn't quite see you and you moved…

One of the riders still unleashed a stream of invective against him for just being there.

The other made a hand signal that he didn't recognize right away.

Then he did.

She meant for him to turn back. Well, he wasn't going to listen to *that*. She wanted him not to have access to the woods that had once *belonged* to his people.

Robin Hood was a woodwose.

That was even what it meant. Woodman. Even if they'd forgotten the man part.

So, he kept moving, ignoring the retreating backs of the riders and the swishing tails of their horses.

He jogged toward the old quarry, fenced off because foolish children of all species would dive in.

He was not expecting what he would find there.

They were holding the young woodwose upside down over the quarry. From her squeaking shrieks, he could determine gender, or at least sex.

From her size, she was a teenager.

The right thing to do was growl and snarl and run forward, but two things stopped him.

The first was that he was a civilized woodwose, and if this got back to his boss or the young man he hoped to make his mate or the guy who served him his beer, he wouldn't be a civilized woodwose anymore.

He would be a feral one, who not only didn't deserve a job or beer, but didn't deserve to live.

The second was that if he startled them, they would drop her, and that was a bad fall.

He was not proud of the fact that the first thought he had was the first one when it should have been the second. This was what humans did to you.

This was what being civilized meant.

It meant not being violent even when it was justified.

They were going to throw her in.

The civilized thing to do was walk away, but Melville wasn't going to walk away.

He was going to help her, but to do so he had to...

...and if woodwoses smiled, he would have smiled. He stepped back farther into the trees and made a *hoo-hoo* sound.

It was the exact sound he'd always heard humans make when they wanted to mock woodwoses and bigfoots and sasquatches.

It was the stereotypical sound an ape made, and he flinched inwardly as it passed his lips. To these people, though?

It would say they had other prey, and perhaps, *perhaps* they would leave off torturing the girl.

Two of them came toward him. The other two still had the girl, but they had stepped back. If they dropped her now, she would not go over the edge.

That was—had to be—good enough for him.

With a snarl, he charged.

He didn't intend to hurt them, mind. Well, no, part of him did, knowing the police would do nothing.

Nothing but arrest *him* for daring to threaten humans. They knew it, but it's hard to stand your ground.

One fled.

The other tried to punch him. He stepped to the side, and saw his startlement; nobody expected a woodwose to be fast.

The girl was taking the opportunity to break free. Her clothes were torn. In fact, her *fur* was torn. She looked at him.

He jerked his free thumb, and she ran off into the woods.

Then he devoted himself to the task of scaring these men such that they would never try it again.

Of course, that didn't mean they wouldn't tell everyone.

It didn't mean he might not be identified.

Unfortunately, humans *could* tell woodwoses apart.

Most of the time, that was a good thing.

Now, now it was not.

Her name was Blythe; like most woodwoses, her parents had given her a name even more English than the typical English human. She had gone out on her own.

The people who grabbed her had used a League slogan. They were hanging out in forests hunting woodwoses. The second horseback rider might even have been trying to warn him without her bigoted companion knowing.

Not all humans were bad. Far from it.

Blythe was more shaken than anything else. He did the gentlemanly thing and offered to walk her home. She accepted and led him out of the park and along the road, carefully. There was very little traffic to avoid.

He told her his name, but other than that, they walked in the kind of half-companionable, half-awkward silence of people who don't know each other and aren't comfortable with small talk.

Small talk was also a human thing, though, but there *was* an awkwardness to this. He'd managed to damage his shorts in the attack and he wanted to take them off, but he knew he couldn't. Not until he got home.

Humans would even think he was coming on to the child, but even if she *had* been the right gender for him, she was far too young to be considered as a mate by anyone except a pervert.

Of course, humans thought all woodwoses were perverts.

They thought anyone who didn't think like them was a pervert, including a good number of other humans.

He got her safely home, then considered his situation. The best thing to do was to drive straight home, get rid of the damaged clothes, and pray that he hadn't been identified.

Yes, that was definitely the best thing to do, but he hesitated, looking at the little cottage she and her parents lived in.

It was a nice place, a quiet place. A place where people didn't have to rush to work.

Maybe one day he'd live in a place like this.

He drove straight home, got rid of the damaged clothes, and prayed that he hadn't been identified.

Being no fool, he stayed in on Sunday watching an American streaming show in which the sidekick was a bigfoot and was actually played by a bigfoot, not a human in an ape suit.

He was still the sidekick and existed primarily to make the hero look good, but he supposed it was some brand of progress.

He watched all of the unwatched episodes. He ordered Chinese food, ate it in front of the television, and decided that he really did need to talk to his crush, in the hope that something might come of it.

Knowing his luck, the other would turn out to be straight, but if he never pushed, he would never find out.

The encounter with the thugs had shaken him, he supposed. They hadn't had guns or knives large enough to get far past his coat, as well-groomed as it was.

But they could still have done some damage if they hadn't been cowards who went after children. He wasn't exactly *glad* they were cowards who went after children; he would prefer such did not exist at all.

He also spent some time planning for the eventuality of losing his job. He sent out a few resumes, for what it was worth.

He thought of that cottage.

If he could find somebody who would let him work remotely, maybe he could live somewhere like that.

Not right there, of course. Humans got nervous about too many woodwoses in one place.

Maybe it was time to let the humans get nervous.

The next day, he groomed, bathed, and went to work. Nothing happened and he began to relax.

The end of this week was the end of the pay period. His boss was so old-fashioned, he still paid by check.

He sent out a few more resumes. Half-heartedly. He wanted a new job, but he *needed* the job he had. People didn't extend credit to unemployed woodwoses.

He needed the job, so he wore the suit and groomed and tried to look like a human with extra hair.

On Friday, he opened his pay envelope.

Something pink fell out.

He should have been angry. He had gotten into a fight. His crush hadn't shown up all week to be asked.

Now he didn't have a job.

But as he picked up the slip, it occurred to him that that didn't just mean he was broke.

It also meant he was free.

When he got home, there was an email waiting for him.

An interview next week.

And when he went to the interview, the person on the other side of the table was a woodwose, and he knew he was home.

About the Author

Born in Nottingham, England, Jennifer R. Povey (she/her) now lives in Northern Virginia, where she writes everything from heroic fantasy to stories for Analog. She has written a number of novels across multiple subgenres. She is a full member of SFWA. Her interests include horseback riding, *Doctor Who,* and attempting to out-weird her various friends and professional colleagues. Find her on Facebook at or Mastodon at @NinjaFingers@universeodon.com.

LADIES FIRST

by David Rider

We first met Silas bathing in the stream near our cabin. This was weeks before the heat wave baking the rest of the country set upon Illinois, so the morning air was chilly. Grae noticed him first, silhouetted by the rising sun through the trees. Staring past me, he said, "Esther." I turned to see a black-haired boy splashing frigid water over his body. He saw me doing the same, nodded, and waded to shore to get his clothes.

Grae said, "Boy."

"Yes, I see," I said and went to put on my overalls.

Grae stepped into his, going shirtless like myself. He fussed with the bib, saying, "Button." While I helped fasten his buttons, he squinted warily through his good eye at the other boy. This was the year after Grae tripped and fell on a butter knife he'd pilfered from some rich picnicker's silver tea service. It went through his left eye and into his brain. He yelped like a puppy. That was the end of the Grae I knew. Once I plucked the knife from his socket, a different best friend took his place—still warm, still loyal, but he now spoke in single words.

"Brown," he said.

Not every word made sense. Sometimes I had to search for clues.

The boy had donned blue trousers and a dirty shirt that was once white. He had bronze-colored skin.

"Yes, he is." I straightened his straps. "C'mon, let's get to chores."

We walked barefoot to the path leading up the embankment.

The boy approached the same path. It was the easiest way into the woods and wide enough for only one. We got there at the same time. He bowed and gestured. In an accent I'd never heard, he said, "Ladies first."

I said, "I ain't no lady."

"I insist."

Grae said, "Go."

I glared at the boy. I didn't know his name. I didn't know he'd been watching us even before the stream. I didn't know how much we had in common or that we were kindred spirits. That all came later. What I did know was his smile coaxed one out of me I didn't know I had.

It was 1936.

We were twelve years old.

The three of us became fast friends that week.

We had a name for our club the week after that.

And then a dark killer came to put an end to us before a month had passed.

Grae and I were homeschooled by his mother, my Aunt Geraldine. She left to seek actual work in Utica, at first, then Chicago. The Depression had been rough. Her chances of landing a job were slim, she being a woman with no civilized-world skills to speak of. She taught us to hunt—and did a crackerjack job—but that wasn't going to translate into secretary work. I couldn't tell her that, though, seeing as she took me in at eleven and asked nothing in return other than feeding their chickens. Anyway, she'd pound the pavement for a few days, return to check on us, and head back out. Her time away grew longer and longer. Upon seeing I could care for poor, damaged Grae without her, she must've decided not to come back.

Silas had an absentee caregiver too. Our new friend told us he had come from Guadalajara and came to Illinois by way of San Antonio. His daddy was murdered when they crossed the border—which he explained by saying, "Because of what he was." He completed his journey riding the rails north, knowing only the location of an uncle's cabin. It happened to be a mile from ours. That uncle left a note saying he'd return in a few weeks and for Silas to make himself comfortable.

The three of us clicked, pure and simple. I looked forward to nights spent hunting together. Grae felt the same. He liked Silas, and Silas didn't take long learning to handle Grae's shortcomings.

One evening at dusk, after a sweltering day when the weather first hit ninety, we sat cooling porch-side watching fireflies lighting the forest.

Silas placed a marble in his slingshot's pouch, pulled the band back, squinted an eye, and took aim. "I could tell much from the way you hunted rabbits that first night. You're speedy. Grae's strong. If he was quick like you, he could take down a deer. You ever tried?"

I spotted the firefly he was targeting between its blinks, nocked an arrow, and fired my shot before he released his. Its severed, lit bottom half drifted to the ground like a dropped match. "I can take down any game he can. Or you, for that matter."

"I'm talking without weapons."

"So'm I."

"Then consider this a challenge."

"July fourth?"

"July fourth it is."

We shook.

"Cool," Grae said, getting out of bed.

"It is." I reckoned the morning temperature was twenty degrees colder than yesterday. It was the first of what'd be a three-day reprieve from the heat wave finding its legs. "Good day for a long walk."

"Silas?"

"Think he'd like the Rock?"

"Yeah."

I pulled off my nightshirt and reached for my overalls. "Let's get him."

We headed north to collect Silas, telling him we were going for a two-hour hike. He asked if he needed sandals. I said, "If'n ya have bitty baby feet." So he didn't wear any. We took the trail west, along the southern bank of the Illinois River, and pointed out wildlife. He was stunned seeing his first bald eagle soaring across the sky. This led to talk about the fabled Thunderbird. Then he told us about Quetzalcoatl, and we blathered about myths and legends for a spell.

"If you think about it," Silas said, "that's what we are."

"Myths or legends?"

"The more I think about it," he said, "gods."

I cocked an eyebrow. "How ya reckon?"

"Take you," he said, lifting a lank of my hair. "Imagine a dark-haired, dark-skinned caveman family telling stories under the moon..."

"Moon," Grae said, looking up.

"...Then *you* suddenly step out of the darkness. They wouldn't know what to make of your golden hair or blue eyes. You don't think they'd worship you?"

I scoffed. "They'd hunt me. You're a dang fool for thinking otherwise."

He brought up the subject of being hunted with some frequency. That might've been when we realized he tended to look behind him a lot. At one point, Silas pointed toward an island in the middle of the river. "If we're ever hunted, we could hide out there for a few days."

"We can go even if we're not hunted." I skipped a stone so far it hit the island. "Grae and I camp there once or twice a year. We go when it's colder cuz the bugs bite something fierce."

Silas suggested we camp there that night, assuming the weather stayed cool.

We spent the day exploring Starved Rock.

Grae discovered a troop of churchgoers had left their bus unattended. He returned to our hiding spot with a stolen sack of ham sandwiches. We ate half and drank from one of the canyon waterfalls. When we passed the same church folk on one of the trails, Grae heard one of their flock griping about hunger and wanting to get back for lunch. He offered the woman a sandwich wrapped in wax paper. She touched the side of his face where his eye was missing. "May the Lord bless your sad soul."

Grae said, "Alms?"

The woman took in the state of him before fishing a coin from her purse and handing it over.

He gave her the sandwich. After they were out of earshot, he flicked the coin in the air and grinned. "Quarter."

"Wanna stop at Macaskill's General on the way back? Been a while since we had Coca-Cola."

"Coke," Grae said, nodding.

"They got Coke down in Guadalajara?" I asked Silas.

"I don't know. We didn't go to town. Stayed on our ranch. We only left because men came and burned it down."

We walked in silence, wanting to hear more, but Silas wasn't much on sharing feelings. Not that Grae and I were, either. Again, peas in a pod.

Macaskill ran a general store located on the main road tourists take back to civilization. He was a beady-eyed Scotsman that saw everything punk kids did after traipsing through his jingling door. He was known to rough up shoplifters and once slammed a girl's face into the wall. Luckily, he did a good amount of trade and was usually too busy to see sticky fingers at work—but he *did* see us coming. He eyeballed us from behind the counter, saying, *"You two."*

"Quarter," Grae said, holding up the coin and passing it to me—as if that would ease his mind.

Faking the voice of a woman of means, I said, "Where might we find bottles of yon beverage called 'Coca,' my good man?"

"I've no time for yer nonsense, lassie." He tracked our progress toward the rear aisles. "And I've eyes on the both o' yas."

Other decent, paying folks entered, with Silas coming in behind, so Macaskill drew his attention elsewhere.

Grae wandered toward the fruit bushels. He could gnaw an apple to its core in a matter of seconds while pocketing fistfuls of hard candy, so I left him to it and split away.

Silas didn't like enclosed spaces with only one exit. His nerves were calmed by his excitement at the number of goods on the shelves.

"Haven't ya been in a general store?" I whispered.

"No," he replied, staring at the book covers on a rack.

Macaskill finished ringing out a customer and checked our whereabouts. When I saw him looking for Grae, I called, "Hey! How much *is* a Coke, anyway?"

"A nickel. But ya don't open a single bottle till ya pay!"

I went to a horse trough loaded with Coke and flashed Grae the signal. Silas headed to the door. I grabbed the bottles and approached Macaskill at the register. The wooden countertop was wide. Poor planning on his part. It allowed me to put the quarter close to my edge where he could see it was real but not reach it. He'd mounted an opener on the customer side. Presently, I began snapping off caps. Not seeing how many I had, he eyed me when I put the first bottle on the counter, then over to Grae at the second. When he saw the third bottle and realized Silas was reaching for the door, his eyes bulged.

"Now!" I cried, scooping up the quarter and bottles.

Silas yanked open the door.

Grae blurred behind me.

Macaskill lifted the hinged door to come from behind the counter while grabbing a baseball bat.

My heart raced with a heady mix of excitement and fear. The only time I felt more high was running through the woods at night, chasing down furry prey. It twisted my guts in the most pleasurable way.

Silas almost ruined it by gesturing out the door and saying, "Ladies first."

I slowed and started to say, "I told ya, I ain't no—"

"Go!" Grae shouted, with Macaskill on his heels.

We flew off the store's porch and hit the gravel at a sprint.

Macaskill was too big and too slow to brain us with his bat, so he hurled words. "Ya better run! Ya thievin' pack o' rascals! Ya better run and not come back!"

Bottles clinking in my grip, we disappeared into the forest, leaving behind the sounds of our laughter. When we finally stopped running, breathless and hysterical at the thrill of it all, I passed a bottle to each of my fellow rascals.

Silas held his to the sun, studying the brown, carbonated liquid with curiosity.

"Trust us. It's good."

"Good," Grae said.

"Then we need to make a toast," Silas said.

I thought a second before raising my bottle. "To the Thievin' Pack!"

Silas echoed, "To the Thievin' Pack," with Grae chorusing, "Pack!"

We drank and our little gang became official.

The Thievin' Pack lived up to its name again at dusk when we stole a skiff from a dock. Grae manned the oars and fought the river's westward current. He's powerful strong, and in no time we reached the island's muddy bank. After pulling the boat up among the weeds, we gave Silas a tour of Bitin' Bug Island. The cool day had turned into a cooler night, so the bugs weren't a problem.

We found our old campsite between the raised roots of the tallest tree and built a fire. Grae emptied his pockets. We took stock of the loot: three apples, six butterscotch candies, ten pieces of licorice, and a pack of Black Jack chewing gum.

Silas reached behind his waist, asking, "Do either of you read?"

"I read some. Grae used to. Why?"

He took a book from his waistband and handed it to me. It was hardbound, like a schoolbook, with a green burlap cover featuring a boy's gap-toothed face. I opened it and read the author's name. "Mark Twain."

"There are pictures," Silas said.

"Pictures," Grae said, scooting closer.

Between pages and pages of words were glossy, colorful paintings. Together they told the tale of a boy close to our age. I'd seen books before, but never anything with beautiful art like this. I asked Silas, "Do ya read?"

"Not English."

"Want me to read this, like a campfire story?"

Grae nodded. "Story."

"We can follow the pictures," Silas said.

So I read aloud about an orphan named Tom and his friend Huckleberry and their adventures in Missouri. Grae and Silas nestled into the crooks of my arms, loving the words and pictures with equal measure. The stars came and we munched the last of our sandwiches before moving on to the sweets. My voice grew hoarse after a spell, but by then we were tired. We fed the fire once more, then curled up together for warmth, and our pack fell asleep with full bellies.

It'd been a good day.

Dark ones followed.

The strange thing about stories is how their words haunt you once they're over. That's how it was after reading Mr. Twain's book.

I'd spaced out our nightly readings over two weeks. We usually started on the porch. Grae would lie flat, hands behind his head, waiting for me to nudge him when a picture came up. Silas rested his chin on my shoulder from behind. The heat brought mosquitos. When they got to be too much, we went inside where there weren't as many. Then I hunched in bed with the book in my lap. Silas followed the words above my finger as I ran it along the page. He said it helped him learn. Toward the end, the story gave him nightmares.

He'd pretty much moved in by then, staying the night rather than walking back to his sad, empty cabin. Our thin bed barely held three for sitting, so when we slept, Silas curled on the floorboards. I'd hear him thrashing in the middle of the night. These bizarre fits came after the chapter, "In the Lair of Injun Joe." I'd crawl onto the floor and press my hand to his chest to calm his pounding heart, thinking maybe his brain was stirring up bad memories the way a stick stirs up pond muck. Turns out it was worse.

He felt ashamed at causing such a fuss. Not long after finishing the book, we were walking in the moonlight, checking rabbit traps, when shame compelled him to explain a thing or two.

"Among my other gifts, mi madre told me I have what you would call *the sight.*"

I'd never heard such a term. "What's that?"

"I dream things and they come true."

I laughed in spite of myself. "Grae used to dream the moon would make him explode."

Grae nodded, glancing upwards. "Moon?"

I studied it. "First quarter."

He looked doubtful.

"Not for eight days, on July fourth," I told him and turned back to Silas. "You were saying?"

"I once had a dream our cow died, and it did."

"How long after?"

"No more than ten days. Usually less. Then on my last birthday, I dreamed mi madre would go missing. She took it seriously. For nine days, she wouldn't leave home except to fetch water by the stream. On the tenth day, we found the bucket but she was gone."

"Gone?" Grae whispered.

"And before *los soldados* came to burn our ranch, I warned mi padre. That was the only reason we survived. We watched it burn from the safety of the woods. We could no longer stay in our country and had to come north."

"And your dreams now?"

"A dark man is coming for me. The one who killed mi padre. Death rides with him."

"Death for who?"

For the briefest of moments, I saw Silas's eyes flick in Grae's direction—and, lordy, didn't *that* make my skin crawl? "I see only fire and smoke and blood."

"Ten days, ya say?"

His dreams had started two days before. It didn't take more than simple 'rithmetic to figure how much time we had left.

Death came sooner.

Two days into July, scrounging breakfast outdoors on a cloudy morning, Silas lifted his head to sniff the breeze. Grae and I did the same. Something was burning to the north.

The three of us landed on the same idea the same instant.

Silas dropped his squirrel carcasses and tore in the direction of his uncle's cabin.

We chased after, feet pounding grass, keeping pace as best we could, but he moved mighty quick. He leaped over logs and sprinted faster than I'd seen.

Grae wasn't built for speed and fell behind. I kept up, begging Silas to wait, cuz I sensed something the closer we got. I never professed to having *the sight*, but what I did have was animal instinct aplenty—and now it warned me of danger.

Right when we burst into the clearing where his uncle's cabin was situated, I tackled him. We rolled all tangled into the meadow's tall grass. He struggled to his knees but I pulled him down, whispering, *"Don't ya sense it?!"*

After a short spell, he did.

Grae crawled into position next to us, also sensing it.

We peeked our heads above the grass.

Off to the right of the burning cabin, upwind of the curling smoke, stood a man in black.

From the way Silas's breath caught, he recognized him.

The man was dressed like a cowboy, hat to boots, clothing black as pitch. A holstered six-shooter hung on a belt. Standing next to him was an ebony horse. It snorted at the flames. The man struck a match on the saddle and lit a cigarette. He smoked till the cabin's roof gave way with a *whoomph*, sending a shower of sparks skyward.

Given the heat wave, if it hadn't started raining at that moment, there'd been a real chance of a wildfire finding its footing. But no amount of rain would stop the cabin from burning to the ground.

The man turned to swing his gaze 'round the clearing—we ducked when he did—then mounted his horse and took off north at a gallop.

Silas said, "That was the man who killed mi padre." He staggered across the meadow.

We followed. The rain soaked our clothes even as the fire tried to dry us the closer we got.

When Silas spotted his uncle's charred corpse inside the doorway—an uncle he hadn't yet met cuz he'd been with us—he dropped to his knees and shook with sobs. He raised his face to the rain, crying, "I have no one now!"

Grae and I held him tight. "You got us. You got your pack. And we got you."

Silas vanished the next morning.

He left a note, but it wasn't a proper goodbye. He couldn't write his own words in English. Instead, he scribbled words in pencil copied from the end of Twain's book, from something Huck said to Tom about trying to civilize him:

I like the woods, and the river, and hogsheads, and I'll stick to 'em, too.

He signed with the letter S.

I'd read the note to Grae when a knock came.

My nerves were frazzled and became more so when I saw the man in black peering through our window.

I opened the door.

The man was broad-shouldered and filled the doorway. He had a firm jaw covered with stubble. His eyes glinted but their color wasn't clear cuz they were set in a permanent squint. They studied us, judged us worth not a whit of courtesy, then scanned the room. He spoke in a Texas accent, his voice sounding like cemetery wind. "Man of the house about?"

"My Aunt Geraldine is out hunting."

"Hunting," Grae echoed.

"She'll be back with her twelve-gauge soon enough."

This didn't concern him none. He regarded me again. "Mind if I come in, little lady?"

At that, my heart took to thumping something fierce. I gritted my teeth and steeled my gaze, wavering between urges: spit in his face or launch myself at him.

He noticed. An amused look crossed his face. He moved to push past me. I'm tall for my age, but by my measure, he was a head taller and had to stoop coming through the frame.

I staggered backwards, balling my fists. I spoke in a shrill voice that sounded weak even to me. "Hey! Y-you're not invited, mister!"

After two steps, he was standing in the middle of the cabin floor. He checked the corners for hiding places. "I'm looking for a boy."

"There ain't no boy here! Now get—"

"He ain't what he seems," the man interrupted. "For one, he ain't a naturalized 'Merican citizen. I been trackin' him since he and his pa crossed the border. We can't have that. Can't tolerate it. No one invited his kind."

I wanted to say no one invited my nana or papa to come over from Norway, but here I stand with no one hunting *me*. I wanted to ask why it was better to cross an ocean than a river to get here. I wanted to call him out on being a murderer for killing Silas's daddy. But any of that would've tipped my hand.

He wandered over and found Silas's note atop the Twain book.

Grae and I froze.

He picked it up, read the line, saw the letter S, and glanced at the book's cover. "Who here reads Samuel Clemens?"

I'd never heard the name. Didn't know who he meant. I had no answer.

He snorted to himself as if thinking, *Who're ya kidding? No one here can read.* He went out the door, saying, "You kids stay away from that abomination. I'll put him down."

We waited till we saw his horse galloping away, then Grae and I got dressed to find our friend.

Silas wasn't anywhere in our woods or Bitin' Bug Island. On July fourth, the second day of searching, Grae spotted a marble on the trail to the Rock. Farther along, we came across campfire remnants and a hare carcass picked clean.

Fresh horse tracks headed the same way.

We quickened our pace.

Grae pointed out a beautiful sight toward the shimmering horizon: with another six hours of daylight left, the moon lifted over the trees. Seeing its full circle tickled us to no end—not only for the usual reasons but cuz it held the promise of light aplenty after sunset.

Upon reaching Macaskill's, the thermometer outside said it was the hottest day yet, with the needle nudging one hundred.

By and by, we came to a fork. To the west was a shady path where the mud hadn't hardened. Hoof prints, fresh as you please, headed to the French Canyon. We went east, uphill, toward the scenic overlook that'd widened Silas's eyes before.

It was a good call. We found him at dusk, at Eagle Cliff. He sat crouched at the edge, holding his knees, gazing down the drop-off at the river below.

He hadn't heard us coming, so he was startled when I called, "Why'd ya leave us?"

He turned, bearing streaks on his face left by tears. "To keep you safe. Everyone around me dies. If I'm to die, best it happens to me alone."

Grae and I knelt on either side of him. "Everyone leaves us, Silas. But not you. That's not s'posed to happen. We're your pack. We got nothing but each other. And we protect our own till the end."

We held each other, bawling like bitty babies.

We were so wrapped up in our feelings, god curse 'em, that we weren't minding our surroundings till we heard a shout.

"Step away from the boy!"

We scrambled apart, startled, and found ourselves standing before the man in black. He'd left his horse down the trail a ways and had snuck up and trapped us with nowhere to go. In his hands was the cocked six-shooter, the barrel aimed at Silas.

"Time to die," the man said and pulled the trigger.

I'm fast but Grae was closer and he jumped in front of Silas before I could.

The bullet thunked into Grae's chest, dead center. He turned to me and looked down at the blood pooling 'round the wound. More trickled from his mouth. He said two words for once—"Ow, Esther"—then he stumbled backwards and tumbled off the cliff's edge.

"Grae!" I screamed, tracking his descent and pulling Silas behind me.

"Goddammit," the man said, shocked at this awful turn of events. He raised his smoking weapon again.

I put myself between it and my friend.

The barrel wavered, a clean shot denied.

I whispered to Silas, "Does he shoot me?"

"No," Silas said. "You're not his target. But that's where my vision ends—with you making a choice."

"All I need to know," I said, stepping forward.

"Stupid girl!" the man hollered. "Ya don't know what he is!"

"He's our friend! Of *course* we know what he is!"

"Stop right there!"

I crept forward, my hand out front, waiting for the gun to go off but trusting Silas's visions were true. "We know what he is the same way he saw what *we* are since the morning we met. Like draws like."

His trigger finger tightened.

I snatched the barrel, yanking the weapon backwards and upwards from his grip. His finger broke with a snap. I tossed away the gun.

He held his injured hand and looked dumbstruck by my strength.

"Sun's down," I said and undid my straps. My hair from below spread up my belly and chest, coating them with a fine, blonde pelt. As my torso expanded, I dropped my overalls. The hair on my head joined the sprouting fur on my shoulders, working its way down my spine. Razor-sharp claws pushed out to replace my fingernails. My calf muscles shifted in their painful, pleasureful way as the growing bones went crooked-like and raised me up in height. Then came the grinding push from my chin and nose as my snout lengthened. Long fangs poked through my gums. My human teeth bounced like pebbles off the rock at my clawed feet. The sounds of the woods came louder when my furry ears stretched into points above my head. My vision changed, eyeballs allowing in more light and turning the sunless world bright as day.

I stepped closer, now just as tall as the man. He took in the sight of me. I heard his heart a-thumping and smelled the fear wafting off him like a foul funk. I snarled a curse word in my other language he couldn't hope to understand.

Silas joined me. He'd assumed his monthly form as well, one with black, shaggy fur. It was easy to figure why we hadn't seen him that first night as he tracked us.

I heard a sound from my other side. Grae had scampered back up the cliff. The bullet hadn't been silver. It'd pushed out from his chest when he changed, but he couldn't work his buttons. His overalls were fit to bursting over his broad chest covered with brown fur streaked through with gray. He could speak better in wolf form, asking, *What do we do now?*

It was a good question. The three of us hadn't ever killed anything other than small critters before. Then I remembered the bet I'd made with Silas—the one about who could take down bigger game.

He had the same thought. His muzzle curled in a snarl as he stepped up to the terror-stricken man. Then he turned to me, gestured with a bow, and growled, *Ladies first.*

I ain't no lady, I replied. *And this man killed your kin. He's yours.*

Grae said, *But we're a pack now. It's only right we do it together.*

Together, Silas agreed.

But they didn't move, still unsure.

So I went first anyway and plunged my fangs into one side of the screaming man's throat. Silas took the other. Grae slashed open his belly.

We fed well.

We ran through the canyons—racing toward our home grounds—growling and howling and having a grand ol' time. Come daybreak, we'd bathe in the stream, scrub off the blood, and go about our usual nonsense. Like Tom and Huck's robber-pirate gang, we swore to stand by one another, and never tell the pack's secrets, even if we're chopped all to flinders, and kill anybody that hurts one of the pack.

Nothing would ever be the same. We'd tasted flesh and found it to our liking. In doing so, I also realized something Silas was right about—something I saw in the man's eyes before we devoured him. Anybody in these woods not showing proper reverence will suffer my wrath, cuz for sure I ain't no lady.

But I *am* a goddess.

About the Author

David Rider grew up roaming the alleyways of Calumet City, Illinois. Like most Gen X kids, he lived an unsupervised, feral existence of dreaming and fighting. He currently lives with his wife, kids, and dogs in a rural Midwestern town surrounded by farmland. He still daydreams, but saves the fighting for dark entities lurking within the cornfields.

He is a member of the Horror Writers Association. His stories have appeared in various anthologies from Sinister Smile Press. He has published two novels, *We Are Van Helsing* Books One and Two as well as a short story called *Tweakers, Crane Girl and the Semi-pocalypse*.

https://www.davidriderauthor.com/

THE SACRIFICES FOR OUR CHILDREN

BY ZACHARY ROSENBERG

When my daughter was born, I wrapped her in silken blankets and held her with all eight of my arms. I knew from her first day of life there would be sacrifices I would have to make for her.

My name is Sara Tano, and I am a Jorōgumo. By day, I work as a computer programmer at a prestigious company. I am friendly with my coworkers, few knowing I am a single mother like my mother before me. I pay my taxes, enjoy movies, and every few months, I lure men home to consume them. I never knew my father, nor does my Akari know hers. She was born almost to the day of my twenty-third birthday, far earlier than when my mother bore me. Once, I valued my freedom and independence as a passionate predator. Now, I am a mother who must provide for her child.

Tonight is the night of her first change, and I am bringing home a man for her. I bid her relax as I left, that I would be home soon. Akari needs the nourishment only a strong man can provide, and I will benefit as well from my daughter's fulfillment and happiness. Once, I would have hunted solely for my own gratification. Now, I must both feed and educate my daughter.

I know a mother is not supposed to ever let pessimistic thoughts intrude upon maternal bliss, but having Akari limited many options in my life. I arrange my schedule around her completely. When she cries, I must awaken at night to comfort her, which often leaves me exhausted for work the following day. With her own change coming, she had been especially needy. I got no sleep whatsoever on Thursday evening, and a day of reports and writing code has left me dead on my feet.

It took all my energy to drag myself to the bar and wait for the right man to approach me. Someone strong, handsome, and brimming with confidence and vitality. His hair is the black of the hallway shadows, skin tanned from the sun. His smile is wide and pearly, his forearms thick. One finger bears a pale ring of flesh against darker skin; the ghost of a marriage past, or one he wishes to forget for this evening. I believe the name he proffered somewhere around the third beer was Joe.

I remove my coat before I lift a finger to my lips at the first sign of his drunken chuckle at the pictures on my nightstand. Akari is in my arms, her luminescent smile immortalized in the photographs. Not represented by my smile is the anxiety that hid behind it.

Motherhood is not a road we walk upon, but an ocean we navigate. I am the captain of a solitary vessel that sails those fraught waters, tossed by unruly tempests of anxiety. I worry over finances. I worry about schooling. I worry about her future, as the daughter of a first-generation American whose name is foreign and who will be objectified by the men around her. I worry we will be discovered for what we are. I worry she will surrender to her instincts and be seen feeding. I worry for her safety and for her health, with all those fears leaving almost no room for the concerns of my own life and the loss of the freedom I had once taken for granted.

I structure my life around her. Are mothers not supposed to do that? I dread the day we inevitably argue as I did with my own mother. I value my self-control, but the fear dwells in the back of my mind that in a moment of heated fury, I will snap at her that she was unplanned, that I truly contemplated if I was ready to be a mother as she grew inside me. I love Akari beyond words, my beautiful little blossom of a girl. Unplanned or not, she is my very world now. I make sacrifices for her, again and again. Tonight is just another example of that. I feel almost no resentment.

Almost.

"Make yourself at home," I tell Joe, avoiding using his name in case my memory is inaccurate. I brush my hair back, looking at myself in the mirror. Do I really look so tired now? My hair is still sleek and black, but there are new lines on my face and bags under my eyes. I never considered myself vain, but now I can see myself aging. The stress of motherhood is no small thing. "Please keep your voice down, though. My daughter is ill. She's sleeping over in the next room."

"Got a kid?" he asks, his voice slurred with alcoholic ecstasy. "Don't mind. It's kinda hot." The smile is lascivious. His hands are strong and quick, his movements swift. Even if I was to back out now, I strongly doubt he would allow it. I have been in this position with insistent men before and know how they behave. The assertive ones often make the best prey. That is a lesson I must teach Akari as well. Hunting is something that is natural to us, but the finest hunters are the ones that learn their lessons from their mothers.

"Yes. She was asleep when I left her," I answer succinctly. There is no need to inform him of more than he requires when he will become acquainted with her soon enough. Loathe as I was to leave Akari alone for several hours, asking anyone to watch her could have proven disastrous with the state she is in. "It's just a childhood illness. Very common."

"Chicken pox? I had that as a kid." He does not seem truly interested in hearing about Akari whatsoever, sliding toward me with all the stealth of a shark closing in on a seal. His tongue runs across colorless lips to moisten them, his eyes fastening to my own. His hands brush over my shoulders. He is admiring me, less as a person and more as a sculptor running his hand along priceless marble.

His hunger and lust roll off him in waves, mingling with the fragrance of alcohol in an olfactory assault. I dodge away from his grasp nimbly enough, chuckling all the while. "Not here," I chide him. It has been a while since I played hard to get, but it comes back to me so easily. I was wild in my adolescence, to my own mother's perpetual despair. I frolicked and drank and devoured to my heart's content, days that I try to tell myself again and again were not the happiest of my life. I am a mother now and the happiest days can only be dated from Akari's birth and onward. My old life was just another sacrifice.

"My daughter might hear. She's sick, remember? This way." I lift a hand, crooking a finger and bending it toward my smile. My breathing quickens and I step back through the modest little house my salary and my mother's investments bought us. I stop to rest by a door that is painted a bright pink, festooned with little pictures of unicorns and smiling stick figures that remain standing thanks to pieces of tape. "Here."

My hand closes on the metal of the doorknob and twists gently. The door swings back, without so much as a creak of protesting hinges, and Joe is on me. His mouth seeks mine, his hands groping at my back. I pull him closer, trailing my lips against his face. There is no passion within me, but I feign it well enough. I kiss along his cheek, his jawline, his throat. I sink my teeth into his neck, making him yelp when I pull away. He laughs softly, a low chuckle that begins in his throat.

"Minx," he grunts. His hand goes to his neck and comes away with a coating of blood that he suddenly cannot stop looking at. Red blood and a dark and viscous fluid that shines like polished onyx in the light of my home. He looks at me, lust melting away to surprise. Confusion. I place myself out of his reach, sliding back into my daughter's room. The farce is at its end.

My daughter's bed has not been slept in. The pretty pink sheets are drawn up neatly. Her dolls and stuffed animals are sealed away safely in the cupboard. Plastic sheets cover every inch of the room. I turn, seeing my daughter at the same time Joe does. He tries to scream, but my bite is doing its work well.

The veins in his neck turn black, his panic and the frantic beating of his heart only speeding up the process in which the venom works through his body. His legs give way, his voice slurring. His tongue is paralyzed and soon his muscles will follow. I walk to him and grab him by the wrists, easing him gently to his back so he does not fall and crack his head. He is heavier than I thought, but I am stronger than I look. I pull him into the room. "If it is any consolation," I say, knowing it is not, "it won't hurt. I'm sorry, but you must be conscious for this."

It is an apology that feels right. He is a thuggish brute of a man; one whose hands seem harsh and used to dealing pain. But he is still a living being and my heart is not stone. But my daughter is hungry for her first proper meal, just as I was at her age. Did my mother think the same as me, even then? Did she fret and worry behind her austere veil of maternal perfection? She never said, and I have never asked.

There is a sickness that afflicts all our kind the first time we blend between our shapes, and the only cure is a fresh meal. Behind me on the wall, Akari rests in a web of pale silk. She sits in the center, so beautiful and perfect. Her shining carapace bears gold and red blossoms set upon black chitin. Her eight red eyes burn bright below the black hair that remains fastened with a red ribbon. Her mandibles clack together, dripping with her own venom, eight legs twitching with hunger. Joe is unable to move or speak, but his eyes are wide with horror, lips trembling. I put a hand on Akari's head and lean in to plant a kiss just above her eyes, a physical demonstration of the feelings in my heart. She runs her head against mine, nuzzling there with all the childish adoration she has for me.

I am her everything. Protector and provider. Her love for me is unconditional. My precious, perfect girl. How could I ever resent her? I am ashamed I even considered it. She is every bit the best of me, in ways no one would understand save only other Jorōgumo and the few we trust with our secrets. "Akari." My voice is gentle but stern. "Prey is never to be tortured. Never to be tormented. They are living things. Kill and feast. But do it swiftly. Your instincts will tell you what to do."

I step back as she descends the web. She looks to me, seeking approval. I offer only the tender, loving smile that my mother offered me back when I thought she was without fault. We quarreled many times as I grew older, though I still love her. I wonder if it was the same with her and my grandmother. I suppose it might be the same with Akari and me in the future.

She lands upon the plastic. With predatory grace, she scuttles toward Joe, mandibles clicking with hunger. He will feel no pain, but that is scant relief from the obvious terror. I was quite wild and reckless as a younger woman, taking pleasure with my prey more than once. I must do my best to teach my daughter to be better than me. "Akari." I leave no room for debate, not one scattered fleck of dissent. "Quickly." All he has been, all he will be, is irrelevant. This night, he is now just another sacrifice.

Her fangs sink into his throat, her own venom injected with digestive juices so she might begin to liquefy his organs that are so much more nutritious when the prey yet breathes. It is a quick and clean kill. Even if she has seen me prey on others in the past, she takes her meal with the skill of a veteran hunter. My daughter is a natural, and my heart pulses with the fires of pride to see it.

I watch long enough to be satisfied with her progress, the plastic taking care of any traces of blood. I will dispose of the desiccated husk later, as I have done with my own meals. Akari is now engrossed in her feeding like a human child lost in a sugary haze of endless ice cream. She no longer seeks my approval, draining the vitality and life of her prey. My sacrifice to her.

I leave her to finish her meal, closing the door behind me. I walk to my favorite chair and take my laptop from the table. I look at my emails, seeing the assignments I must handle on Monday. I try to focus on the work but soon lose interest. It's night and the weekend, with nothing here that cannot wait until the workweek. I check my phone, and I see that Beth has sent me several texts to wish me luck. I quickly text her back that luck is certainly not required. My mind is too full of my daughter now. I cannot even take this tiny window of opportunity to pursue any of my own interests. Right now, I don't even want to. I just think of my girl, in the next room, easily taking her meal.

It is not easy to raise a child, let alone one that society would deem a monster. Akari is a sweet and gentle girl, but the hunger was with her since she was born, just as it was with me. I lectured her, ordered her to be abstemious and not to prey on those around her. I shared my kills with her until the change was irresistible. My little girl was so excited for this night, so thrilled to claim the heritage that was hers for the first time.

I am proud. But I am also worried. There will come a day, sooner rather than later, when she will leave the proverbial web. She will grow and finish school. She will get a job and make new friends. Perhaps she will find a family of her own and I will be a grandmother. Will she take my advice then? Will she want to listen to what I have to say? We're all just making it up as we go along, every mother in this world. We do our best, both humans and monsters. My people are ancient, but there were mothers long before that.

Akari soon emerges wearing her blue nightgown. She appears fully human now, her eyes dark and shining. Her cheeks are flushed apple-pink, her feet padding soundlessly upon the ground. I have years left of this. I will see her to school. I will take her to her friends' houses for sleepovers. Will she play sports? Will she want to join the acting club? The school choir? I must teach her not to prey on her schoolmates until college, to be satisfied with the meals I bring home that we will share together.

There are no guides to being a mother. I am captaining a ship to an unknown destination, hoping only for the best while I navigate the choppy waters. Akari smiles at me, hopeful for praise for a job well done. "Can I sleep with you tonight, Mama?"

I almost tell her that she's too old for that. I need my space and privacy sometimes. But she is my daughter, and my life is full of sacrifice and compromise. But at this moment, I wouldn't have it any other way. I send Beth a quick message, telling her what a wonderful night we had and how proud I am of my daughter. Though Akari was unplanned and unexpected, she is neither unwanted nor unloved and she must know that always. "Of course, honey," I murmur, wearing a smile to mirror her love back at her. Privacy is just another sacrifice I make this night upon the altar of motherhood. But she has done so well, I cannot refuse.

The corpse in her room might inform my decision, admittedly. I'll deal with that tomorrow. I've gotten very good at disposing of corpses. It's not exactly a skill one puts on a resume, but stupid monsters seldom survive long.

"You did wonderfully, little blossom." I love to tease her that her red and gold pattern resembles a flower. Her face is alight with joy as it ever is with the nickname. "Bed in five minutes. Mama will sing to you."

"Hug first?" she asks, eyes wide. I know exactly what she wants and open my arms for her after adjusting my shirt to let my body change. "I love you, Mama!" She rushes to my embrace, received by me. It is a tableau repeated throughout untold ages. Civilization may be ancient, but there were mothers to hold their daughters long before that.

"I love you too." My words are the tender reflection of my heart, no less tender for being pushed through a mouth unsuited to speech. My mandibles click together in something akin to a human lullaby. I pull my little Akari close, deciding on the song I'll sing her to sleep with as she is wrapped within my arms.

All eight of them.

About the Author

Zach Rosenberg is a Jewish horror and SFF writer living in Florida who crafts horrifying tales by night and practices law by day. The latter is even more frightening. His works have been published in various magazines and anthologies, including Seize the Press and Dark Matter Magazine. His debut novella, *Hungers as Old as This Land* was released by Brigids Gate Press, and his upcoming books will be released by Off Limites Press and Darklit.

BAR

THE LAST DAYS OF MONSTER PARK

BY BERT S.G

They leave Dracula Three in the desert to die, and I'm just sitting here, sucking down bottles in The Tomb, trying to pretend I don't feel a damn thing. None of the regulars have turned up yet, so it's just me and Bernice and the TV above the bar, and beneath her rasping coughs the newscaster sputters on about "the last days of Monster Park." Bernice reaches up with one bandaged finger to roll the volume down. I take another swallow and think about Dracula Three, twisting and screaming, burnt up like a rag under the endless sun.

"Probably for the best," Bernice says. A cigarette rolls between her lips, two orange smears stained around the gauze slit of her mouth. "After that stuff with the Blood Blob kids. Poor, ugly bastards."

I shrug. Those kids were a fucking menace, but what does it matter? Everyone hated Dracula Three, and now he's gone. The circle is closed. Time to worry about bigger, messier things.

The news takes a break and we get a commercial for the newest hit show, *Teen Mummy: Boy Detective*. Bernice snorts and sneers. I hear dust rattle in her lungs, centuries of derision. "Look at that putz. All that plastic, all that schlong. They call *that* a mummy?"

"Yeah, well..." I find my legs. I slide up from the stool. "People love a good monster. Till they don't."

She asks if I want another, but I have to finish my rounds. I weave through the empty tables and up the steps. Bernice hollers, "Chin up, Harv. You did the right thing," but I push straight through the door like I didn't even hear.

So: Monster Park. You know about it, right? A monster gets caught, they have to send it somewhere. Big Monsters get sent to the island. Little Monsters get sent to the park. And this is where we all live. Several thousand acres of mid-century aluminum, surrounded by hundreds of miles of sand and shrubs, our own little slice of heaven carved into the radioactive hellscape of the great Mojave Desert. Out here, the whole sky is a sun, brilliant and unyielding, a single sheet of fire that kisses the horizon on all sides. I'm sure if you make it far enough you'll find some kind of fence, sharp and electrified, probably even some heavy artillery on standby. None of us have ever attempted it. None of us knows. See, we're all happy here, give or take a few notables. Beneath these sizzling rooftops, between these sherbet-colored walls, we've made a home for ourselves. A community. And, for many of us, we've found the one thing that eluded us in the human world. We've found a sense of peace.

So my job is, I'm the park manager. Kind of a sheriff of sorts, I guess, only there are no real laws here and everyone pretty much minds their own. Every now and then there's a problem that needs to be solved, some repair work comes up, or a long-simmering conflict calls for mediation. That's where I come in. Most days, the job is pretty cake. I make my rounds, check in on folks, get the gossip, maybe come home with some free drugs or a plate of home-cooked food. Other times, the weight of it is crushing, just grinds my bones to dust. I take it home with me at night and pour it all out on the bed and wallow around in it, eyes open, back throbbing, until morning creeps in, and it's time to get back on the clock.

Like with this Dracula Three thing. But we'll get to that later.

I don't know how I ended up with this gig. I'm not the smartest, I'm not the toughest, and I'm certainly not the oldest. Fact is, us Wolf Men age in regular people years, so while I'm well over the hill compared to most humans, put me up against your average haunted skull or wandering ghoul, and I'm basically still just a wad of unshot sperm. We've got Frankensteins and zombies and prehistoric lizard men; we've got alien brain slugs and sentient mists that exist in 4D space. Who knows how old any of these creeps are? Think about mummies. Like Bernice, man. She's older than any of us. The joke is they built this whole park around her. For all I know, it could be true.

Anyway, it's a real melting pot. Lots of faces, lots of stories. Not a whole lot in common except for one thing: we're all monsters, and we've all done monstrous shit. And now we're here, making a new life for ourselves in this pile of old trailers and dying mesquite trees. We have cookouts and craft fairs and yard sales; we go to bingo night and self-help meetings and weddings and funerals. We lie awake with each other and stare into our ceilings, stare into the sand. We dream of an existence unburdened by the past. We mourn for lost time. We anticipate the future.

We've been living here happily for a long, long time. So of course they want to destroy us.

What happened was this. Me and Dr. Fly and Jimmy the Giant Eyeball were down at The Tomb, maybe about a week ago, drinking ourselves to pieces and just feeling good about life in general. Now, The Tomb isn't an actual tomb, although I can see why you'd picture it as such. The Tomb is an old in-ground shelter house, basically a box of concrete planted in the dirt, one of several scattered around the park in the event of a tornado or dust storm. Years and years ago, long before I ever got here, Bernice claimed one of these spots as her own and turned it into a private lodge, sort of a VFW hall for monsters. Only rule for membership is "Don't Piss Off Bernice," which tends to keep the clientele pretty exclusive. Me and Doc and Jimmy, we do our best to stay on her good side.

So we were there, and so was Bernice, and whatever garbage was on TV got interrupted by a very loud blast of breaking news. Seems a Big Monster escaped from the island, some kind of shrieking, centipedal nightmare, and every city on every continent was raising its fist in high alert. Necks bulged against ties on the UN floor: THIS IS A NIGHT-MARE FOR DIPLOMACY! Spittle-drenched mics at the global press conference: ARE AMERICA'S MONSTERS OUT OF CONTROL? Domestic protestors and foreign ministers were united in rage. Mean-while, the creature had yet to be located. A smiling newscaster promised to keep us informed of the ongoing crisis.

"Good on him," Bernice said, but Doc and I shared a look, and I could tell we were thinking the same thing: *Monster Park is doomed.*

See, any time some monster-related disturbance upsets the balance of peace, the pressure mounts. America needs to take DECISIVE AC-TION, they say. America needs to get TOUGH ON MONSTERS. How else can we set the public's mind at ease?

Thing is, Monster Island is safe. No amount of grandstanding and tough talk will ever change that fact. Big Monsters give America leverage on the global stage. Big Monsters operate as a strategic reserve. The threat of our country unleashing a Big Monster attack keeps the rest of the world in line, keeps the wind blowing our way. If the government wants to get tough on monsters, make some grand gesture to soothe the international psyche, they won't start with Monster Island. They'll start with the noise in the closet, the shadow in the lake, the thing under the bridge that eats goats. They'll start with Monster Park.

That's when the phone rang and I got the news. Bernice handed the receiver to me across the bar. I could hear screaming before it even touched my ear. It was Blood Blob Mom. Her kids were missing. Something horrible happened. It just *had* to be Dracula Three, it just *had* to. I handed the phone back and ordered three shots, one for me, one for Doc, and one for Jimmy.

"Where ya going?" Doc buzzed.

I grabbed my hat. I put it on. "Guess I'm working today after all."

I tell you I'm a Wolf Man and you know: I've done some bad shit in my time.

I'm not proud of my past. This isn't a weird brag. I'm not going to embarrass either of us with details or excuses. Let's just say I've hurt a lot of people. Some of them deserved it. Many of them didn't. And the hurt wasn't always physical—I've torn just as many hearts as I have throats. It never felt good, but I couldn't control it, and I couldn't escape it. That part of me was always there, that monster part. That wolf. I was ashamed of what I did, of who I was. And that shame terrified me, and that terror angered me. And that anger brought the monster out, over and over again.

Then Doris came along. For a while, things got better.

Sometimes, I think about writing to her. Check in on her life, see how the kids are coming along. Tell her I'm sorry for all the pain I caused her, all the wreckage I left behind. Let her know I'm all right. Tell her things are good, lie to her, make us both cry. But I never quite pick up that pen. What would it matter? There's no mail service out here in the park. Besides, she'd probably just throw it away.

Not many of us come here voluntarily. Most are caught mid-rampage and brought in by force. It wasn't like that for me. I knew the only way I could stop hurting people was to leave them all behind. I had to remove myself, either by bus or by bullet. I chose the bus, and the bus brought me here, and I've been working on myself ever since. Talk therapy, group sessions, meditation, lots of journals, lots of weed. I've gotten to where I hardly notice the wolf anymore. But I know he's still in there, and I never let my guard down. I never stop doing the work.

Blood Blob Mom was a wailing mess when I finally got to her. I could see her billowing through the porch screen, sloppy, gelatinous heaves. It took the better part of ten minutes to get the story out of her: the kids were gone, they left on their bikes the night before, they never came home. She was convinced Dracula Three had gotten to them. I tried to be reassuring. Maybe they'd been out stealing freon from air conditioners all night? Wouldn't be the first time. Maybe they stayed late blowing up jackrabbits with homemade fireworks? I don't know. Those Blood Blob kids, they were always up to no good. But my own words failed to convince me. I knew she was probably right.

"I'll go pay him a visit," I told her, but it wasn't exactly that easy. See, you don't just go walking into a Dracula's home and start raising hell. You've got to be invited. That whole "vampire code" thing, it actually goes both ways; they can't come in unless you ask them to, and you can't drop in on them unannounced. For an ageless crew of undead parasites, they can be pretty uptight about the rules. So I had to get the other Draculas to do my dirty work for me. Since it was still daylight, there wasn't much else I could do. I made a sweep of the neighborhood, scoped out the usual places, poked around Dracula Three's overgrown yard. Came up with nothing. I steered my cart back to The Tomb and used the phone to leave a message on Dracula One's answering machine.

If Bernice made an expression under her mask of clay skin and bandages, I couldn't tell. She passed me a beer and said, "Troubles, Harvey?"

I sucked foam through my whiskers. "Fucking Dracula Three. He finally did it. He finally ate the Blood Blob kids."

Dracula Three also came here voluntarily. He'd been a musician out in the world, back in the sixties, pumping out a string of monster-themed novelty hits. Songs like "Do the Drac" and "Bloodsucker's Ball." You remember that stuff. Everyone does.

For a hot minute, he was on top of the world. Talk shows, groupies, sponsorships. But the mood passed, as it always does. The public grew bored of him, then turned on him, and after that he was just another monster. Dracula Three saw what was coming and he didn't like it. Rather than face an eternity of hunting and hiding, he dropped out of the scene and settled here in the park. That should have been his happily ever after. It wasn't.

The other Draculas took him in, tried to show him the ropes. Took him to events, introduced him around, did their best to make him feel welcome, to feel accepted. Only that wasn't good enough for Dracula Three. He didn't want to adapt. Didn't want to let go of the old habits. Didn't want to do the work. Everything was a problem for him: the blood rations, the heat, the crowded conditions. I mean, that shit sucks for all of us, but we're in this together, so we've got to make the best of it. Dracula Three didn't think so. He started to self-isolate, started to lash out. Floating around windows at night, picking fights at parties. We tried reaching out because that's what we do. But there are only so many times someone can flap their giant wings and hiss at you and spit blood in your face before that spirit of goodwill dissipates. After a while, even the other Draculas pulled away.

Looking back, what happened seems inevitable. Dracula Three's monster-ness was a threat to the park, to the balance we had struggled so hard to maintain. How long before we were corrupted by his influence, by his refusal to change? No one was talking, but everyone felt it. It was in our voice at every meeting, in our matched gazes, our shared laughter, at the bottom of every glass. All of us thinking the same thing: *Dracula Three is doomed.*

This thing with the kids had been building for a few weeks. Dracula Three vanished for a while, went off the radar—then reappeared, like some kind of malignant fog, creeping around the edges of the park, watching the playgrounds, lurking in vacant lots. Always with the Blood Blob kids nearby, either not knowing or not caring that they were getting skeezed on. Now, these kids—and I shouldn't call them "kids," really, because all three of them are old enough to get dusted and clear out a party with their shitty freestyle rap game—they're just large blobs filled with blood. Clearly a guy like Dracula Three is going to have certain thoughts about that. Blood Blob Mom had been lighting me up to do something about it, but the fact was I could never catch him in the act. All I was getting was a bunch of hearsay through the phone receiver. Dracula Three obviously wouldn't answer the door when I knocked, and those damn kids would just call me "dog dick" and throw rocks at me from their bikes every time I tried to ask them about it.

So I blew it off. Figured the situation would eventually fizzle. I think we already talked about how I'm not always the smartest guy in the park.

Dracula One caught up with me shortly after sundown. Told me he and the other Draculas would look into it.

Fast forward twenty-four hours: Doc and I were back in The Tomb, falling into this black hole of a news report about the ongoing threat of monsters in America. Congress would meet soon, the news explained, to discuss what to do about it. What to do about *us*.

A call came through and Bernice answered, "Harv's office," before handing me the phone.

"Vee found zee bikes," Dracula One said. "In zee trailer, zee bikes."

"Ah, shit."

He said the four of them—Draculas One, Two, Four, and Five—stopped by for an impromptu visit. Figured the direct approach would be best. He didn't act surprised to see them, didn't try and make a run for it. Just let them in like it was any other day. And right there in the kitchen, stacked between the sink and a TV tray piled high with crossword magazines and old IV blood bags, were these three bikes. Dracula One said they noticed them right away, he hadn't made any effort to hide them. So Dracula Five was, like, *You seen those Blood Blob kids lately?* And he just broke down. Didn't admit it, didn't deny it, just started crying, sobbing out all his torment, and he told them to kill him already, to go ahead and get it over with, go ahead and let it all end.

Each word of this conversation made my headache progressively worse. By the end, there was a void of pain behind my eyes wide enough to drive a fist through. I pressed a finger to my temple and began to rub. "This is a problem," I said.

"Vee take care of eet?" There wasn't any breath on the other end, just voice. "You vant?"

Overhead, Bernice had switched from the news to one of those old cowboy movies, the kind where people lived in the mud but no one ever got dirty.

I told him, "Just make it go away. I don't care what you do. I just don't want it to be a problem anymore." I hung up the phone and pushed it over so hard that it fell next to Bernice's feet and shattered all over the floor.

On the TV, one cowboy shot another cowboy, and the shot cowboy fell down dead.

I swallowed bourbon until I didn't have to think anymore, and then I was back home, I was in my bed, and Doris was there waiting for me, as always, reaching out from that eternal space where memories breathe and burn.

What happened between us wasn't her fault. She thought she could tame me, and I thought domesticity would cure my wildness. Keep the beast away, once and for all. I wasn't always a Wolf Man, see. No one ever starts out that way. You always get turned by someone, somewhere, and then the lifestyle takes over, and you just get worse and worse. Blood on your hands every morning, the kind you can't ever scrub off. Echoes of screams, rattling behind your eyes, a shame-soundtrack that follows you everywhere. Always wondering what you did. Always worried if you'll do it again.

Doris wasn't worried about all that. She could see the man I was before, said she felt the goodness in me. She really believed that shit, and she made me believe it too. She was so beautiful. Big ass, giant eyes, kind smile. When I think about her, I always remember her fingers, the way they felt against my forehead, against the back of my hand. Just the lightest touch would soothe me. I would have followed her anywhere. I gave her three good years before I started killing again.

And so I came here. And I've thought about her every night since. About the gap in her teeth and our little house behind the bowling alley.

I wonder if she still stacks produce at that grocery store. I wonder if the twins are giving her hell. I wonder if they remember me, if they ask about me, and I wonder what she tells them when they do. Does she say I left so that I wouldn't poison them? So that they'd have a chance at something better? Does she tell them I loved them too much to stay? Or does she stay silent and let the memory lapse, exorcising me to nothing more than a spectral awareness, something warm and lost that nudges them in dreams?

So, here we are, back at the start. I'm leaving The Tomb, and then I'm in my cart, I'm making my rounds. The day recedes behind me. The usual folks are in their usual spots: Gill Man, cooling off in his wading pool; Skeleton Family rising from their graves for the night; Spider Lady, rebuilding her web from the evening before. Everything is where it always is, where it always will be. Existence continues unperturbed. I know this is all bullshit, but it feels comfortable, slides on like an old pair of slacks. We're all fine here, just fine. No surprises. No conflicts. No regrets.

I hear the kids before I see them. That grunting, pig-snort laughter is impossible to mistake. The wheels under my cart turn to wet concrete and slowly churn to a stop.

The whole world catches in my chest. A single dot swells at the end of the road, draws closer, divides itself in three. If this were a movie, right now the camera would do that cliché zoom on a panicked face while the rest of the scene stretches out beyond sight, beyond reason. The dots assume shapes, features, names.

BLOOD. BLOB. KIDS.

Their voices reach me, but I can barely hear them over the roar of veins bursting in my head.

"Dong blower!" one of them shouts. "Stop looking at my ass, dong blower!"

"I'm not a dong blower! You are! You're a dong blower!"

I whip the cart around, blocking the road. They barely even acknowledge me enough to stop.

"What are *you* looking at, dog dick?" the big one sneers, and the smaller ones snort in admiration.

I let out a growl—a *real* growl, full-throated and fierce, a sound that hasn't passed from my belly to my lips in decades—and they stop cold. No one in the park sees this side of me, this monster side. A little peek behind the mask is all it takes to set these little pricks at full attention. I gather them into my gaze and hold them there.

"Where have you been?" I ask them. "Don't fucking kid me. This is a serious question."

The three of them look at each other, as if sharing a thought. After a pause, one of them hands something over to me. A cassette tape. I squint to read the label. I feel like I stepped through a hole into another world. None of this seems real. The handwriting is splotchy, the ink has smeared. But I eventually focus on the words *Blobbin' N' Knobbin'*.

"Demo tape," the big one says. "Been working on it for days."

"Demo tape?" I don't even recognize the voice coming out of my mouth.

"Yeah, we're gonna be famous rappers. Set up a studio in one a them old shelter homes. Just been chillin' down there, droppin' beats, spittin' bars."

"Studio?"

"Yeah, Mr. Dracula helped us out. Been hanging with him a lot lately. Dude knows his shit."

My teeth, grinding.

"Mom says to keep away cuz she thinks he's a chomo, but he's not. He just hates talkin' to people."

My fist, clenching.

"Anyway, he let us borrow some gear, but we hadda leave our bikes with him as collateral."

The tape, bursting into shards.

"Yo, dog dick, what the *fuck*—?"

And then I'm howling, pouring everything into it, the past, the future, every second of every year that I've been trapped in here, trapped with myself, trapped in this park, bursting every stitch that ever held me together, that ever bound me to this world, all of it, all of it pouring out of me, out of every crack and seam, every life destroyed, every face forgotten, all of their pain comes up through me, screaming, *screaming*, and that sound is bottomless, it has no end, it shakes the desert, shatters the windows, an echo of the whole world caving in on itself, crushing us, ending it forever, and it keeps coming and coming and coming until I'm raw and ripped and weak and empty.

That night, the Draculas come.

I'm washing my skivvies in the sink, trying to talk myself out of running, just hopping in my cart with a can of gas and taking my chances in the wild. I could dig myself a cave and break off from polite society forever. No conversations, no complications. Just unlimited sand and the sweet release of starvation. Then I hear a familiar knock at the door and I think, *Oh, good, maybe they'll just kill me. Save me the effort.*

Instead, they bring a tape. And some beers. I grab my old boom box from the rumpus room and kick open a few lawn chairs for us.

They tell me Dracula Three left a bunch of recordings behind. Apparently, after retreating from us, he retreated into himself. And his banjo. And while the rest of us wasted energy wondering what sort of crazy shit he was plotting, he was busy pouring his heart into homespun ballads about the high, lonesome, vampire lifestyle. Dracula Four thought it would be hilarious to sit around and give them a listen. I figure, *Why not?* and pull a fresh can from the box.

Only there isn't any music on this tape. Instead, after some garbled audio hiss and a cluster of pops, Dracula Three clears his throat and begins to speak.

"Once people decide you're a monster, there's no going back. Sure, sure, they always say they WANT you to change, but really they don't. I mean, think about it... Once you change, they have to adjust the narrative they've established, and that takes effort, right? You're supposed to be the one working, not them."

That first beer goes down fast, real fast. I reach for another. The Draculas lean in close.

"And what's it matter anyway? There's always gonna be some ancestor of some villager who comes crawling out of the woodwork, raising a red flag over you about some shit they know nothing about, probably has no effect on their day-to-day life, just so they can keep sucking their own dick about how righteous they are.

"Sometimes I just want to scream at everyone here, you know? It's like, why bother? Your reputations are sealed, man. Your fate has been determined by groupthink and microaggressions. Why keep pretending? You ARE the monsters! Just BE the monsters! I mean, I came out here so I could be around other monsters, and I'm STILL the only one. Still all alone."

He goes on and on like that for a while, but you get the gist of it. The tape spins out about five beers in and ends with a sudden click. We ease back into our chairs and sit in silence, staring into that watercolor sky, turning words over in our minds.

Finally, I say, "He's wrong, you know."

Dracula Two is nothing but eyes, two floating red specks that shudder with laughter. "Congress begs to differ, my friend!"

"Eh, who cares what humans think?" My thumb traces a seam in the side of the can, pushing a thin trail through the condensation. "Their brand of assholery is set in stone. We've gotta change for *ourselves*, see. Otherwise we're just proving them right."

"Yes, vell..." Dracula One rises, stretches his back, and waves for the others to join him. "Tell zat to zee ashes, ah-ah-ah!"

You always expect a crash of thunder or blast of white smoke, but it never comes. One second, you're surrounded by Draculas, laid bare and helpless under their ancient eyes. The next, *gone*, just a mechanical chitter and a puff of tiny wings, disappearing into the night. And then you're alone.

And that's all there is. No ending, just waiting. I kill the remaining beers and stare into those twisting sands, into that great desert of un-knowing. Will they really pull the plug this time? Or will it turn out to be more bluster, just something to occupy the airwaves until the next Great Outrage comes along? If so, how will they do it? Gas us? Bomb us? Cut off our rations, try to starve us out? Good luck with that. Some of these guys have been around for literal centuries and need absolutely nothing to survive. Maybe they'll bring in one of the Big Monsters from the island and force them to trample us or spray us with atomic fire. That would be poetic. Part of me hopes it goes down that way. Just one giant lizard, tears in his eyes, committing a final, damnable act of violence in hopes of getting kicked up the social ladder a notch. Good job, buddy. We're real proud of you. Here's a really large medal. Now get back to the island with the others.

A breeze whispers loose, dragging my empty cans across the dirt. I watch them rattle away and I think about Doris. I think about the twins. I wonder: do they understand? I wonder: do they worry?

When I was little, I had a pet toad. It got caught in the window well one spring and I rescued it. I was probably four years old at the time, not older than five. There were these older kids in the neighborhood I used to play with, and one day I decided to show this toad to them. I was so proud of myself for nurturing that thing. It was the first time I really loved something.

I won't tell you how that story really ended. I don't like to think about it too much. When my head goes to that place now, I lift my arms to them, I open my hands. The toad takes two bulbous breaths and hops away. I chase after it and the other boys don't follow, they can't come with us, they'll never have their chance to pour the cruelty of their world into me. The toad keeps hopping, keeps leading me, and I follow it, my tiny legs pumping, my heart drumming with each kick. I am crying, I am sorrowful with joy. And it pulls me away from that world, from this world, from the person I became, from the monster that I know.

About the Author

Bert S.G. grew up in a trailer park, escaped to the wild, and survived several decades as a painter, musician, and troublemaker. He currently spends his days herding cats and hoarding VHS tapes in the greater Kansas City area.

ANY
COMI

His Little Helpers

by Alex Wolfgang

Frigid gales swept through the village the day of Julaften, but they did little to deter its residents. As they had each year since the festival began, the older folks spared no efforts in making the day as special for the children as they could. The scent of candied nuts wafted from wooden bowls. Echoes of bells sunk into snowbanks. Most of the young ones had been sewn new coats, hats, and gloves, leaving only their puffy red cheeks exposed to the wrath of northern winter. Anders thought little of the cold, even less of the day's pleasantries. His mind remained fixed on what lay ahead.

When the gloaming made way to night's swallowing darkness, the festival's most crucial tradition began. In a procession marked by torches and nervous chatter, the adults led the children to the edge of the forest to see them off.

Anders's hands sweated in his gloves, but they remained steady. While the other kids basked in the festive atmosphere, he steeled himself to find answers to the question that had burned so long within him.

The night before, he'd slunk from bed at the sound of his mother weeping from downstairs. She'd been just visible from the banister. A huddled mass on his father's lap, her yellow curls obscured what must have been a tear-soaked face. His father grimaced and patted her on the back, making futile comforting sounds as she tried to stifle her wails. Dim light from the fireplace cast dark valleys of shadow on his face.

"We'll never see him again," she choked out, "and it's all our fault."

His father had no response. Anders watched and waited. He rubbed at the little bump on his head, the one his mother told him came from being dropped as a baby. It always itched when he was anxious. Moth wings fluttered against the walls of his stomach.

Anders was old enough now to understand some things. To be Julenissen's little helper was noble, but perhaps dangerous—tearing through the countryside in a goat-led sleigh, delivering presents before morning, sneaking into strangers' homes with their parcels. Their fear was well-founded. But everyone he'd asked had said he was no more or less likely than any other child to be chosen.

His heart pounded against his ribs as he tried to focus on his task, tried to search his mind for answers.

No adult had ever helped him. He'd tried. Asking his parents only upset them. He'd stayed after church one day to ask his pastor, but it only resulted in a bland retelling of the story of Julaften.

"But what makes us different?" Anders asked. "Why do we go into the woods each Julaften? That isn't in the storybook."

Pastor Hansen responded first with a tense smile. He glanced around to see if the two were alone before proceeding, but the church had already emptied.

"The villages in Fjærringer have a special relationship with Julenissen. We are in the far north, and Julenissen needs a child to help him deliver the gifts as he moves south. One day soon, he'll choose a member of our village to be his little helper."

"Has anyone from our town ever been chosen before?"

The old man gave him a strained smile and took time to think, as though deciding whether his own memories were to be trusted.

"No, but he has chosen children from other towns, and we're quite sure that he will visit us very soon. Any year now, I would say."

Hansen said nothing further, but Anders had many more questions. He'd wanted to ask why Julenissen needed a new helper every year, why he hadn't picked any of the kids in their village for so long, and why they needed to go into the forest to find him. And what about the younger children, the ones who watched with glassy eyes as only those born his year set out each festival? Hansen sent him away before he could press for more answers.

Now the time for departure had come, and despite his determination, cold fear trickled into his blood. He did what he could to ignore it. As he and the other children lined up along the wall of dense trees that partitioned the woods, he clenched his lantern in his fist and gritted his teeth. Yes, his mother was right. It would be him. He wanted to be chosen despite her constant worry. Even if pursuing a greater purpose meant leaving his life behind, he would make her proud.

The adults watched, fear and excitement in their eyes—more so, it seemed, than in previous years—as the kids set off. His mother buried her face in her father's shoulder. His father could scarcely meet his gaze. They hadn't said much to him that day, but their expressions spoke volumes.

They think I'm weak, he thought. *They've always thought I was weak.*

Always pulled from school at the slightest cough or queasy stomach. Always doted upon for weeks when he felt the least bit melancholy. He never felt more fragile than the other children. No matter. Tonight, he would prove them wrong.

As he made for the woods, the blanket of snow and the dense trees soon drowned out the mix of weeping and cheering from the adults, and Anders found himself alone with his lamplight and the darkness. The other children existed only as spheres of yellow that dissipated as they set off in different directions.

Within moments, his solitude was complete. The surrounding abyss was that of the night sky—silent, still, black, eternal. His breath and pounding heart filled his ears with nothing to drown them out. He sought something, anything external, but the trees and snow sucked away distant sounds as they emerged. A buzzing insect. A hooting owl. So quiet, he couldn't be sure if they were real or in his mind. With each step deeper into nothingness, his determination receded further. All he could do was focus on his light. He let it guide him deeper into the forest's void.

The lantern soon flickered, pitching him fully into darkness for the longest moment he could imagine before returning. He nearly cried out and dropped it. The orange glow was weak, but it was all he had. It offered solace in each step, even if the one following was always in question.

Something cracked beneath his foot and he stifled a wail. Just a twig snapping under his weight, yet he couldn't shake the image of a broken, cast-aside human bone. When another cracked, he imagined himself stepping through a forgotten cemetery, one where nobody had bothered to dig the graves and bodies lay rotting until the black void left only skeletal remains.

This was no place for Julenissen. No place for joy or life. It was a sick inverse of the festival. The adults had tricked them with warmth and joy. Had they lied about Julenissen too? He remembered now why he'd never made it farther than a few steps in previous years. The mind could shut this place out when he wasn't immersed in it. Now there was no escape.

Time dilated. He sought the moon through the spindly treetops, but not even the stars offered guidance. He could have been walking for ten minutes or for hours. Tears leaked from his eyes, furthering the fuzziness of his lamp's glow. They threatened to freeze on his cheeks.

Panic rose, a building pressure with no release. He closed his eyes, drew in a slow breath, and held it. Eyelids still squeezed shut, he tried to place himself elsewhere, somewhere sunny and warm. In a far, southern city surrounded by people. For a moment, it almost worked.

As if drawn in by his fear, a sound emerged behind him. A huffing breath, labored and thick. Anders trembled, afraid to pry his eyes open.

It isn't real. I am alone.

Eyes bored into him. Breath continued steadily, heat emanating from its source. Moist clouds of vapor caressed his skin, thick with the stench of decay and rot, of animal fury and curiosity. The heat drew him in instinctively, offered respite from the icy night. When he was too close, the abhorrent odors rushed through his nostrils and made him kneel and retch. Anders finally opened his eyes and flailed his lantern about. His light illuminated nothing but surrounding snow and trees.

He was overcome with the desire to run back home, but he didn't know which direction he'd come from. He'd never made it this far, this long. From his pocket he pulled a small compass and illuminated its face with his lantern. The dial spun erratically, deciding three different directions were north before reversing course and seeking it out again. Anders shoved it back into his pocket and kept moving in what he hoped was the right direction. It didn't take long to lose his nerve again, and he chastised himself for it, but it couldn't be helped. He hoped his mother was wrong. He no longer wanted to be chosen. He wanted to go home, to leave some porridge for Julenissen and be done with it.

A burst of glacial cold slipped beneath his glove, too abrupt and aggressive to be natural, and Anders dropped the lantern into the snow like it had been pried from his fingers. It extinguished. He whimpered, then went silent, listening again for the labored breathing.

It soon resumed—it had never left.

His lips formed a word his voice couldn't muster: "Julenissen?"

Ingrid hadn't stopped crying since Anders walked into the forest. She had prepared to never see her boy again, but it didn't make it any easier when the time came. It had gotten more painful each year, but now it was no longer a rehearsal. Bjørn did his best to comfort her, but he had nothing to offer. They sat before a crackling fire in their living room.

"Can't we stop it?" she sobbed, knowing the answer. "Can't we fix this?"

"No." Bjørn lightly rubbed between her shoulder blades. "I don't think so."

He'd done his best to remain silent throughout the years. There were never any fair objections for him to raise, even if each look into his boy's foreign eyes destroyed a little part of him. It could have destroyed their relationship, but he never stopped loving her. He even came to love the boy too. After all, it wasn't the boy's fault nor Ingrid's. For nearly a decade she'd searched for a lost part of herself, the woman she used to be, and he felt it his duty to help her find it. Even if he didn't know how. Even if it wasn't possible.

While Ingrid wept, he shut his eyes and watched the milky-red fire dance through his eyelids. He thought back to that Julaften when he'd found her in the stables. The horses were spooked, all lined up against the walls and patting at the loose wood in fits. His wife lay on the ground, screaming inconsolably, covered in blood and dark, matted hair. Was the blood hers? Was it human? He never knew. He carried her inside and cleaned her up, held her until she exhausted herself of tears and finally slept. She couldn't remember how it happened. She hadn't even glimpsed her assailant. But her clothes were untorn, unremoved, and there was no pain where there ought to have been. Even so, she sensed the stirrings within her almost immediately.

The town bells had rung early the next morning. Every door was smeared with blood—some claimed to see a pattern in it, something like a goat's head. They all knew what it meant, though they'd prayed they wouldn't see it in their time. The pact had been broken. Their protection was over.

The men met in the town hall that day, but no one confessed. Bjørn remained stoic. He knew that it would do them no good to know it was Ingrid. To kill the thing inside her would kill her too. And perhaps that... thing... would return for vengeance.

The blood marks didn't fade for a year. It didn't matter what they scrubbed them with. But on the next Julaften, they were gone.

Twenty-five babies were born that year, more than any year prior. Each one of them was inspected carefully after birth, but the town doctor could never pick out the black sheep of the bunch. Little Anders was perfectly healthy, perfectly normal, so much so that Ingrid and Bjørn began to doubt their own memories of that horrible night. But deep down, they knew.

So much went unspoken that year. Both Ingrid and Bjørn could see pain and anguish on the faces of their neighbors but, feeling they were the cause of it, said nothing. Pastor Hansen decreed every baby born behind a blood-smeared door was under suspicion. When the sign was gone, however, they all but gave up their search. Hansen said there was only one way to proceed. If no one would confess, they'd have to send them all and let the beast find his child on his own.

Anders had no choice but to follow the sounds of whatever lurked in the darkness. Slowly, his fear faded, and he sensed something enticing about the presence. Something not-so-malicious as he'd initially thought. If the beast wanted to kill him, it could have done so easily. Instead, it was guiding him somewhere. Perhaps to Julenissen.

He followed it for another hour, taking short and careful steps through the unseen trees. Eventually, he heard other sounds, saw faint glowing in the distance. Splintered twigs and crunching snow from all directions. Whimpers of curious fear. Then, dead ahead, a yellow sphere flickered on the horizon. Fascinated, he walked toward it as it cast a dim glow on his surroundings. Other children's silhouettes moved toward the light. They staggered as if they saw God in it, intoxicated by its power. Like it was a spring of fresh water and they hadn't drunk in days.

When he was close enough to make out the licking flames and shooting embers of a fire, he also saw the cabin behind it. An ancient-looking thing nestled in the forest, its details so obscured by darkness that it appeared ethereal. A gangly, hunched figure stood beside it. The beast's horns thrust upward, reflecting the glow. Its fur shone black. Its mouth twisted into a grin, exposing gray teeth. It beckoned them closer. The other children closed in together, and he fell in step with the crowd. Their expressions ranged from terror to awe, but the promise of warmth, light, and an end to their journey was too much to resist.

Something human lay hiding in the thing's eyes. Something loving, inviting. Anders felt the last of his fear trickle away from him. Warmth radiated from the beast, this time not just its rank breath. It opened its maw and trumpeted a soft cry like an elk in heat, a sound Anders had heard before in a distant memory or some half-forgotten dream.

The children came together around the fire, then fanned out in separate directions. Anders continued toward the cabin, following where he was called. The others were instead fascinated by stretches of firelit forest that looked to be unoccupied, but they made their approaches to nothingness with the same reverence that he did to the beast. As if they could see something there he couldn't.

He approached the thing, trembling not from fear but from an almost religious psychosis. The pupils of its eyes darted back and forth as it gazed at him, wet with human emotion and an unmistakably feral ferocity.

"Julenissen?" His frozen lips barely formed the name.

The creature leaned its long head backward, hacked up something like laughter. Anders felt it should frighten him, but he instead found it infectious. He laughed too, his numb cheeks coming to life.

It raised a hairy paw toward Anders and lightly caressed his cold face with the back of an ink-black talon. There was a spark of familiarity in the touch.

He looked around at the other children. All were facing away, transfixed by whatever was before them. Couldn't they see that Julenissen was right here? How could they expect to be chosen if they would not even look at him?

The creature bent and examined the boy closely. It shifted its head up and down as if measuring his body. Apparently satisfied, it lifted its talon to the top of Anders's head, plucked off the cap, and probed around in his hair. It caught on something—the little bump that had been there all his life. The talon punctured a hole in his skin and, with a gentle tug, the beast pulled downward from his scalp, making the boy's head buzz.

Flesh split apart down his face, unzipping like a jacket. He knew it should have terrified him, but instead it felt victorious. He was being chosen. His parents would never see him as fragile again.

In the last moments he could still use his eyes, he saw the other children being unzipped by unseen forces. He wasn't the only chosen one. This might have bothered him before, but as his steaming insides emptied onto the forest floor, melting the snow at his feet, there was too little humanity left within him to care.

Ingrid couldn't be sure she'd slept at all, and when dawn broke the next morning, there were no more tears left in her. She and Bjørn did not speak as they prepared breakfast in a rehearsed routine. They did not know what was next, what their fates held in store for them.

These worries were short-lived.

Joyous sounds drew their attention. Distant laughter—both young and old—echoed through the early morning air. They looked at each other, then rushed to put on their coats and boots to investigate.

The bright dawn had brought with it a miracle. As they followed the sounds, they glimpsed joy in the other adults' faces. Dread and hope battled in their minds. Had they not yet noticed Anders's absence, or were they too caught up in the relief of their own child's return?

But then a familiar face made their hearts soar. When they reached the edge of the forest, Anders emerged with a self-satisfied grin. While Ingrid rushed to scoop up the boy in her arms, Bjørn quickly counted the children. They must have returned together, for all twenty-five were present.

Fear melted away. They didn't understand how it could be possible, but they didn't care. The texts were wrong. The pact hadn't been broken after all. Perhaps the beast was more forgiving than they'd thought.

Bjørn looked at Anders's face, *his* boy's face, as if seeing it for the first time. A part of him felt ashamed for thinking ill of his origins for so long, but the pleasure of being wrong overpowered the shame. Mixed with triumph and joy, Bjørn also saw forgiveness in his eyes, though he knew there was no way the boy could have known how he'd been perceived all his life.

Bjørn didn't see the tuft of dark hair sticking out from the boy's belly. When Anders returned home and undressed, he folded it back in under his skin. He hoped the others hadn't been so careless. Less than a year remained before the next festival—the final festival—and there was much work left to do.

About the Author

Alex Wolfgang is a horror author from Oklahoma City. You can find his work in Cosmic Horror Monthly, Nocturnal Transmissions Podcast, and the anthologies *Howls From Hell*, *Bloodlines*, *Collage Macabre*, and *Fiend in the Furrows III: Final Harvest*. When not reading and writing horror, you can find him drumming, hiking, playing tennis, and watching movies with his wife. You can follow him on Twitter @alexwolfgang, on Instagram @alex__Wolfgang, or visit his website:

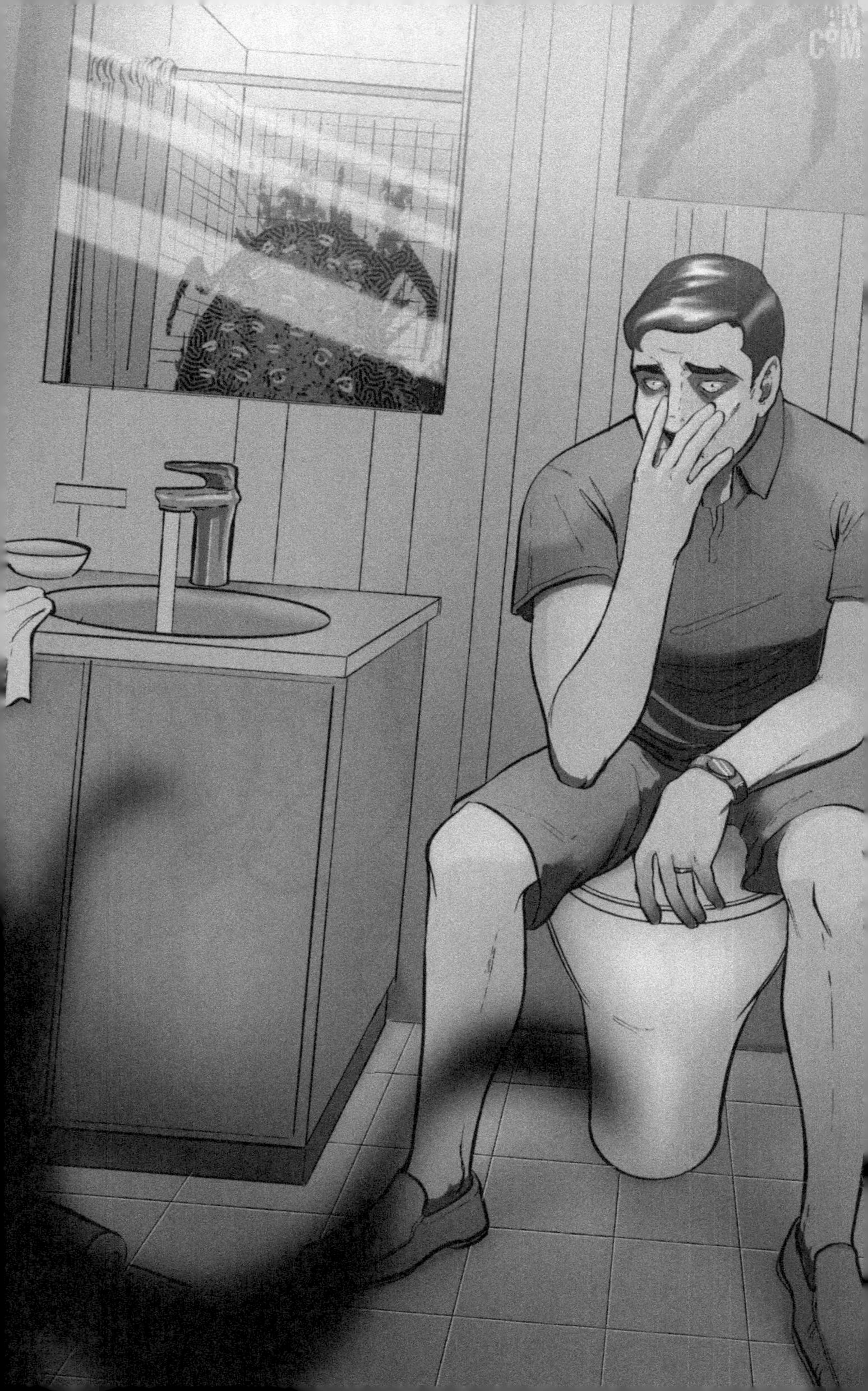

MOUTHS TO FEED

BY T.M MORGAN

The boatsman, his skin burned orange from a lifetime of sun, manned the outboard motor. The elderly couple huddled mid-boat had faces that could have been expressing ecstasy or terror. As if reading the husband's mind, the boatsman pointed and shouted, "There. It is the resort." The line from his finger and across the water terminated at four abnormally tall palms, conveniently forming an A and a V.

Terrance felt stupid for not seeing them before. "The ride across the bay is longer than I expected," he yelled back to the boatsman.

The man nodded with a trained smile.

"Terrance, oh my God, it's happening. I think I forgot my..."

The wife, Letitia, sat in the kind of elegant posture only a woman with six decades behind her could, even with the rambunctious boat beneath them. She placed her hand on his leg so he could clearly see it. But Terrance lost track of her words before looking down because he already knew what he'd see: an almost imperceptible two-inch slit lengthwise on her wrist. No blood. As thin as a strand of hair.

"Did you—" But at the moment he spoke, he jostled and tipped precariously over the side of the boat as it hopped and bounced across the open, choppy sea. Letitia snagged his jacket at the collar to pull him back.

"Good Lord," he said, righting himself. "I thought I was going in." His wife tensed beside him, and her face locked into a grimace of pain.

"I left it at home. I'm sorry."

His gaze fixed on the expanse of water still to go. He couldn't get it out of his head that sharks hunted here.

He turned from his place on the wide patio. "We have to—"

She put out her hand. "Please, Terrance. This will be the last time I can enjoy myself. You'll take care of it? Like you always do, my love?"

A breeze like warm water flowed from the bay and made his skin tingle. Eight floors below, the open restaurant and bar shot live music upward, an exotic threesome of drums and off-kilter stringed instruments. But nothing felt right: the resort, the bay dotted with small islands, this moment with his wife. *The last time,* she said.

"Yes, of course. I'll handle it."

"You still love me?"

"Always." He kissed her with a gentleness that came from four decades of marriage. "Let's get something to eat."

"Perfect. Can we use the dancing bit? I'm so weak anyway. And it's the only way I can get you to dance."

"Of course," he said. "Whatever you need."

The open-air restaurant bustled with people. It wasn't ritzy—string lights hung from the rafters—but it was cozy. With evening on its cusp, the sunset was one of the most beautiful things Terrance had ever seen. It was as if every anxiety and fear melted away. He was weightless. The steady roll of waves on the beach mesmerized him.

"Thank you," Leticia said.

He offered a half-smile that only grew as he looked at her. "What choice do I have?"

Her chin had a buttercup glow from the candle set between them. "Still. I know you're probably thinking 'How could she forget again?'"

He didn't say that he had a hard time hearing her with the other, over-lapping conversations and clanks of plates and glasses. So, he nodded. Maybe this was heaven encased in isolation—no worries to drag down the soul—and this small moment could exist forever.

The bar area filled, guests talked loudly, booze flowed, and people began to gesticulate when they spoke. Two women took hands in a small, open area. They spun in a traditional waltz though there was no music. Leticia squeezed Terrance's hand, and he led them to the floor, and they too waltzed to an imaginary "Blue Danube." *Da da da da-da, bum-bum bum-bum.* He hummed the melody quietly at first and then let it grow until it seemed everyone at the bar joined in, the choir gaining strength with each phrase. His cheeks went flush.

She collapsed on cue. It looked as if her energy had drained away, and her legs buckled. Terrance tried to hold her upright, but she was droop-ing in his arms; and then he muttered, "Oh, God," and she muttered unintelligibly back. A young man at the bar wrapped his hands around her from behind, pulled her to a stool, and looked into each eye as she smiled back.

He turned to Terrance in a way that implied secrecy. "Her eyes are dilated."

Terrance stammered. "Well, she's... we'll—"

"They probably are," she said and placed a warm hand on the man's cheek. "I'm okay. It's the medicine. I get a little tired sometimes. And I had a drink."

The man put two fingers on her wrist, all signs of the slit now gone. His focus snapped into place. "Your pulse is thready. We should call—"

"No. I just need to lie down." She removed her hand as if backing it away from a flame. "Can you help my husband? My legs are still wobbly." Now she leaned to the man and implied this was also secrecy. "He still thinks he's thirty."

The other guests, who had stopped the boisterous singing, watched with quiet concern and nursed their cocktails. Night had come fully; bits of starlight lay speckled across the calm sea.

"I suppose so, yes," the man said.

"Thank you. You're kind to help."

"Of course. Now, each of us to a shoulder?" The man dipped himself under her right arm leaving Terrance to take the left, who shrank down as they trekked along the winding path to the hotel's back lobby doors.

In the elevator, the man said, "I'm going to get my bag to check your vitals. Can you manage the rest of the way?"

"So, you're a real doctor?" Leticia said. "I thought you were just playing up the part for my benefit."

"A surgeon. I do cleft repair surgery for children in the orphanages here. My fiancée's arriving tomorrow for a needed vacation."

"Oh, look at you." She poked his arm. "Such a good man."

He stepped off at the fifth floor. "Just doing my part. What room are you staying?"

"804," she said.

Once to their floor and inside their room, with the king-size bed facing the open patio, Terrance helped her head fall back onto the pillow before he flicked on the bathroom light and stared into the mirror. The husk of the man looking back terrified him.

"Are you sure?" he said.

"He's perfect. And without—"

A knock came at the door. Terrance opened it, and the man entered with a movie prop of a doctor's bag: black leather with a wide, foldable opening. He retrieved a stethoscope, pulsometer, and blood pressure cuff.

"What is it?" he said.

Leticia pushed out her chin. "Pancreatic cancer."

"I'm so sorry." He slipped the pulsometer on her finger. The man was precise, each movement like that of a concert pianist. "How's the pain?"

All the digits of her left hand showed. "Five out of five."

Outside, poolside guests erupted in laughter. It didn't fit the room, and Terrance pulled the glass doors shut.

"Dear, can you get this young man some water?"

Terrance noticed how close the doctor sat to her, his thigh almost touching her ribs. After he stepped into and then back out of the bathroom with glass in hand, the doctor waved him off.

"No, thank you. I'm good. I'd suggest not drinking the tap water."

Leticia laughed softly. "Always a doctor!" She gripped his collar and yanked him toward her face, lips pursed as if she might kiss him. But her mouth went to his ear.

"Can you do me a favor?" she whispered.

The doctor's eyes shifted from left to right—from Terrance *there* to the woman grasping him *here*.

"What is it?" His voice was on the verge of quivering.

"Only one thing. I want you to take my husband down for a drink. Don't let him say no. I don't want him shuffling around here while I rest. He needs to have some fun."

"What if he doesn't want to?" The doctor glanced over his shoulder at Terrance.

She gazed absently through the patio doors. "I only have a few months left before I'm stardust. It makes me more curious than ever." Her mouth brushed his ear. "Have you ever wondered what causes us to meet the people we do? Is it random, or is it fate? Terrance and I met on a jungle road in Vietnam when I was twenty-two."

She waved her hand as if giving some authority to the story. "Meet one person and your life changes amazingly; meet another and it goes horribly astray. How is it that we met tonight, the sickly old lady and the young doctor at The Alta Vista? Please, for a dying old woman, do me this favor as if you were meant to do it."

The doctor shrugged. "I helped someone in need. No mystery to that. But I'll do it."

Terrance threw open the patio doors and walked to the railing. The doctor, surprised by the outburst, nearly fell off the bed from spinning around.

"He needs a drink badly." Leticia poked the doctor in the ribs.

He followed Terrance to the railing. "She asked me to take you down for a drink." He was taller than Terrance: built, with a prominent chin. The shirt's collar came to a fine, sharp edge. "A round of Macallan on me. The twenty-five year. To new friends." The doctor smiled with impossibly perfect teeth. "Honestly, I'd enjoy the company."

Terrance looked at his wife. Her head still reclined at a forty-five-degree angle; her curled hair bunched at her temples; her hands lay limply at her side; and her eyes pleaded with him *to go*.

"All right," he said to the doctor. "Maybe make it two."

"Great! Let me swing by my room first and meet you down there?"

In lieu of an answer, Terrance shrugged and led him to the door.

"Much appreciated," Terrance said. "See you in a few."

Once back by Leticia's side, he heaved a too-long-held breath and gripped her hand.

"I don't want to do this."

She placed a warm hand on his cheek. "You know what will happen. Wanting has nothing to do with it. If we had the syringes, we could—"

He shot up. "You haven't done this in a long time. It never crossed my mind."

"Well, you'll need to improvise. You used to think that was the best part." A nostalgic smile turned up to him. "And think about if you don't."

"Of course. At least I brought my pills. I love you." He kissed her on the cheek with her head held delicately by his hands.

The bar had morphed into its nighttime persona—candle bowls every five feet and low, New Age music playing. Terrance sat on a barstool next to the doctor while the bartender poured two glasses. Once he had his Scotch in hand, Terrance inhaled deeply with his nose poking over the glass's brim. A lightness grew in his chest. When the doctor leaned forward to tell a joke to the bartender, Terrance, in a sly motion, tore open a small baggie and dumped white powder into the doctor's drink.

"To new friends." The doctor turned and raised his glass.

Terrance clinked and took a slow sip that trickled across his tongue, causing his eyes to close from the perfection of it. Every thought wiped away leaving only a cloud to envelope him.

"It must be hard," the doctor said too loudly. "When was she diagnosed?"

Blurs of crystal light crossed Terrance's vision, the reflective effects of a newly stirred disco ball. "It's been—my God, I never thanked you. How can I repay you? I don't even know your—"

Before he could finish, a young couple arrived with a baby and caused a stir from a group near them at the bar. Wrapped in a pink blanket, the infant looked to be no more than six months old, her skin so much darker than the people around her that it shocked him. But, as if the little one possessed magical powers, once in their presence, the group gathered 'round.

"We wanted to say goodnight before she goes down," the mother said, leaning forward so that everyone could see the little thing in her arms.

The baby girl herself dozed. Terrance couldn't follow what else they were saying. Observing, however, he saw the physical closeness of the group—bodies touching, hands on backs and shoulders—and surmised the two sets of older people must be grandparents and the others maybe siblings and spouses. The mother passed her baby, and then one by one, each took a turn to cradle the tiny creature with delicate care. The doctor stood behind the last young man to get her, with the baby nestled into the crook of the man's left arm and her legs poking out from his right armpit. The doctor placed his index finger under the baby's big toe, put his thumb on top, and squeezed so hard it almost burst like a grape. The baby screamed so suddenly and so piercingly, the bar stopped. A few, bare moments of silence followed the first shriek as she gasped for breath. The next scream chiseled into Terrance's ears.

"Oh, God, what did I do?" The man with the baby held the little thing out as she writhed.

"Oh, my poor dear," the mother said. "It must be time for her to go down."

As if a secret confessee, Terrance got a good look when the doctor faced him with his temples relaxed, and for the briefest moment their eyes met, and a black chasm opened into the depths of the doctor's skull.

Then a smile erupted, and the man danced a sloppy jig. The young family strolled toward the hotel: the mother cooing, the baby's cries fading.

The doctor slugged back his Macallan. "Another. You deserve it," he said and gave Terrance a brotherly punch to the shoulder. "God, it's terrible what's happening with your wife."

Terrance nodded. "Thank you. That's kind of you."

The bartender set two glasses on the counter. The liquid had an even more golden gleam than before. The doctor motioned for another toast. This time Terrance's swallow went down bitter.

The doctor chatted with two attractive women, leaving Terrance to watch him work, the muscles under his temples tensing when he clenched his jaw. Not a single drop of sweat on him; the sleek hair was of an impossible jet black and the skin mask pulled across his face was like stretched cellophane.

"Have you meth my new friendth?" he said to Terrance with a stoned swagger and turned to the women. "I shaved hith wife earlier."

The women turned their attention to Terrance as the doctor laughed too loudly and bumped Terrance's shoulder again with a fist, this time strong enough to knock him off-balance.

"Righth, my new friendth? Thith ith Therranthe, ladieth."

"Do you shave people often?" the blonde said and sipped her colorful drink.

"You know, I-I think," Terrance stammered, "it's past my bedtime, after all. Thank you for the drinks. And doctor—would you—oh, never mind. Enjoy your night."

When the doctor offered a handshake, Terrance pretended he didn't see, then walked with precision until, out of sight, he weaved through the back patio area. Inside the lobby, the concierge looked up, head moving like a lizard's; the glow of the chandelier lights carried the brightness of a sun. Terrance squinted and hunkered down on his way to the elevators.

Once off on the eighth floor, he dug for the plastic key in his pocket and ran. Inside the room, he flicked on the bathroom light, and Leticia stirred.

"Is that you?" she said weakly.

Stars floated in front of him when he vomited into the toilet. Seated on the floor with an arm laid along the rim, his face hung below the event horizon. It took a half dozen heaves before his stomach settled. After rinsing, he stumbled to the bed, sat beside her, and began to cry.

"What's wrong?" she said and rubbed his back. "Where is he?"

He put his head on her chest. "I can't do this—"

"What? Go get him." Her lips folded back to reveal teeth starting to show their roots. "For me."

He could see the open water through the deck railing and thought of the sharks and how close he'd come to falling in. He and his wife seemed to float together in silence, with her expectant face moving close to his.

Sudden pounding rattled the door. When Terrance didn't move, she shoved him.

"Get that, it's him. We might get lucky."

"Quiet."

"What are you doing?" She swiped his forearm away.

"I'm not letting him in." When she readied to call out, he covered her mouth. "He'll go away. He's not a good one."

She smacked his hand away. "Answer it. He's perfect."

Terrance walked silently to the peephole. The doctor stood on the orange and black carpet with a hand on each side of the doorframe. He leaned forward until a quivering pupil darted in the hole.

Leticia slung her legs to the floor. "I'm coming then."

"No! I'll do it," he whispered back.

Music echoed up from the restaurant and bounded across the court-yard and pool. Time slowed. In its way, the universe trembled. Leticia stood as tall as she had in weeks, her spine locked into a rigid column. A scent like oranges escaped her skin that made Terrance shudder. The doctor knocked incessantly. The same man who terrorized a baby. A bad man. Terrance gripped the handle and turned.

"I shthink—" the doctor said before stumbling into the room. His momentum carried him past Terrance, and he fell at Leticia's feet.

"Get him in the bathtub." She unzipped her dress, letting it fall to the floor. This left her in only panties and bra. Up her left leg, the one facing Terrance, a blue vein bulged from ankle to hip, with two-inch fissures in a perforated line along its length.

He pulled the mumbling doctor by his heels into the bathroom. The body drooped going over the tub side and, since it couldn't lay flat, it instead crumpled at the middle. The head rested against the back wall, and the feet twisted into the space between the spigot and handles. The chest rose and fell with the slimmest of motion, barely a slow wave. Terrance folded the arms and brushed back the hair, which felt surprisingly soft on his fingertips.

"I'm sorry, but you're going to have to be awake for this."

The man stirred from finger flicks to his cheeks, with eyes sprung wide and moans of desperation rising in his throat. A cool night breeze blew in when the bathroom door opened. The doctor squirmed upon seeing what walked through.

"Monther!" His breathing stopped and caught in lurches.

Terrance shook his head forcefully. "Look around you, doctor. Look in the mirror. Every day... monsters. Who are you to judge? My wife didn't ask to be who she is any more than you did. It's out of our control. Now, this will be extremely painful. I'm so sorry."

The thing that had been his wife staggered in and nudged Terrance to standing. Its skin was covered with what at first looked like too-large chicken pox scabs. Then the mounds parted to reveal piranha-like teeth and stub tongues waggling within. Its actual mouth took the entirety of the face, the other features pushed into folds of skin. The area between its legs spread down the inner thighs and disappeared inward like the entrance to a cave. Once Terrance saw that all was in its proper place, he shut the door and walked to the patio. The bar sent up bursts of laughter, and the outside dance floor swirled with lights and people. Youth and joy. He remembered such days.

The door burst open, and she emerged barely able to stand. Water clung to her hair. Nothing remained of the mouths. It was only Leticia left naked and weak. He ran to her. Watery footprints marked their path to the bed. The green and lavender comforter exploded with dark blotches. When she grasped at herself in spasm, her hand left a water smear down her belly. He folded the wet comforter over her naked body.

"He wasn't a good one," she mumbled and gave a knowing smile, then waved him off. In the bathroom, the tub—other than showing a few ringlets of blood—was empty. He used bleach wipes from his luggage to detail the crannies. After an hour's worth of elbow grease, the tile was spotless to the naked eye.

"See, you do always plan ahead." She strained to see him with her head pushed back into the pillow.

"I bring them everywhere. Now, we need to get packed and ready to leave in the morning."

She jerked as if he'd slapped her. "I don't want to leave! Don't take this away from me, Terrance. You'll figure something out."

He interlocked his hands and paced. "I think this place is heaven too. But you know he won't be enough to—"

"No! I want to live, not wait to die at home. I want to taste until I can't. Please, for me."

He raised a hand. "I will do whatever you want."

"I'm sorry," she said. "I forget that you still have fears too."

He pushed open the patio doors and strolled to the railing. In the low moonlight, the bay looked like boiling tar. Air filled his lungs. *Forty years,* he thought. Of course, he'd do whatever she asked.

The next morning, the lobby bustled with people. Leticia's excitement at getting the extravagant breakfast buffet—caviar, cava, Italian cured meats, a long table of fresh fruit—almost made Terrance forget the young doctor. He loved to see her beam, the stunning sunrise lighting up her face. The bay churned with whitecaps. On the beach, a few people lay on towels, the women's tops thrown to the side. The view seemed to mesmerize her.

But as they sipped coffee after eating, her body went into convulsions. Not enough to draw eyes to them, but Terrance immediately jolted to see her hands grip the table as if trying to crush it in her fingers. Crippling pain showed on her face. A mouth appeared instantly—no initial slit, no slowly moistening lips—on her wrist. The little thing split open and showed its chomping, hungry razor teeth. He clamped his hand over it. Blood oozed between his fingers when it bit into his palm.

With as much grace as he could muster, he stood, took her by the elbow, and led them toward the hotel lobby, only to see the manager, standing in red trousers and a white jacket with gold buttons, trying to calm a young woman whose voice crept louder with each word. Terrance couldn't hear any of it but knew immediately who she was.

"It's the fiancée," Leticia whispered behind clenched teeth. Her eyes watered from the agony coursing through her body.

A path diverged into the surrounding jungle, one of the half-dozen guest walkways. With Leticia hobbling beside him, he veered down the darkest path. The mouth bit a second time, this time sucking down a chunk of flesh. Pain like a live wire shot up his arm.

"It's the cancer," she muttered. "I'm so weak. I can't control it even with the meal last night."

"I know. We'll figure it out." But even as he said this, another mouth formed on her neck just above the collarbone. It opened and closed clumsily like a fish mouth.

"I need it, Terrance. Please. I'm so hungry."

They stepped onto the soil, and their feet sank toe-deep into the jungle mulch. Large, heart-shaped leaves brushed their legs as they made their way to a thick patch of undergrowth. She shivered and sat with her back against a trunk.

"Get that fiancée," she said. "Her life will be misery anyway. It's for the best."

"I'll try," he said, on the verge of tears.

On the path back, he wiped his hand with the handkerchief in his pocket and then balled it into his fist. If he kept it wrapped tightly as if gripping a baseball, the quickly saturated cloth stayed out of sight.

When he reappeared at the hotel's back patio, the fiancée stood alone. A rush of anxiety darkened her face. When he approached, her eyes were wild.

"Ma'am, excuse me. I couldn't help but overhear earlier. You're looking for your fiancé? The doctor, right? I had drinks with him last night. I might be able to help."

It took her several seconds to bring him into focus. "What? Yes, please. No one here believes me. It's not like him to just—"

"We should hurry. I saw him go into the jungle last night. That way. That path."

Her eyes narrowed. "What did he say last night? How did you end up talking? Why would he wander off?"

Terrance held her elbow and began to lightly guide her toward the path. "He was drunk. I only talked to him for a bit at the bar. Excited to see you, I know that. Kept on about getting some fresh air and finding some ruins nearby. I was going to head that way this morning anyway."

He skillfully kept her walking until they were at the edge of the jungle. "I had a scare with my wife once, and it turned out she'd gotten lost in a cave. No worse for wear. Have hope that it's just one of life's bloopers."

"Yes, you're right. Show me the way."

Her footsteps on the wooden walkway clanked behind him. The jungle now looked horrific; caws and chirps rang out in a shrill choir. He ducked when a red bird swooped above them. The air thickened with humidity. Sweat coated his neck. He let her catch up to keep an eye on her. She looked feisty, like Leticia when she was young—eager to hold her own in the world.

"How far is it?"

"I think only a half mile or so. It's on the brochure."

The spot where he'd left Leticia approached on their right, and the thick clump of growth stood out. Leticia ripped through the fronds like a leopard, down on all fours and leaping forward. The mouths chomped with wet, sucking sounds. The fiancée froze, her finger pointing forward, and her legs beginning to take her backward. But Leticia was on her with speed, slurping the woman's head into her wide mouth and swallowing her screams. The other mouths latched onto the arms and legs and held them tight, and then the same with the torso. With Leticia's body arched over and bent at the knees, the crevice between her legs began to slurp up the woman's legs. The tiny mouths on the body sucked like ticks, draining blood until the woman's skin turned gray. The head popped off inside Leticia's mouth, and the rest of the body disappeared up the cavernous hole. Only a few drops of blood spilled on the walkway.

Leticia stumbled to the ground, the mouths fading until no blemishes were left. Her face realigned itself. Terrance swatted the large leaves and searched for her summer dress. It lay where he'd originally left her, the zipper down the back split open but otherwise intact.

"She was pregnant," Leticia said as she fell back against the tree trunk. "We did that fetus a favor."

He nodded, but his hands trembled. Even as she spoke, a mouth appeared on her breast, gaping open where the nipple should be. The air's thickness stuck in his lungs. He knelt and kissed her forehead.

"I love you."

"I love you. You'll know what to do, my love? Like always?"

"Of course," he said.

A grapefruit-sized rock made of cooled lava lay against the tree trunk. He snatched it and struck her on the temple, ready to follow with blows until her skull cracked open. She lay unconscious with a flow of blood that ran down her cheek and across her lips. Mouths popped open across her skin. The odd, local music flittered through the trees, sounding so far off it might be miles away. Terrance stood and staggered toward the hotel.

The manager was on the back patio when he returned. Terrance strolled past him with his gaze fixed on the horizon. At the dock, several boatsmen waited in their crafts of varying sizes. One, long and covered, a water taxi, took up one side of the dock. Two smaller ones floated on the left. The same boatsman who carried him here waved.

"Sir, you go to mainland?"

"Yes, that sounds good."

The bay offered a hard chop, sending the boat high atop each wave. Terrance kept a firm grip on the side while his chest thumped.

"Are you enjoying your stay? Where is your wife?" The boatsman still talked in his pitchman's voice, eager and pushy.

"She loves it here," Terrance called back. "I don't think she wants to leave."

One of the water taxis passed, the seats filled with local children. They hooted and waved their hands, broad smiles on their faces. The boat seemed too small, too many of them on it. Terrance pictured it capsized, their shouts replaced by terrified screams as the water bubbled red. But they continued speeding across, two dozen or more of them. It was their turn, he thought, for whatever awaited them at The Alta Vista.

About the Author

T.M. Morgan has other work published in Vastarien, Lamplight, podcasts at The Wicked Library and Sley House, and in the upcoming anthology *Vinyl Cuts* (Scary Dairy Press). He lives in southern Maryland near the Chesapeake with his wife and children.

TINY
COMICS

TAKE MY HAND

BY CHRISTIE HANSEN

I'm visiting the neighbors when a big splash comes from above. My salamander friends flit fearfully amongst the pond weeds of my garden, none longer than my finger. I tell them not to worry as if they can understand me, and look up toward the canopy of withering water lilies and fallen leaves that filter the sun on the surface of my swamp. I am unsurprised to see the old, leaning birch on the shore has finally surrendered, but something else is there amidst the bare branches. It is the silhouette of a body. My heart races, but the figure sinks slowly, arms and legs still, and I blow sad bubbles. My first ever visitor, and it is dead.

I kick off the bottom, leaving my little cousins to their feeding, and a flick of my tail curves my path to approach the tangled branches from what used to be below. I dig through the gnarled mess until I reach the body. I think it might be human and give its ankle a lick.

Yes, definitely human! And even better, it convulses and gags a torrent of bubbles. It's alive! I've never met a live human in person! The closest I've ever come is the taste of the water that comes downriver. I wonder where this one came from. Their nearest lair is days away.

I extricate my surprise guest from the sinking tree and rocket them off to the little island in the middle of the pond. I'll deal with the debris later. For now, I spread the human out on its back. It twitches and jerks like a cricket in a web, and I lean in to search for what's wrong with it. I may know little about them, but humans can't be that dissimilar from trolls.

The human is small and skinny, only as high as my chest. We are both widest at the hips, suggesting it is female too. Oh, I hope it is! I hope we have lots in common.

It has no tail, and its arms and legs are stubby. Its skin is the deep brown of good loam, but if it has any patterning, it's hidden under a faded black dress and pale blue apron. I swallow a laugh, for I am the inverse: vibrant black and blue, and wearing an old leather tunic.

The human's face is bunched up like a baby, with a mouth so small I wonder how it eats anything bigger than a tadpole, and its unfocused eyes dart like firebugs. I hunger to learn more, and loom over it as its breathing steadies. Cold water drips off my hair and onto its cheeks.

Its eyes focus on me, widen, and its breathing quickens again. I blanch, becoming conscious of the fact I've been doing chores all day and haven't so much as washed my face. I must look absolutely dreadful, and dive back into the water to preserve some mystique while I claw the knots out of my hair. I resurface when I am as presentable as I'm going to get, stopping just when the water is lapping beneath my eyes.

The human is sitting up in a shivering ball. I frown. Is it that sensitive to the temperature? Sure, the autumn frost has been creeping over the pond in the mornings lately, but I won't start feeling it until the winter freeze sets in. Is human skin that much thinner than ours, or are they just big babies about the cold?

The human has noticed my return and is staring. I bob in the water, watching it watch me. Hesitantly, it raises its head and emits a series of pleasant but meaningless sounds from its mouth. I gurgle and croak a greeting, but human ears must not be sophisticated enough to comprehend trollish tongue, for it just stares more.

I am at a loss until it uncurls itself and haltingly crawls toward the island's edge. It's making the first move! I should have done that! My heart quickens, and I dart forward to meet it. Gray clouds paint the calm surface of the water, offering me welcome concealment as I come to a stop an arm's length away, looking up at my much smaller visitor. It offers me a shaky smile, and I return it, the corners of my maw peeking above the surface. Its eyes dart again, and its smile falters. I am blowing introductions!

This is my swamp. As hostess, I need to take the lead. I raise my hand out of the water, palm down, fingers spread, and offer it to the human.

They meet my eyes, looking uncertain, but bend down and briefly press their lips to my knuckle.

I huff, blowing bubbles at the human's rudeness. I realize I'm flubbing things a bit, but I've done nothing to warrant such a cold response.

The human jerks back, clutching their hand to their chest. I huff again! The audacity! Are all humans so ill-mannered? This one seems properly shamed by my snorting and finally extends its hand for a proper greeting. Palm down, fingers closed. That's a bit of an overcorrection, but graciously, I accept it.

The human is indeed female, and from the communal lair up the river. She is also back to being extremely rude, screaming and thrashing about on the little island as she swaddles her bleeding stump in her apron. I roll my eyes and chew, sheering flesh off of bone with my first row of teeth. I tuck the meat into a cheek pouch, grind the phalanges between my molars, and the blood trickles down my throat; a feast of information. We are close in age; I taste the drought of my fourth winter deep in her calcium. She works often with herbs and was picking them before she fell in my pond. Blackberry plant is sharp on her fingertips, and chamomile is embedded deep in the grain of her palm. Her blood has a subtle, sour tang. She had a cold a few weeks ago, but is in good health now. I roll the elements of her around my mouth, each movement yielding more details of her life.

Nothing yet to explain her surliness, though.

I offer the big baby my hand to eat again, and this time she kicks me! I nearly spit out her finger fragments and retreat further out into the water. She flails around on the island, continuing to scream, and I have had enough. Being a good hostess does not mean I have to suffer this humiliation or abuse. I swim to the main shore, toss a biting comment about manners across the water, and head into the undergrowth. I have work to do.

It's already past midday, and cloudy in the first place. A chill breeze puts a sharp edge on the homey smell of composting leaves. I shed my irritation in half-conscious grumblings as I hike my tending trails, and I have pushed the human from my mind by the time I reach the sick grove. The trees here have developed some sort of disease that's turned their wood dark and brittle, and I can't have it spreading. I settle in next to the elderly oak I've been chewing through for the better part of the last week and get to eating.

My guts turn as I get started. Not from the disease; it would be impossible to keep up with my dietary needs if a little wood rot was enough to make me sick. Rather, it's the monotony. I've been working on this grove for weeks already, and I'm not even halfway to my goal of clearing the infection before spring germination spreads the disease further. I wish I had help, but I have no one to call on.

We are solitary by necessity. The balance of earth, leaf, and beast is always shifting, and even two adult trolls sharing territory can quickly cause a cascade. My territory is bountiful, and I am young and have only two stomachs yet. But still there have been winters where I tasted a thinness in the flesh of the earth and the blood of the trees, and known that I had to diet through the spring. We are solitary by necessity. Not by preference. Even visits must be few and brief, and so their quality must be superb.

I have been preparing for years in anticipation of the honor of hosting a visitor, and when I finally have one, they are a rude, vicious little ingrate.

I have always wondered by what magic humans could afford to live in their communal lairs without desolating the land around them. Now I wonder by what grace they do not tear each other apart.

A chunk of knot catches in my teeth, and I dislodge a scrap of flesh in picking it out. I slap myself on the thighs and rise to my feet. I cannot give up on my first guest so easily. If humans can stand each other every day, they can't be completely uncivilized. They just... have different ways of doing things, surely. We've gotten off on a foul taste, but I can still make this work! I swallow a mouthful of bark and hurry back to the trail. The sun is against me, but I have an idea of what to do.

The human is still on the island when I return, stirring the water around her with a long stick. There's something she's trying to fish out, but she stops when she notices me emerge from the ferns. I give her a big smile and wave to show her what I've brought before slipping into the water. If there's anything that can bridge the distance between two strangers, it's dinner, and I've brought the best my swamp has to offer.

The human scoots to the far edge of the island as I approach, giving me room to deposit my spread. She has torn off part of her skirt while I was gone and bound up her wrist stump, plus a tight band around her upper arm that I worry is cutting off her blood flow. I frown, but remind myself that humans must have their own customs. Surely she knows how her own regeneration process works better than I do, and I made a point of picking foods full of good fuel for regrowing a hand. I lay out yams, half a dozen varieties of mushroom, an entire bundle of okra stalks, and a selection of snakes and lizards. Lastly, gurgling my own fanfare, I present the crowning glory: the big turtle from the southern pond.

The human stares at my bounty, and I beam. She can't decide where to start! She looks to me for a suggestion, and I crack some okra in two. The pods have long since rotted out of season, but the stalks are still nice and crunchy, and I pile half into her lap. She stares as I wrap a snake around one, securing the head by impaling its fangs in the stalk, and down the delicacy in three bites. I gesture with another snake, offering to set one up for her, too, since she's still down a hand at the moment. She waves the offer away and starts to nibble the end of her okra while eyeing the mushroom stack.

Delicately, she prods the pile apart and sorts them with a stick by species. She frowns at me, for what reason I can't fathom. I spear a few from different piles on my claws, and pluck them off one by one: button, conk—she inhales sharply when I eat the dapperling for some reason—and russula. She keeps staring as I take seconds, so I push the rest toward her. She grimaces, but takes a few buttons, swishing them thoroughly through the pond water and wiping them on her apron before taking a bite out of one. She smiles, rubs her stomach, and groans.

I force a smile, but this is a disaster. Why isn't she eating? I snatch up yams and pile them into her lap, snap more okra into smaller, bite-sized pieces even though she hasn't finished her first. I pick up the turtle, my centerpiece. Holding it upside down and making sure she's watching, I give the breastbone a punch. I mean to show off my finesse, cracking the plate open without damaging the shell, but I am panicking now and strike too hard.

The human recoils as bits of bone and gut splatter over us both, and I am mortified. She turns, glancing over her shoulder at something in the water, and I catapult myself over her head to retrieve whatever it is. It turns out to be a large wicker basket, half-sunken and full of sodden plants. Maybe this is what she wants to eat? I snatch it and return to the island, depositing it in front of her and retreating back up to my eyes in the water again in case I've somehow further mucked up.

She stares at me again, as if I'm the inscrutable one here, and babbles something incomprehensible. She spreads her apron over the ground, then digs into the basket with fervor. She sorts the contents over the cloth, gingerly sopping excess water with the corner. Soon she pulls out a small, metal bowl from the basket, and my curiosity overtakes my embarrassment. I creep closer to the island as she mixes bits of different plants and something from a crystalline bottle in the bowl. She produces a pestle and tries to grind the contents together, but the bowl keeps slipping from between her ankles. She grumbles and winces as she tries to brace the bowl with the side of her stump, but nearly tips it over again.

She is turned sideways to the water and is so focused on her task, she doesn't notice me until I tap her knee. Then she nearly throws herself off the other side of the island in surprise. Fortunately for her, my hand is quick, and I catch the bowl before it spills. I pull myself chest first onto the island and hold the bowl out for her. She blinks at me, gradually settles back onto her knees, and begins to grind the contents. Slowly at first, building speed as my grip proves unshakable. My curiosity grows deeper, and I pull myself further out of the water to see what we are mixing.

The mixture has become a watery slurry. I dip a finger in to taste, but the human squeals, so I reluctantly honor her secret until whatever condiment this is has been finished. She takes the bowl from me and looks around, settling her gaze on the root end of the collapsed birch that started this whole mess. She turns to me and points to the tree imploringly. I shrug. Birch isn't my favorite, but if it's what my guest wants to eat, a good hostess obliges. I slip back into the water and return with an assortment of roots, bark, and sticks.

The human discards the roots and peels the bark into thin strips, mounding them up like a bird's nest on top of the remainder. Holding one of the thicker sticks between her thighs, she digs a little knife out of her basket and sharpens the end. I watch her, perplexed at what purpose any of this serves, and only more so when she hands me the sharpened stick. She picks up another, and after a few false starts, I understand that she wants me to roll it back and forth between my hands.

I don't understand, but all right, I guess. She guides the tip of my stick into the nest of shredded bark and holds her face close, alternating between chanting and blowing softly on the scraps while I roll the stick. I frown at the sky. Night is starting to fall, and the human's tone is becoming more strained. She pounds her remaining fist on the ground and shouts at the stick, so I twist faster, so fast that I smell wisps of smoke coming off the bark. I want to stop, but the human gasps and she repeats one sound over and over, slapping me on the leg. I grimace and, against my better judgment, keep going.

The shredded bark bursts into flame. My eyes widen. I shriek, swipe the tiny blaze into the water before it can spread, and the human screams. She hits me and shouts in my face, and I roar back.

Am I supposed to be sorry for saving our lives?

She grabs her bowl and shakes it at the mess of sticks and bark floating away from us, sloshing the contents all over the place.

Did she know that was going to happen? Was that what we were *trying* to make happen? Did she actually *want* to make fire?

WHY?!

She screams again and turns away, hunkering down on the ground with her back to me. She quakes, either consumed by anger or by the nighttime cold that's quickly settling over us.

I grumble and gather up the remnants of my failed feast, dumping it into the human's basket in case she changes her mind later. She snatches one of the yams out and chucks it into the pond, then tries to go back to ignoring me. I give her a disgruntled snort to match her childishness and move in front of her. I point to her and mime a swimming motion. Can she swim?

She sneers and waves her stump in my face, which I take to be a no.

I hand her the basket and, glancing away, she allows me to pick her up. With her cradled in one arm, I catch her eye and take an exaggerated breath. We don't have far to go, but with such a tiny body I don't know what her lung capacity is like. She obliges, but as soon as we dive in I may as well not have bothered, because she loses half of it in a stream of bubbles when I head for the bottom. I guess she thought I was taking her back to shore, but it's much too late to send her off. She can stay at my lair tonight.

It has been a week since Human came to stay with me, and I am increasingly distressed. Her hand hasn't made a bit of progress in growing back. No wonder, as she adamantly refuses to eat more than a few bites of anything I bring her, if she eats at all. Every day I try ranging farther and farther out in search of something I haven't brought her yet, something that will kickstart her regeneration, but all she will eat are the same few specific plants.

She always wants more of the herbs for that concoction we made the first night, though. I help her mix a new batch every evening, and then she slathers it on her stump and wraps it up in a fresh strip of her dress. She keeps trying to get me to take her back to the surface, but it would be reprehensible of me to cut her loose before her hand grows back. Besides, she hated getting down here in the first place.

My home is brilliant. I got the idea from the beaver dens I used to pillage as a tadpole in the nursery valley. Its entrance is at the bottom of the pond, hidden through a garden of water weeds, and its top is the little island in the center. Inside it has three stories, with the living space in the center being the biggest.

Human is making noise early this morning, and I poke my head into the guest room to find her working in her laboratory. She has built several contraptions out of sticks, sinew, and stones that I've brought her, and has used each in one way or another for making her stump juice, but the results never seem to satisfy her. My collection of shiny rocks and neat shells is piled in a corner where she swept them off their shelf fungus displays. The luminescent lichen that shares the nurse logs embedded in the wall now sheds its soft glow on her stock of potion reagents instead. She is sitting on the edge of the bed—layered carpet moss and furs—bent over the log I gnawed in half for her workbench, and muttering into her good hand.

I creep beside her to take a look at what she's doing. Her work always fascinates me, even if I have only the broadest understanding of what any of her devices do. She has the one that spins her metal bowl around in circles on the table in front of her, and a batch of sludge splattered over everything.

She leans into me and drops her head against my shoulder, letting out a distressed groan. I gurgle reassurance and rub the top of her head. Usually she likes that, but she pulls away, looks me square in the eyes, and mimes the fire sticks.

I hiss my absolute refusal. We are not having this argument again. I have no idea what she wants fire for, but I'll have no part in it. I withdraw to the living room, and she follows, chattering angrily and pounding on my back. I collapse onto the middle of the floor and stretch out beneath the intricate pattern of colored lichens that spiral down the walls, following each variety's preferred host wood. Human drops heavily onto my chest, arms crossed, and glares. I throw my hands up. Fire is dangerous. What it touches doesn't grow back. We're having enough trouble getting her hand back as it is, we don't need to risk burning it off forever!

She points from me, to herself, to the ceiling. She wants me to take her outside.

I growl and roll onto my belly, ever more tired of this discussion. But she stands to walk up and down my back, which actually feels pretty nice until she starts bouncing on my butt. I swat her off with my tail, and when she lands beside me, she thrusts her stump in my face.

I look from it to her and blow a defeated raspberry. Fine, but I'm not letting her out of my sight.

Human gulps for air and crawls on shore as soon as we surface. I thought she might handle the trip a little better this time, but she just lies there shivering. I roll my eyes and pick her up. We'll dry out and warm up faster if we're moving. It's bright and sunny this morning, and I nudge her toward one of my foraging trails. I've found a good source of some of her potion herbs near the good fishing spot in the river, so we'll start there.

I use this path frequently, so it's nice and smooth and broad, and easy for Human to follow. She runs ahead, and I casually lope along on her heels, but she tires quickly and settles to a walk with a sigh. We reach the river soon, and I show Human where I found her herbs, then go to gather fish while she forages. The salmon are running, and the river looks more like a scarlet carpet. The banks are rich with those that have exhausted their lives this breeding season, some still plump with unspent eggs when I collect them; a sad, but delicious treat. My basket is only half full when I hear Human shriek in the distance, and I drop it to tear off after her. She must have gotten lost looking for more herbs because she's much farther than I left her.

Our sense of smell is not as sharp as taste, but after a week in my lair, she has picked up a familiar scent. A helpful wind carries it to me. Two familiar scents, actually, though I can't put my finger on the other.

I am swift on all fours and find her in moments, crawling backwards away from...

Another troll! Two guests at once? I can't believe my luck, at once grand and terrible. I can't possibly afford to host a second guest, but then, Human does eat so very little...

Human looks up at my arrival and scrambles behind me as the other troll emerges fully from the surrounding foliage. This is certainly the other scent I was picking up. She is much older than me and much larger. We never stop growing as long as we have enough to eat, and she is a breathtaking behemoth. Nearly twice my height and thick with fat and muscle beneath shiny black-and-yellow skin, and a particular undertone to her scent. I won't be sure until I can actually taste it, but I am very excited if I'm right!

She smiles at me and gurgles hello. She was looking for this fine territory's keeper.

I can't help but squirm at my elder's praise. Drawing myself up to full height, I bow to her and offer my hand. Palm down, fingers together, eager to impress.

She chuckles as she gently spreads my fingers apart, biting off only two with one clean snap.

Human gasps behind me. I shoosh her, cheeks burning. Do not embarrass me here!

The other troll offers her hand, so much larger that I can only handle her outermost digit and have to bite twice to break through her powerful bones. No sooner does her blood touch my tongue than I taste my suspicions come true.

She is family! An aunt from my father's side, down from the mountains far to the north. I cannot contain my joy and bound around her like a hatchling to her laughter.

Human stares, mouth agape, and my auntie turns to her.

Auntie offers her hand to Human, and all the color drains out of Human's face.

I slip between them and tell Auntie about the trouble we've been having regrowing Human's hand, showing her the stump as evidence. It has made no progress at all, and Human won't eat to help it along.

Auntie furrows her brow and tugs Human's bandage off with a flick of her nail. The wound is still sticky. Meanwhile, my and Auntie's fingers have already scabbed over. They'll be regrown within a day or two.

Auntie asks me how much contact I've had with humans, and I confess that this is my first. She nods and asks if Human has tried making fire yet.

I tell her yes. How did she know?

She nods sagely. She tells me that humans and trolls in the north tend to avoid each other, but she knows some things. She says that humans worship fire, and will not eat without first sacrificing a portion to it.

I gawk at Human, who is rewrapping her stump. She looks so small and vulnerable next to me and Auntie, yet her kind tempt death with every meal? Why would they do that?

Auntie shrugs. Humans are strange people, she says, fearful and reckless at the same time. But if my Human will not eat, perhaps that is why.

Human finishes bandaging her stump. I squat down in front of her and, hardly believing I'm doing it, mime the fire sticks.

The three of us spend the afternoon preparing for this lunacy. Auntie clears a spot on the pond shore while I follow Human through my trails, collecting whatever she points at. By the time we return to the water, I am hauling a dozen branches from the sick grove, a sheave of cedar bark, and a basket full of yams, fish, and herbs. Auntie has scraped a wide expanse of shore down to the dirt and built a tall ring of rocks in the middle, and Human sends me back to the lair for her tools while she gets started.

By the time evening is setting in and the light is fading, I am twisting the stick again against a mountain of cedar shavings. Auntie hovers over my shoulder, curious about the process but not wanting to be near it, while Human is bent down, chanting to the shavings.

Auntie asks me if I'm sure about this, which is a ridiculous question at this point. Of course I don't want to do it, but I have to.

I look at Human, fretting over the kindling, hand tapping my leg to speed up, stump cradled against her breast. This is my responsibility.

Auntie nods approvingly, but retreats to the water. She wants to be nowhere near this if we get it working.

I take a deep breath and twist faster. I catch a whiff of smoke and grit my teeth. Human's voice and patting grow more excited. The smoke builds and my entire body tenses, desperate to spring for the pond. I set my shoulders and snarl to myself, twisting as fast as I can while Human blows, digs her flimsy little claws into my leg, twist, twist, twist, and...

There's a burst of hot, orange light at my knees and I launch myself into the water before the twisting stick hits the ground.

Human screams for joy and starts piling the smallest bits of wood into the blaze, gradually building it up larger and larger until it is half as tall as she is. She dances around it, whooping.

Auntie and I are treading water halfway to the island, and I can still feel the heat on my face. Auntie gurgles. This was as much as she signed up for and she still needs to eat more tonight if she doesn't want to fall into torpor before morning. I wish her good hunting as she swims off.

Human gestures for me to join her. I swallow a lump and swim closer, emerging behind her. The heat washes over me, drying out my skin and parching my eyes, but I creep closer for whatever it is she wants me to see.

She has built a pyramid of small logs, open on one side, that roars high and hot. There are yams piled up in its heart, while fish are skewered on sticks set in the ground. To the side, she has gathered a bed of coals, and her metal bowl rests in it with a fresh batch of the herb slurry, bubbling and popping.

The rest of the food we collected is still in the basket beside her, and she makes no move to eat it. Does she have to wait until the fire fully consumes her offering before she can?

She plucks one of the skewered fish out of the ground and, holding the stick between her knees, gingerly presses and squeezes the flesh, then hands it to me.

I turn it over and over. What am I supposed to do with this? Does she want me to participate in the sacrifice ritual? I look to her for an answer.

She snickers and pulls another fish from the fire. She checks it too, then, to my horror, takes a bite out of the belly. I gag, and she scrunches her face and wriggles her toes. In seconds her fish is reduced to bones and she is starting on a second. She catches me gawking, holding my fish at arm's length, and laughs at me.

I flush. Fine! I bring the fish to my lips, sniff it, and give a tentative lick. *Eugh!* It tastes like smoke. But Human is beaming at me, so I force a smile, take the tiniest bite I can manage, and retch onto the ground. All I can taste is the fire overwhelming everything else. I dunk my head in the pond and swallow until the foul flavor fades, and when I come up, Human is on her back cackling. She wipes a tear away and tosses me a raw fish from the basket, which I snap out of the air. I chew slowly, savoring the taste of actual food while I give her and her crimes against nutrition the stink eye.

She stirs the contents of her bowl periodically, and by the time she rakes the first yam back out of the fire, the potion has thickened up into some kind of paste. She sets it aside to cool on the rock ring while she eats the yams, which have turned into something more like the inside of cattail reeds. She offers me one, but I am perfectly happy with mine being properly crunchy, thank you.

When the fire is dying down, Human peels off her bandage and smears the cooled herb paste over her stump. She shows it to me and smiles, finally satisfied with the results. I'm just glad to finally have it done, and she allows me to splash water over the firepit to put it out before we return to the lair.

Auntie leaves in the morning. We're both sad that her visit couldn't last longer, but now that Human is eating, I definitely can't afford to have them both here. We nuzzle a long time, trying to store up enough affection to last until the next time either of us meets another of our kind, and she leaves me with one more tidbit of advice about humans. She says humans are like bear cubs: if one goes missing, a bigger, angrier one is bound to come looking for them sooner or later, and then you have to eat a whole bear by yourself.

Not as boring as eating an entire grove by yourself, but I take her meaning. We embrace once more, and then she continues her southward journey to the ocean. It tears at my heart that I will never see her again, and perhaps Human senses my pain because she holds my arm tight and strokes my hand until I stop sniffling. When I do, she points to herself, and then to the north. Toward the human's communal lair.

I shake my head and hold her stump up to my hand that Auntie ate yesterday. My fingers are halfway regrown, while even with her poultice finally completed, hers is still a stump.

She touches my fingers, points to herself, and shakes her head. She points north again.

I sigh, understanding. Whatever humans need to regenerate, I don't have it here.

I have to take her home.

We build another fire on the shore that afternoon. It's much faster with the pit already set up. Now that I know what she needs, I leave her tending the blaze and her horrible food-burning process while I forage more wood and raw ingredients. On the bright side, fueling these fires has taken a great bite out of the sick grove, and by evening, we have stocked up baskets full of burnt food that Human wraps in hides. She is directing me to store them in the branches of a tall tree by the water for tomorrow's journey when I hear shouting.

I turn as a new human jumps out of the brush with its face scrunched up and an ax in its hands. It snarls at me, and several more burst out behind it, similarly equipped. I rear back, overwhelmed. I'm definitely unable to host this many guests at once, but my human comes to my assistance. She steps between us, arms up, and shouts at the newcomers. They pause and lower their tools. My Human goes to embrace one, a big, muscly one with gray hair on its face.

I look the group over, trying to get a sense for what distinguishes one human from another. They are all the same color, no stripes or splotching to speak of, and about the same size. Their hair and clothes are the most distinct differences, but if I look really closely, I can start to pick out some details. That first one that jumped out has a notched ear on one side. The one to its left has a trio of deep grooves in its cheek. And the one my human is hugging has only one eye, despite... having... two sockets.

The gray-haired human sees my human's stump and starts shouting again. It points its ax at me, but I'm already reeling. It... is it possible... that humans don't regenerate *at all?*

My human steps between us again and all of them are shouting now. She raises her hands again, and my eyes fall on her stump. I taste its echo and my stomach turns.

The other humans go to push past her, but I am already in the water. I dive for the bottom, trailing bubbles. I need time to think, to reevaluate all our time together. I hear my human's voice, muffled by the water between us, and curl into a ball amidst my garden weeds. In time, everything goes quiet, and when I come back up at night, all the humans are gone.

It is a month later. The first snows are on the ground, and on the roofs of all the little dens in Human's great communal lair. I have been lurking around its outskirts for the last week, and have determined that hers is one on the west side of the cluster. I wait until the night is dark and the moon is high before I creep closer, through the streets, up to her door. I push, and there is some resistance, but after a small cracking sound it opens and I manage to wedge myself through.

Any doubt that this lair is hers is overwhelmed by the pungence of dried herbs and old concoctions in the air. The scentual assault leads me to a room on the first floor where the walls are covered in racks upon racks of bottles. There is a large table in the center and one of the humans' foreboding fire shrines in the wall, along with an awesome array of tools and devices. I can only recognize a few by the cruder recreations still filling my guest room.

I start gathering my ingredients, which is difficult both because I'm not used to the size difference, and because I can't smell any of her reagents through the bottles. I knock half a wall's worth of crystal on the floor trying to find and finagle the willow root out of its slot. I freeze, bottle dangling from my claws, and that is how Human finds me when she stalks in with a cleaver in her hand. She stops when she sees me, and slowly sweeps her head around the room to witness the mess I've made.

She approaches the table and looks down at the poultice I've nearly finished but for the burning. She shakes her head, sets down the knife, and shakes the bowl at me to ask what I think I'm doing.

I huff. Frankly, I think I've done a pretty good job, all things considered. I hand her the root powder and load up the firepit over her protests, then go looking for the twisting stick.

She sighs but smiles as she comes around the table, and takes a pair of stones off the mantle. She hands them to me and mimes a striking motion at the firepit. I mimic it, and sparks fly off of the rocks.

Once I've calmed down enough to pick them up again—and she stops laughing—I get the fire going. We wait for the poultice to thicken in quiet, but not silence. She waves from the bowl, to me, to her stump, and throws her hand up. What am I doing this for? She brandishes the stump at me. It's healed over, as far as humans are concerned, which amounts to nothing more than skin forming over the wound. I show her my hand. I amputated it recently, and the new one is only about the size of hers. She frowns, not understanding. That's fine, it'll be easier to just show her. I go back to cleaning up bottles.

When the poultice is ready and cooled, I bring her to the table and have her lay her shortened arm out beside mine. She frowns, but does so. I gurgle, pleased. I estimated well.

I pick up the cleaver she set aside earlier and, before Human can stop me, chop my hand off right below the wrist. She yelps and babbles as it flops on the table. She grabs my arm and reaches for the poultice, but it's not for me. She looks at me, eyes frantic with concern, but I just smile as I take her stump instead, and lift it to my mouth.

She realizes what I'm about to do a moment too late, and I cleanly shear off just the skin at the tip. She hisses in pain and I dunk her wrist in the poultice, then grab my errant extremity. I timed my regeneration just right, and my wrist fits to hers almost perfectly. She struggles, but I hold her still until I feel the ends stop trying to slide apart from one another before I let her go.

She staggers away and wheels on me, fury seething between clenched teeth, and she berates me as if I could understand anything more than her tone. She shakes her fist and wags her finger, only becoming more irate as my smile spreads until she has backed me into a wall. I sink to the floor and she points her finger in my face again, demanding to know what I'm smiling about.

I tap her on what used to be my knuckle, and she gasps. She hadn't realized which hand she was using.

I'm bringing the last cord of firewood from the sick grove home when I hear my neighbors on the shore, and take off running. I am not stealthy at a sprint, and Human is already laughing when I burst out of the brush to snatch her up in a hug. She returns it, arms barely able to close around my back, and I become aware of the other humans with her only once she has let go. She brought Notch Ear and Crushed Leg today. All three are still sweaty from the long walk in the summer heat. Leg is wearing shorts, and rivulets run through the dusty coat that further blurs the distinction between his original flesh and my donations.

Ear is carrying a pack full of flasks and gauze, and Leg's is full of those fluffy blocks humans make by putting pans of slop in their fire shrines and somehow it comes back out solid.

I stuff one in my mouth and chew slowly. The language of the humans' burned food is still a challenge for me. The earth that grew the wheat and the cows who gave the milk are only the faintest aftertastes. But I have learned over these last few years to taste other things. I taste the permanence of the shrine and the patina of the pan. I taste the towel over the proofing basket, and the warm afternoon that raised it. But most of all, I taste the hands of many people who played a part in making it.

Ear and Leg add my cord of wood to the rack outside the cabin, then head inside to put their things away while I settle a comfortable distance from the reinforced firepit, delighted that they'll be staying a while.

Human arranges the bottles and bandages to one side of me, and the bread to the other. I hum happily and take another as she produces a knife and joins my harmony. She has to reopen the incision on my wrist three times before the bottles are all filled and the bandages soaking, by which time it is dark and the bread is nearly gone.

The others have long since fallen asleep beside the fire, too weary to drag themselves the few paces to the cabin, but Human is nestled in my lap, still humming as she ties a bow around my healing wrist.

I chuckle. We both know the gesture is superfluous, but I am full with bread and warmth and happiness. She turns my hand over so it rests comically in her much smaller one and strokes her thumb across my palm. The skin where her hand joins her wrist now blends so smoothly from black to brown that I would hardly know it hadn't always been hers if it hadn't been mine first.

I split the last loaf with her as the fire burns down to embers. Human leans deeper into my chest, her breathing matching mine. In the quiet of the night, sharing the meal between the fire and the water, I marvel at my luck.

I am the first troll to ever learn the taste of community.

About the Author

Christie Hansen is a dungeon master, cookie witch, and emerging author from Washington state's South Sound. She writes queer fantasy with an eye for inclusivity, sex positivity, and rad monster girls.

MeetUP.
The Mothman

SWIPE

BY CM TOOLSON

Lilah clacked her long nails against the wooden desk and sighed deeply. She was bored. Another low growl vibrated from her abdomen, her stomach twisting painfully. Bored and *hungry*.

Her gaze lazily drifted to the smartphone on the corner of the desk. She reached for it, eyes scanning quickly across the neat rows of apps before her sight rested on one brightly colored icon. The dating app. It was how Lilah had procured her last meal. Her thumb snaked out almost robotically to press it open.

Lilah looked with disinterest at the list of men.

Swipe right.

Swipe right.

Swipe right.

She matched with them all; she didn't care. Whichever one of these clowns would get her next meal was all that mattered.

Her swiping finger abruptly halted, lingering millimeters above the screen. This one made her pause—her curiosity piqued. The profile picture was in shadow, only the silhouette of the man visible. He appeared to be wearing a long coat of some kind along with a brimmed hat, but it was the wings jutting from his back that had caught her interest. They weren't shaped like a bird or angelic being, but rather like those of a flying insect. The only color visible in the photo were the glowing red eyes emanating from where his face should be. His profile name simply read "The Mothman." Lilah tilted her head with delight.

Swipe right.

It was only a few minutes before the notifications dinged: **1 New Message**. Lilah opened it and read the simple greeting.

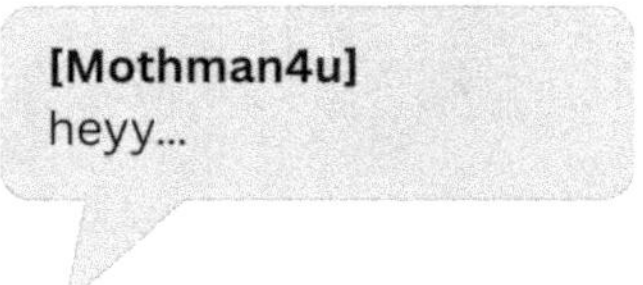

Lilah slowly typed out a response, careful not to let her long fingernails hit any incorrect letters.

Almost instantaneously came the response.

Lilah assumed he was trying to be cute. She hated cute. Contemptuously, she considered closing the app entirely before her rumbling stomach gave her pause. *This guy better not be wasting my time.* Steering the conversation away from the usually dreadful small talk, she wrote:

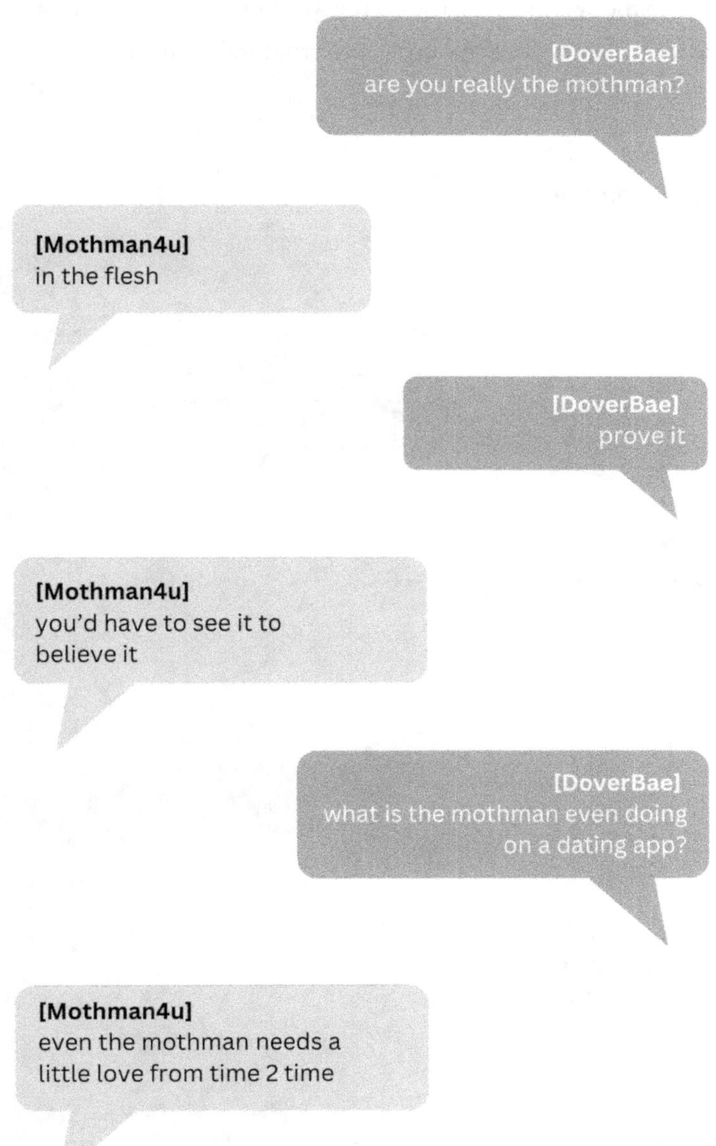

That left Lilah amused. She checked the location on his profile again. Boston, Massachusetts. Less than an hour's drive by car from her. She pulled up the Wikipedia article on the Mothman, quickly scanning over the information written about the preternatural creature.

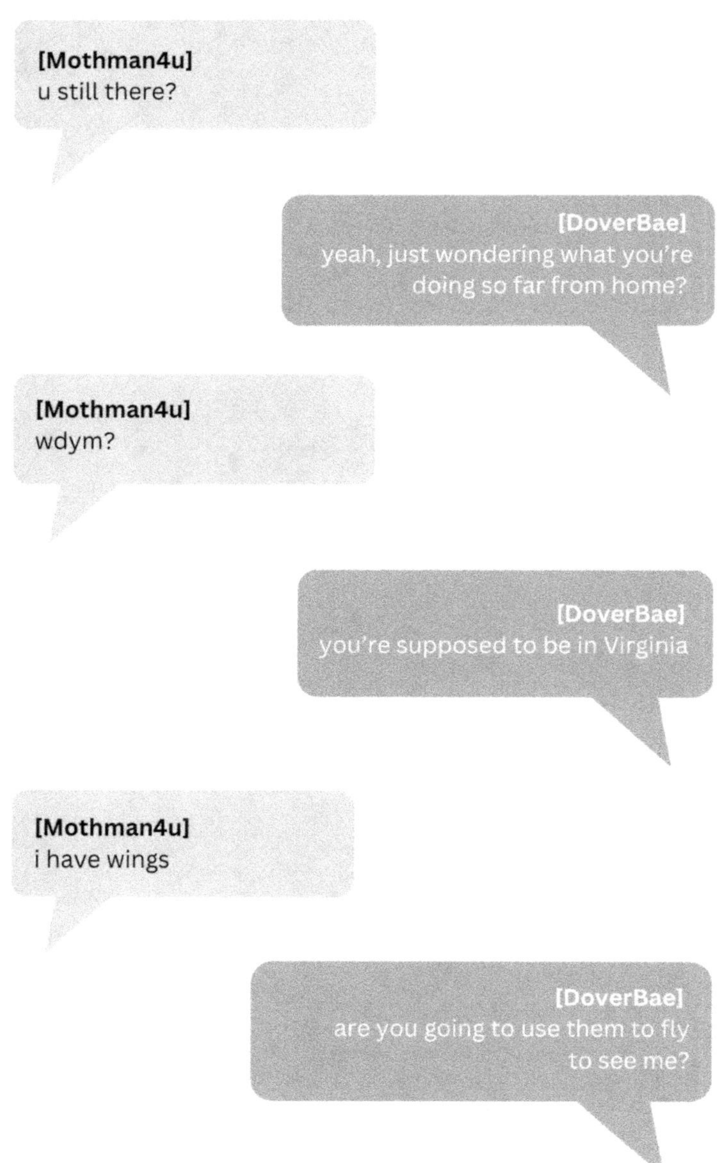

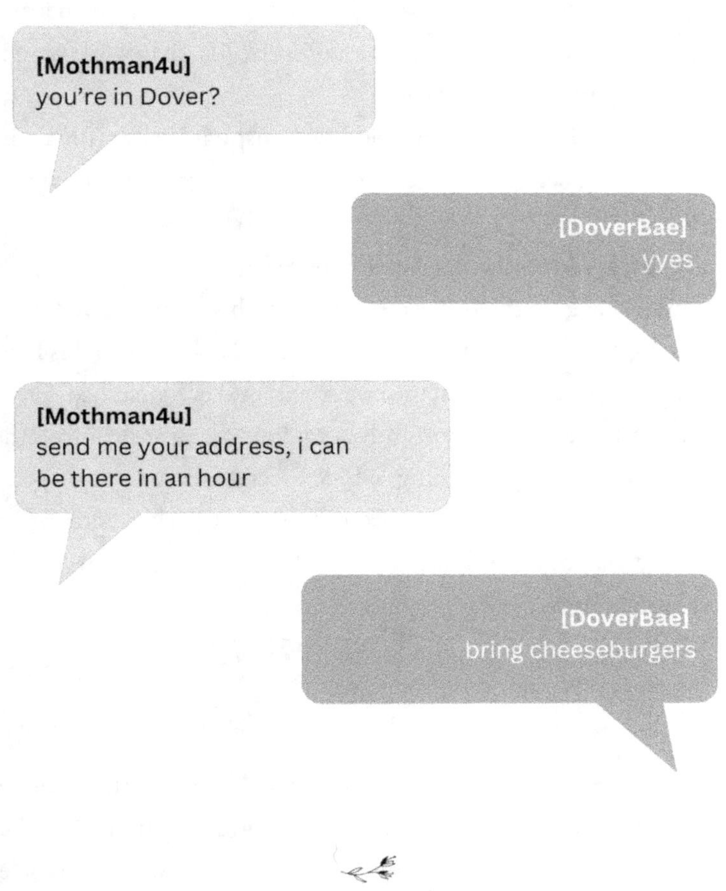

Jackson closed the app and smiled to himself. Another success.

His first dating profile, the *real* one, had gotten him nowhere. No woman wanted a casual hookup with Jackson Reed, a college student living in Boston, Massachusetts. At 5'7" (on a good day), slightly overweight, and borderline socially inept, there was nothing to set him apart from the thousands of other men in his area he was competing with.

It was his buddy Duncan, fellow Econ major, who had originally given him the Mothman profile idea. Jackson had been complaining, yet again, about swiping endlessly with no matches when Duncan had pulled out his phone and showed him his profile. "The Slenderman" it read, with a grotesque photo of a tall, stick-like man with octopus tentacles protruding from his back.

"The bitches dig it," Duncan told him conspiratorially with a wink. "They love to be scared. They don't know who's going to show up at their door."

And thus, the Mothman profile was born.

DoverBae was going to be his third hookup this month, and it was all thanks to a giant insect wearing a trench coat and fedora. And this Dover chick was hot too. Maybe even the hottest girl he'd ever matched with on the site. Her profile had copious full-body shots in tight-fitting clothes, no strategic camera angles aiming to hide a secret gut.

After quickly using mouthwash and deodorant, Jackson grabbed his keys on the way out the door. "Remember to get cheeseburgers," he muttered to himself.

Jackson knocked again on the front door for what had to be the fifth time in as many minutes. He double-checked the address he'd been given. The street name matched. The house number matched. He was in the correct spot. He opened the app, intending to send a message. Before he could press send asking where the fuck she was, he received—

He twisted the knob, and sure enough, the door swept open with no protest.

"Hello," Jackson called out, stepping into the darkened entryway.

No response.

Jackson shut the door behind him. From his vantage, the initial rooms of the house appeared small but well-kept. None of the lights were on, but he could see well enough from the streetlight coming through the windows. He wondered why his date wasn't here, at the front door, to greet him. Maybe she was pissed that he wasn't *actually* the Mothman.

A ding alerted from the still-open app on his phone.

Jackson's eyebrow quirked. This was a little kinky, but he was down for just about anything. Based on his exterior view of the house, there were only a few possible rooms she could be hiding in.

The living room and kitchen turned up empty of all signs of life, as were the two rooms upstairs. Jackson even checked the bathroom, going as far as pulling open the shower curtain and the cupboard under the sink. *Shit.* That meant there was only one place left.

The basement.

By this point, he was getting a little creeped out. Creeped out and *annoyed* that the greasy bag of burgers in his hand had long since gone cold. But he wasn't going to blow the thirty miles worth of gas he'd spent getting here, the hour of his precious time, or the fifteen bucks he'd spent on fast food just to turn back now.

Jackson located the one door in the house that he had yet to open. As he turned the knob and pulled, he was immediately accosted by a pungent odor.

"Oh shit." Jackson's free hand flew to cover his nose and mouth. *Oh shit, literally.* The smell reminded him of when the septic tank used to overflow at his own childhood home. She'd better not have invited him over expecting free plumbing services.

Jackson began his descent down the stairs, one foot slowly in front of the other, the aged wood creaking with each step. He was glad he left the door open at the top; the light that seeped down was the only source of illumination. His ears pricked to a soft scuttling sound from the far corner as he took the final stair, emerging into the pitch-black room.

It better not be fucking rats, he thought to himself. Placing his palm flat against the wall at his right, he swept it back and forth while he tentatively took small steps, hoping to brush against the light switch. As he made his way forward, the scuttling seemed to grow louder, more urgent. A low moan caused Jackson to freeze dead in his tracks. *Could rats fucking moan?*

His hand windmilled frantically against the wall until finally, *fucking finally,* his fingertips brushed against something protruding from the smooth surface. Flipping that coveted light switch with perhaps more urgency than he'd ever before experienced, the sizzle of the one, lone fluorescent bulb hit his ears at the exact moment that the dim glow flashed, causing his eyes to squeeze shut; the sensation almost painful after spending so much time in the dark.

Fighting against the automatic reflex to keep his eyes shut, he saw her at last. *DoverBae.* The object of his desire and the cause of this entire evening. But she didn't quite look how he was expecting.

The bag of cold burgers dropped with a soft plop from Jackson's left hand as he stood transfixed at the sight of her. Her long, dark hair, so vibrant and bouncy in her profile photos, now lay greasy and lank, plastered flat against her scalp. Wandering strands twisted down around her face like vines. Her tanned and glowing skin now appeared pale and anemic. She seemed to have lost weight, her cheekbones hollowed and her eyes sunken into her skull. And the smell. *Oh, God.* The concrete around her was darkened in a wide pool of her own excrement. Half-eaten remains of rotting produce and days-old fast food piled by her elbow in a lazy heap. Her large eyes stared transfixed on Jackson's, and she moaned again from behind the dirty rag tied around her mouth.

Jackson shook himself from his state of shock and shot across the room with frantic urgency, kneeling beside her to tug the gag down from her mouth. His hands moved next to the rope that bound her wrists behind her, connecting them to the radiator against the wall. The ties had dug into her tender flesh and were slick with blood.

"What happened to you?" he asked in a hushed tone, fingertips wrestling futilely against the iron knots.

She struggled to answer him, her voice coming out as a feeble croak when she parted her lips.

"Shh, it's okay. Don't speak," he told her, feeling like an asshole for asking questions at a time like this. Then he added, "I'm gonna get you out of here." More to convince himself than her as he fought against the knots that wouldn't budge.

Her mouth opened and closed like a gaping fish, still struggling to form words until he finally made out what she was trying to say. "Behind you."

Jackson stood and turned so fast that he almost tripped over his own feet.

When he'd learned about the *fight, flight,* or *freeze* response in his Psych 101 class, Jackson had always assumed he was a *fight* kind of guy. But the scream of horror that died in his throat as he stood motionless and silent, feet firmly planted to the ground—his body's only movement the slight tremor in his knees—now proved him wrong.

A grotesque monster stood only a few feet from him; its own stare locked onto his transfixed gaze. Though the creature stood shorter than him, barely over four feet tall, its freakish presence loomed like a tower. The head was huge and bulbous, shaped like a watermelon, perched atop a lanky body, the neck, arms, and legs lean and spindly, with a child-like torso—abdomen softly protruding. The skin that covered the being was the color of dull rust, dry and matte, pulled taut across its entire form. Long toes like a monkey's molded around the lip of the bottom stair on which it stood, blocking Jackson's one and only exit.

Its fingers were tendrils, each tipped with a shining black claw, one set curled around the railing, the other clutched an object—a cell phone—*her cell phone. The girl tied to the radiator,* Jackson realized with a deepening sense of dread.

It had no features, no lips, ears, or nose, save for its pair of un-blinking eyes, taking up half the canvas of where its face should be. Their inky blackness gave off an eerie, internal glow.

"What the fu—" was all Jackson managed before he cut himself off, hissing as needles entered his skull from every direction, his hands shooting up to swat at them like wasps, but there was nothing physically there to knock away.

You're not who I was expecting, Jackson heard, except not really. He didn't hear the words with his ears. They simply materialized into his head, injected through the invisible needles piercing his brain.

Fighting against the pain, a slow-drip infusion of poison, Jackson managed to answer through gritted teeth, "Who did you expect?"

Rather than words, the creature sent an image to Jackson through its telepathic link: a monster in silhouette, trench coat, red eyes, wings. *The Mothman.* His dating app profile picture.

He wanted to laugh. This thing had really expected another of its kind to show up?

Though Jackson outwardly said nothing, he felt the creature sense his inner mocking and disbelief through their connection. In retaliation, the needles shot in deeper, expanding in width into ice picks. Jackson screamed and fell to his knees, clutching at the hair by his temples hard enough that he pulled out clumps by their roots.

"Stop, I'm sorry!" Jackson gasped between screams, rocking back and forth on his knees as its telepathic connection pulled away once more, the pain receding to a dull hum.

Sorry isn't good enough.

"The Mothman isn't real." His tone was a plea as he looked up at the creature. "You had to have known that!"

I'm not supposed to be real, either.

Suddenly, Jackson's mind was accosted once more with flashes of images: this creature wandering the woods alone, walking for miles alone, looking for shelter alone, staying in derelict buildings and empty houses alone, hunting alone. Always alone. Years and years of alone. Alone. Alone. Alone.

Her name was Lilah. She'd come across humans before in her many years of existence, but she was always met with fear. They ran. They always ran. No one ever tried to make a connection with her. No one.

The "Dover Demon" they had called her, those that saw her, those that heard about her. A demon, a creature of myth. Not real. A wicked, disgusting thing of nightmares. Not one of them stayed long enough to find out how intelligent she was. To them, she was a mindless beast. That was what they thought of her.

His own emotions of overwhelming fear were replaced entirely with the creature's: sadness. Anger. Loneliness. Rejection.

"Please just let me go," he begged, realizing he was crying. The girl tied to the radiator could stay with the creature, he didn't care about her anymore. He just needed this thing to set him free. He needed it more than he'd ever needed anything. Jackson couldn't bear one more second of this.

You want to be free?

"Yes, please," he whispered.

I will set you free.

All at once, the needles were gone. She had released her telepathic hold on him, and his mind was once more his and his alone. The fear came flooding back, but his body still betrayed him. His terror kept him completely frozen in place, not that he believed being able to run or fight would do him any good.

And as she stepped toward him, he realized the old saying was true: *hell hath no fury like a woman scorned.*

About the Author

CM Toolson grew up surrounded by sprawling wheat fields in the small city of Pullman, WA. Home to the National Lentil Festival, she still lives there with her husband and their ferocious tabby cat named Mudballs. Her fascination with the macabre took root at an early age when her father allowed her to watch the movie *Candyman* with him at the tender age of seven. Since then, CM Toolson has been immersed in the realms of horror, harnessing her dark imaginings to craft tales that will leave readers on the edge of their seats.

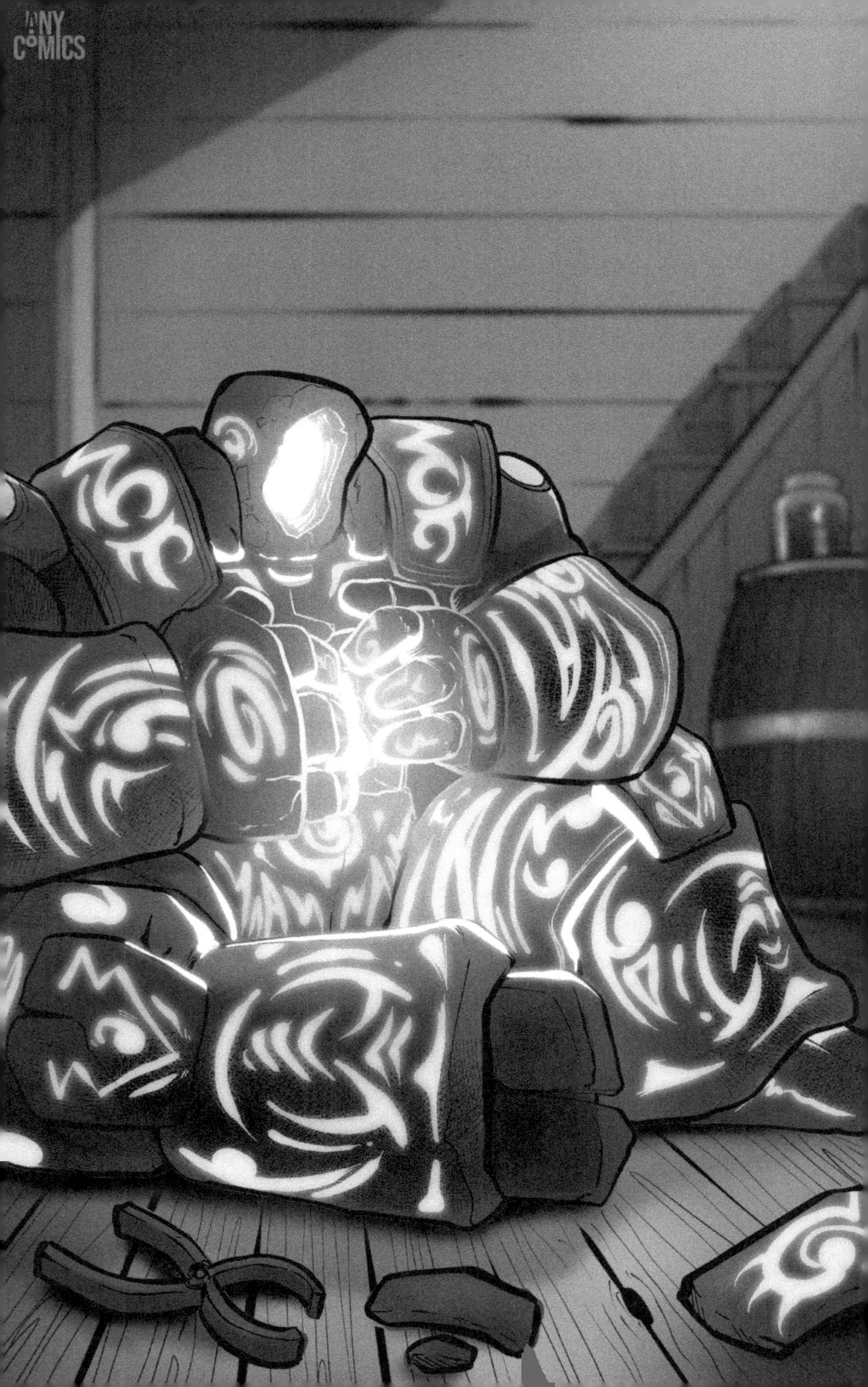

A SLIVER IN THE VEIN

BY J. SYRINGA

Atlas was an animated construct; a relic from a time not even he could remember. But that hardly bothered him anymore. He had much bigger, more pressing concerns. And having tucked himself away into one of his ship's closets, frantic attention turned inward. What he was experiencing now was dangerous. Even more so than the malignant cargo they were carrying. Worse, there was something very wrong with *him*.

Standing in the dark, Atlas dimmed the bioluminescence of his eyes to better feel the room's stillness. It was dark but he had no need for a light; there was nothing to see in there anyway. The space was familiar and the emptiness of the walls comforting. He needed that solace now.

He fought to settle himself past the dregs of adrenaline and the echo of imagined pain still thrumming through his body. Atlas pressed his hands against his chest piece as if the pressure would somehow help, somehow keep the maelstrom contained. It was hard to resist opening his armour again to look back inside. But he already knew what he'd find.

Lining the inside of his armour—his body—were clusters of clear crystals inlaid to key points, all connected by strings of glyphs in a language he didn't know. He'd never met anyone who could recognize the script. And if he were opened, the light of those faintly glowing runes would be reflected back by his gems. Whatever he had that was analogous to a soul was housed within those crystals. It was where his motivations, his memories, and his control of movement were stored. Those baffling, invisible components that made up a self were all secured away into stones that were in turn moored to a large, solid container of metal and clay. But where his body may have been nigh impenetrable, those mineral arrays were much more fragile. Atlas was sure that they embodied his mortality. And maybe then, he wasn't so different from the softer creatures of this world.

He'd been broken, yes. In small ways there were things inside him that were not as they'd been created. But it had never been bad enough to explain what was happening now. No, this was different from the unchanging minor cracks of the past. This was new. And it was getting worse. But Atlas was sure he could keep things under control as long as he kept a level head.

The introspection grounded him. As did the rocking of the ship, vibrating into him from the surrounding womb of walls and floor. Outside, the sea was calm, and he expected a night of smooth sailing. His eyes dimmed further, nearly to black, as he relaxed. Atlas let his mind wander, and only once steered it away from where his thoughts were always so keen to stray. Instead, he thought of the ocean and once more to the mystery of what he was. What he must have been. And now, who it was that he had become.

His earliest memory was of the dark. There had been an overwhelming pressure and an armour-numbing, full-body feeling that he would later learn to classify as cold. He'd come to himself underwater, buried to his pauldrons in silt and decay. Sometimes small, swimming animals would visit, inspecting his faint light. They'd always left soon enough. He'd been of no interest to them, made of earthen stuff as he was. Occasionally, the creatures might've stayed if the currents had dislodged a stray bone from the surrounding muck. But it was never for long. The bones always degraded to nothing, and any flesh or clothing had already gone to rot and floated away ages ago.

Atlas had not questioned the corpses slowly dissolving around him. He'd put them there; he knew that. He hadn't questioned much of anything back then. And after what might have been years, it had occurred to him to move an arm. Eventually, he'd dug himself out.

He'd walked for a long time after that with no destination in mind. He hadn't known where he was so he hadn't known where he was going. He had moved, not because it seemed the right thing to do, but simply because it was *something* to do. Knowing no better, at one point Atlas had walked over the edge of an underwater ravine and trapped himself at the bottom. It had taken him days to learn the concept of climbing, and then days more to perfect it. When he finally made it to land, he'd clambered out onto an unnamed, rocky beach. For the first time he could remember, Atlas had seen sunshine without a veil of water obscuring it. Standing there in the surf, among the sand and small crabs, he'd chosen to start a new life.

A loud thud jarred him from his thoughts. It was nothing to worry about. Likely just the monster in the cargo hold. Easy enough to ignore. The sea was calm, so there was no need to worry about a breach in containment. There came another crash, louder this time. The monster must have been agitated. Atlas sighed—or at least made the approximate noise—though he had no audience. He wasn't keen on listening to the blasted creature having another one of its violent tantrums. Annoyance took his small closet space from comforting to claustrophobic. He'd leave then, and head to the upper deck. It was a good plan and he had a ship to run.

Outside, the sky was twilight, diffusing the horizon and the tall masts of his vessel in a soft, purplish glow. Distant stars were just beginning to twinkle into view. Atlas strode to the edge of the bow, leaning against the taffrail to stare into the black water below. There was nothing to see and yet he couldn't seem to pull his gaze from the darkness. A small, reproachful part of him noted that his mind had been wandering to an alarming degree of late.

When he finally managed to drag his attention away, he realized he was no longer alone on deck. Atlas's mind stuttered and something inside his chest seemed to grind to a stop. Two women were crowded together near the stern. One—their new passenger—had her pale hair loose and her long, even-paler dress billowing around her legs in the faint breeze. The other was Riley, his first mate and apprentice. She had much more practical short hair and was vibrant in a red jacket against the swelling dusk. Riley had her arm around the woman's waist.

Atlas couldn't hear them from where he was, but he watched as Riley leaned over to say something before making a wide gesture. She pointed out into the distance and then threw her head back to laugh. He couldn't imagine what they were talking about; there was nothing out there except more ocean for miles and miles. The two women continued talking in that way, the first with her hands on the railing, not speaking as much but occasionally brushing some fluttering hair behind an ear. As usual, Riley's gestures trended towards being more dramatic. She kept angling in too, smiling while she talked, like they were sharing a secret. And maybe they were.

When Riley reached over to brush some stray hair behind the other woman's ear, Atlas felt unwell. There was shame in the feeling because he really should have known better. He continued to watch though, entranced, as Riley coaxed the fair-haired woman into dancing with her. They looked like they were having fun. Like they were very happy. And that made him feel somewhat better.

The two women were dancing closer now. More a graceful synchronized swaying than anything else. It reminded Atlas of seaweed in the shallows when the tide was in. He'd always found it sort of pretty in its own way. Especially when the light caught, turning the weeds from brown to an undulating emerald. Riley caught sight of him then, over the other woman's shoulder. She gave him a cheeky grin and a little wave, wiggling just her fingers from where her hand was on the woman's neck.

Atlas was proud of her even among the other less pleasant emotions. If he'd had a face capable of it, he imagined he'd be smiling. Instead, he brought up a thick arm to give her a thumbs-up—something she'd taught him years ago when they'd first met. Riley grinned wider at that, and it made Atlas want to widen his own imaginary smile despite the increasing shakiness he felt. He decided to leave them to their dance. Atlas reminded himself that the masts needed reinspection before nightfall. There were instruments that needed monitoring in the wheelhouse as well. He turned away just as Riley spun the other woman in a sudden, passionate twirl. He felt a shift, as if the ship had pitched to one side without him.

Atlas ignored the masts, hurrying past them and all but throwing himself into the wheelhouse. He slammed the door shut behind him and sunk to his knees, pressing his helmet against the closed door. He'd have to check the navigation equipment later, and the masts and sails too. For now, he needed to catch his breath—which was ridiculous as he had neither heart nor lungs. Whatever had ground to a halt inside of him hadn't started back up yet and he felt ill again, unbalanced somehow.

He needed to open himself up; to check for cracks. He knew the frantic compulsion bordered on neurotic, but he had to check again. It felt like the heart he didn't have was splitting open, and that could only mean a fault in one of the minerals hidden inside him.

Gently—and he had to do this gently because he was never designed to be unlocked like this—he pushed metal-tipped fingers into the seams of his body and began to pry apart his pieces. It was slow going, but he'd made mistakes doing this before. A clumsy slip from one enormous hand or a careless shock to his unprotected innards could damage him, possibly destroy him. And then what would Riley think, finding her captain dead and naked, anatomy scattered around the ship's wheel? The thought of her had him sick anew, caught in a wave of vertigo. His fingers wobbled and he forced himself to stop before he made some stupid blunder and hurt himself further.

When he was finally properly opened, he wasn't surprised to discover himself unchanged. The only faults he found were the corruption that he'd always had. When he was younger, in some past life he couldn't remember, he must have damaged himself because he already had some internal tarnish. A few crystals were contaminated with dark veins or shot through with hairline cracks. It was nothing new. He was as he had always been.

It didn't seem right to not be more broken; when every thought of Riley invoked so strong a response. When the soft balm of joy was always accompanied by a sharp, unnecessary pain. The feelings thrashed, an extreme hot and cold that could cause metal to crack. Flayed open as he was on the floor with his back propped up against the instrument panel, Atlas brought trembling hands to cover his face.

How could his precious collection of memories not utterly unmake him? How could the recollection of each individual smile, Riley's profile with her short, fluffy hair, her boisterous happiness, her wild laughter, the way her brow lowered just slightly when she contemplated a map—how could owning these things not break him in some critical, fundamental way? He cared for her so badly. Atlas didn't understand how his body could stand to survive it.

He lay like that for some time, letting the gentle swaying of the craft lull him into a safe fugue. When he finally rose, armour back in place, it was fully night. He did his duties, scrutinizing the instruments, making the necessary adjustments to their course, and then leaving with a light to check on the masts. It was irresponsible of him to have put it off the way he had. Even when he could see in the dark, it was still harder to look things over at night.

When he'd finished his captain's responsibilities, he went in search of Riley. He'd have liked to go over some plans with her and had some suggestions on how they could avoid taxes at their next port. It wasn't strictly legal, but he knew some people. He didn't find her anywhere on the main deck when he descended. And when he checked, she wasn't having a late dinner in the galley either. So he tried her cabin next. Though she wasn't there, he did see her coat resting on the back of a chair.

He wasn't sure where else she might have gotten off to. Perhaps the hold? Unlikely, but then there weren't many other places that she might've been. On his way to check, he passed the room he'd given their passenger and stopped. A giggle wafted gently from under the wooden door, and it was so uncharacteristic of the quiet woman inside, Atlas couldn't help but press a palm to the wood.

The crystals set inside his glove magnified and carried the fine vibrations of sound. Listening with his hand, he could hear a soft, shy voice—the passenger. And then came a louder laughing assurance. There was another laugh, and he couldn't tell from whom this time. The sound of heavy cloth being moved followed, and then there was a breathless little gasp and a pleased noise.

Atlas withdrew his hand. Riley might have been his apprentice, the other woman their rescued passenger, and this might be his ship, but the tender, unfolding scene was likely none of his business. He'd leave the women to their privacy.

He stepped away as quietly as he could on heavy feet. Atlas expected the pain that came next and it didn't disappoint. It flared up and outward, the way a hot drop of blood would melt snow, and then faded, gone again just as fast. He couldn't even place which crystal organ was suddenly stung this time. At a loss, Atlas didn't know what to do with himself. Feeling out of place, he decided to keep on walking.

A ringing thump came from the lower deck, knocking Atlas out of the fog of his stupor. Irritation rushed in to fill its place. It was time to entertain the monster then, he figured. He ought to hush the thing so it didn't disturb Riley or her guest. At least feedings usually did a decent job of calming the beast.

With that in mind, he swung past his large captain's locker. This was where he kept the more valuable trinkets they dredged up from the seafloor. Most were sold or doled out as wages—small as she was, he still had a crew to look after, after all—but some things were saved for their dreadful cargo. Atlas checked a cloth bag and removed a filthy necklace dripping with salt-crusted diamonds. With a grunt, he checked the bag again before closing his locker and heading into the bowels of the ship.

From inside the darkness, Atlas could hear the sound of sharp, stone claws scraping against the floor. He listened as the noise receded, approached, and then receded again. The creature was pacing. The cargo hold was dark, both to conserve power and because the monster seemed less excitable when kept in blackness. Atlas brought the lights up and immediately all sound stopped. A gigantic cage taking up half the hold was bolted to the floor and ceiling, covered in thick curtains. Somewhere within, the monster was waiting.

Atlas dragged a chair over from the corner, dropped his bag, and sat down. There was still no sound from the beast. Various crates were scattered about or stacked against the sloping walls. Nearly all of it was Riley's or equipment purchased on her suggestion. Atlas, after all, needed very little and owned even less.

The part of him that manifested as a cruel little voice whispered that he'd never have the one thing he found himself truly wanting. And in the company of a monster, he let himself indulge in imagining those longings. He supposed he could desire a number of things, really. But some were more complicated than others.

He looked around at the piles of lifeless goods in the store. Tools, equipment, weapons, and chests filled with the remnants of Riley's old life. He had to admit that buzzing at the forefront of his mind like a stinging insect was the yearning to be not so much like a person. Atlas deeply wished that he could be a *thing* again instead. If only so that he might be something to belong to her. If only, sitting here among her other things, he could have been one of her possessions.

Of course it was impossible; Riley saw him too much as an equal. But that, he supposed, was still its own gift. It had taken him so long to think of himself as a person that it was now a bad habit. And one he likely couldn't unlearn any time soon. This was for the best then, and Riley had certainly assured him as much. But it didn't stop him from so badly needing, sometimes. It was foolish thinking; she didn't want him and he couldn't begrudge her that. But it didn't stop her from wanting this blasted monster on his ship, to be kept as a prisoner or a pet. Whatever the beast was to her, he hated it. He knew that it hated him in turn.

He found that his head had been faintly shaking itself from side to side. He stilled. He hadn't meant to do that.

The clicking of claws started again, now drawing closer to the bars he was sitting in front of. There was no sense in putting it off any longer. Atlas stood, and operating a lever, drew the curtains back to reveal the bristling creature they hid.

The gargoyle was huge, the size of a lion. It had an ugly, mismatched, feline body with the muscular arms and hands of a man. Each finger was tipped by wicked claws matching its jaguar hind legs. Its long tail ended in a devil's spade, and the hideous head was made only more so by an expression of undisguised rage. The face was wrinkled and man-like, with a thick beard, astounding in its carved detail, that curled over its chest. From the creature's mouth grew what used to be two long tusks.

Those tusks had been one weapon too many, and before the beast had been allowed onto his boat, Atlas snapped them off at the base. And wasn't it lucky that they'd broken off cleanly. The gargoyle's once-enormous wings received similar treatment, Atlas merciless in rendering them into no more than inert rubble.

The monster's nails scratched against the floor, striking up sparks as it fanned its ruined wings at him, tail lashing.

"Get out!" it shrieked. It had a voice like a boulder splitting. "Get out. Get out! Where is Riley? Get out or I'll kill you. Bring me Riley!"

Atlas crossed his arms over his chest and stood patient, waiting for it to finish its threats and accept that he was its visitor.

The monster didn't like being down here, Atlas knew that. It didn't like being condemned to a single floating point in the middle of an ocean, either. Like him, he imagined gargoyles did not swim. And with its destroyed wings, it would never fly again. Atlas had no pity to spare, however. He didn't approve of the creature being on his boat and liked leaving it alive even less. A fair trade-off between the two of them, then.

The beast only continued spitting and shouting, veins bulging in the granite of its forehead. "Begone, fake man. Unless you've a gift for me, get out of my sight!"

Atlas had had enough. "Riley is occupied," he told it, terse. "She will not be seeing you tonight."

And just like that the gargoyle stilled, expression going sly and awful. A pair of full, sculpted lips slowly smiled, bearing teeth almost human—but not quite.

"Ah," it purred, delighted, spine arching into a cat-like stretch. "I can imagine, yes. That I can. I can imagine exactly what, or should I s ay *who*, she's occupied with."

It leered up at Atlas, sidelong. "With that other woman no doubt. The new one. And oh, but Riley's told me so much about her. Beautiful as anything I hear, voice like a bell, body untouched, and tender, pink flesh full of fresh, rushing blood.

"I'd like to meet this tasty creature who's so stolen our master's attention. Fetch her for me, fake man. It's been too long since I've had a warm meal."

"There will be none of that on my ship," Atlas said, fighting the image as he so often had to, of bending back the cage's bars and crushing the monster's vile head between both his hands.

"I could smell it on her, you know," the gargoyle said, almost conversational now. "She was hungry for the flesh too. Hungry in ways you wish you could sate, don't you? But how can you when you are only a fake man made of rock and clay? How could you hope to offer her anything to slack that particular human craving?" It ran a long, grey tongue over its lips before cackling.

Despite himself, Atlas startled and at first missed the meaning. "Hungry? We still have plenty of food in the stores, cattle and sheep's meat—"

"You stupid, copper shell!" the gargoyle shrieked again, throwing itself against the bars of the cage, sending them rattling. "Dirt man! Clay bones! Moron of metal! For all that you want her, don't you know anything? Lust, you idiot doll. Her hunger is carnal."

Atlas said nothing and waited for it to calm. Yes, he understood his mistake and saw the meaning now.

The gargoyle finally settled with a shake, soothing itself by running its hands over its own stone pelt. "And you, you stink too. Your loneliness is a miasma. I can't smell it only because I'm choking on it. It floods from your joints."

It was all nonsense of course. Atlas produced no odor and the gargoyle could smell no such thing. "I don't care for liars aboard my vessel."

"Then you ought to throw yourself overboard, you overgrown waste of clay, if you tell yourself you don't thirst for her."

Atlas didn't deign to reply. Instead, he said, "Poor behaviour won't endear you to me. And I don't reward liars with supper."

The gargoyle's eyes sharpened, fixing now on the bag resting beside the chair. It sat back on its hind legs, clasping its hands as if in prayer. Atlas warranted it had learned that from the other statues on the church they'd taken it from.

"Please sir," it said sneering, doing a bad impression at piousness. "I'm ever so hungry. And I'll be good. Ever so good. I won't eviscerate any more clergymen, and I'll barely even rip out our master's eyes. Why, she won't even notice. I'll be so gentle."

It bowed its head, further playing at penitence. "Now, now, I see I've touched a nerve in those pretty little gems you keep tucked away. I'm sure we can come to some sort of understanding, you and I." The beast flopped over, rolling onto its back in a display Atlas did not appreciate. "If you like, I'll treat you gently. I'll even let you call me 'Riley' if you care for it."

Atlas stared at the gargoyle for a long minute, and then picking up the bag he'd brought, turned on his heel. Being ridiculed by a monster he'd sworn not to slaughter wasn't something he needed to put up with.

"Wait!" the gargoyle called out, sounding genuinely pitiful this time. "I'm sorry! I'm sorry! Don't go. Don't leave me in the dark with nothing to eat. I'll do whatever you want, you awful abomination. Please."

Atlas turned back around. The creature was clutching one bar of its cage, the other hand outstretched in his direction. It really was a sad sight.

"Swear," Atlas said, tilting his head, "that you will never harm Riley. That you'd sooner break your own arm than hurt any human aboard this vessel."

The gargoyle let out a bitter bark of laughter. "Even if I did, it would mean nothing to you coming from me."

It wasn't wrong.

"Then eat some of your treasures," Atlas said, nodding now toward the nest of jewellery in the corner of the monster's cage. "You're hardly left to starve."

The gargoyle's carved fur and beard stood on end and it flapped its tattered wings in angry distress. "No. No, not my treasures," it hissed. "They're too beautiful. No. You wouldn't understand."

Again, it wasn't wrong. Atlas didn't understand. And he didn't care to.

"And what about this one?" he asked, finally dipping into his bag and extracting a large garnet ring. The stone was chipped and the setting was missing a number of accent jewels.

"Oooh," the gargoyle cooed. It stretched out its hand again, past the bars, for the trinket. Atlas dropped the thing into a waiting palm.

"Yes, yes. This is a lovely offering," it said. "This will do nicely. Yes it will."

Atlas watched as the gargoyle tried to shove the ring onto its too-large fingers, one at a time.

"Not going to eat it, then?"

"No," it crooned, more to the ring than him. "This is worth going hungry for. Shame about the flaws, but the craftsmanship is still exquisite."

It continued its efforts of trying to force on the ring. Nevertheless, no amount of twisting would fit the ornament onto even its pinkie. "Fetch me the file, fake man." It pointed to a crate of tools. "They're over there."

Curious, despite himself, Atlas retrieved the item, bringing it over. In response, the gargoyle stuck its arm back through the bars, pinkie delicately extended.

"I know you haven't the lightest touch," it said with a grimace, stretching out a wrecked wing. "But do try to be gentle, won't you? You've taken too many pieces of me as it is."

Atlas was surprised the creature was willing to trust him with such a small and easily broken body part. But then the beast had little choice if it wanted help in its endeavours of vanity. As an assurance, he reached back into the bag at his feet and withdrew another gem. This one was a cloudy piece of amber.

"Do you want this?" Atlas knew it would.

The monster's head snapped to attention, entirely focused now on the prize in Atlas's hand. "Yes," it hissed. "I do. Very much. Yes. Give it to me."

"You can have this when you return the file, understand?"

The gargoyle wouldn't be able to keep the tool from him if he really wanted to retrieve it, but this did save Atlas the trouble of unlocking the cage. Not that he wouldn't necessarily relish an excuse to throttle the monster, but he couldn't quite promise he wouldn't get carried away.

"Yes," it promised.

Atlas handed over the tool and sat down to watch. The gargoyle turned twice in a tight circle, lowering itself like a cat getting ready to sleep, before it set to work. Atlas remained vigilant. One had to be around monsters like this. But after it did nothing more offensive than slowly file away at its own finger, Atlas felt his gaze going unfocused. As always, much as he tried, his thoughts still wandered devotedly back to Riley.

The gargoyle was only here because she'd asked for it. Well, more like demanded, if he was being honest—and wasn't that so like her? So to the point. So brazen and strong-willed. Riley had such a fire to her. Atlas could do nothing but be warmed before it. And much as he hated the gargoyle, much as he'd been tempted to rip its skull clean off its body the long months they'd been harbouring it, he could never kill it. Not when the monster was her property.

And wasn't that funny, how easy it was for a prisoner to be designated as a possession? Would it be so hard to see him in the same way? Even when he'd go willingly? It was such a pathetic thing to be jealous of, but Atlas certainly wasn't without his own folly.

And just like that, like he should have expected, the cramping agony returned. The pain seemed to fall into sync with the frequency of his crystals' natural resonance, overlapping in a way that was just discordant enough to ache.

He looked over and the gargoyle was purring to itself, lost in admiration for the ring that now fit onto its newly deformed finger.

"Give me the file," Atlas said gruffly. He resisted the urge to try clearing a throat he didn't have.

The gargoyle narrowed its eyes, displeased at being interrupted. Then, using one feline leg, kicked the file between the bars, back towards him. "Now your end of the bargain, golem."

Atlas flicked the piece of amber over to it. The gargoyle caught the stone daintily between its teeth before biting down. Fragments tumbled from its mouth, falling into its beard and onto the floor. Atlas watched in disgust as the beast bent, using its long rough tongue to lick up the crumbs. He'd had enough of the evil company, and left without another word. This time the gargoyle did not call after him.

It was so late it was almost early when Atlas finally returned to the main deck. He could always do another tour of the ship; one more inspection to be on the safe side. But there was a weariness in his articulation and the pain he'd felt in the hold persisted. He'd have rather rested and spent the time in the dark, standing still with as few thoughts as possible. By the time he made it back behind his closet door, there was a subtle shake to his limbs. Atlas dimmed his eyes completely and let the back of his helmet collide with the wall behind him. A dry, strangled noise crawled out of his body and he couldn't tell if it was supposed to be a sob or a groan. Not that the difference mattered.

The urge to pull himself apart again, to diagnose what was wrong with him was strong. He resisted. There had never been any change, and things would be just as they always had been. But it still hurt so acutely. Had it always been this painful? Of course it had. Of course his weak, ailing mind would have thought every new instance was the worst it had ever been. And shame on him for further weakness. He'd already checked himself over twice today. Once more would be more than his pride could take.

He'd fight off the feeling, try to doze until tomorrow. If he still felt as impaired in the morning, then he'd have another look inside. For now, he'd stand still in the dark, and try to think of nothing but the rocking of the waves against the hull. He prayed he wouldn't dream.

He didn't dream. But neither did he rest. The nauseating feeling that ebbed and flowed from his crown to the sabatons of his feet hadn't abated. By the time morning came and he could hear Riley moving past his door for her early shift, he knew nothing would improve until he did what he must.

With a sick anticipation, he began to lever open his cuirass and the vambraces covering his forearms. Immediately he could tell something was wrong this time. The strings of glyphs leading to his largest central cluster were off-colour, their normal glow fading in and out with a diseased, slow flicker. Then he saw the true problem. After so long, after so many of these fruitless examinations, he couldn't help but feel vindicated. Finally, here was the physical expression of all that'd been plaguing him. Things that had seemed so real, for so long, but had always remained unquantifiable—no way to prove they weren't just the ephemeral concoctions of an unwell mind.

It was almost a relief to discover the fissure in the meat of his largest crystal, an inch behind the tip. With a breathy laugh that he couldn't deny verged on hysteric, he carefully brought two fingers to pinch the terminal point of his damaged gem. Then, he snapped it off.

Agony crescendoed as Atlas's vision went multi-hued and then black. He thought he tried to make a noise, but it didn't come. Or if it did, he spoke in a strangled collection of bleeding colours. The world dissolved into a sticky, gripping mess where gravity and spacial orientation meant nothing. Atlas did not even feel himself fall sideways. But when he was roused by a sharp knocking on his door, the corners of the wall were the only thing keeping him upright.

The world was still egg-yolk-soft, and he feared focusing on any solid object would cause it to pop, and start leaking the fluid of its aspect. He was careful not to touch himself as best he could.

"—Atlas?" the voice said again. And then with more concern, "Captain?"

Atlas knew that voice. He loved that voice. And he loved—*what was it that he loved?*

The door seemed to buckle in its frame, like warm toffee laced with miniature screaming faces. He knew those faces. He'd hurt those faces. Something... something wasn't right here. *Who was he?*

The voice had said: "Atlas" and "Captain." The voice knew him. Yes, and it was correct.

With a sparkling sense of déjà vu, Atlas named himself and chose his occupation. He had a designation now, and as a captain, he had a vessel and a purpose. The world started to resolve itself. Those weren't the faces of past victims, they were whorls in the wood. This door wasn't bubbling, because that was not a property that doors had. It was as solid as it had ever been. And the voice on the other side of the door—

"Captain? You better make some kind of sound, mister, or I'm kicking this in. It's not like you to miss a training session."

That was the voice of Riley, the woman he loved. And the woman he'd kept waiting for their morning appointment. He was usually so strict about punctuality.

"That won't be necessary," Atlas said. The sound of his own voice surprised him. It was sure and firm. It was a good voice.

"Finally," Riley said, giving a huff of relief. "Was looking for you, Atlas. You almost had me worried, standing me up and all. This is the first time you've missed something on the timetable. Everything all right?"

"Everything is fine." And it was true. Everything was going to be fine. "Have you had breakfast yet? If not, I'd like to join you."

"I thought you didn't eat."

"I don't, you're correct. But perhaps it would be nice to share a meal together all the same. You can invite our passenger as well." And then, because he was feeling better than he had in a long time: "Maybe she'll prove a better cook than you."

He got a laugh from Riley at that. "Listen, even if they started as eggs, we've got someone in the basement that'll eat the charcoal."

He felt a contented warmth slowly suffuse his body. "We've a true alchemist on our ship, don't we? Turning one thing into another like that. But that's no way to impress your captain, or our guest."

Riley chuckled along with him, and then said, voice disarming in its hopeful tenderness, "You're right though. I think that might be nice."

"I'll see you in the galley, then, in two hours," Atlas told her. "Finish whatever work you've left, and then take the rest of the time off."

"Will do, Cap'n." Atlas could hear the smile in her voice as she stepped away.

It left him alone again, but he didn't find he minded. He took stock of himself, the cotton at the corners of his vision dissolving, leaving the world as stable and three-dimensional as it should have been.

His armour was embarrassingly akimbo, but the script inside glowed with the steadiness it should. Aside from where it was clear the point of one crystal had been broken off, nothing else was out of place. At least nothing that hadn't been for as long as he could remember. Atlas put himself together as the world finished making sense. When he was done, he felt like a new man.

It was then that he noticed the piece of crystal lying on the floor. He picked it up and inspected it by the dim glow of his eyes. This fragment was a dead thing but it was still a piece of who he was. He turned it gently between his fingers, letting the uneven edges catch the light. Had this glittering remnant truly been so powerful? Had it been responsible for all those clumsy, dangerous manifestations in his simple, earthen body?

Well he was free of it now, and this small sliver of himself would be going to a better home. The shape was imperfect, hardly symmetrical, but he would've still liked to make it into something. A ring maybe, or a pendant. The thought soothed some last jagged, stray emotion, and he felt better for it.

It would be a gift. Something Riley could hold onto for the rest of her life. Or better yet, something she might in turn gift to someone *she* adored. And while her life was finite compared to his own, it would allow him to leave her something enduring. Perhaps it would even find its way into the hands of a descendant. Or into the hands of a favourite apprentice should she take one up the way he had.

He couldn't possibly ask for more than to be a part of the love Riley would share with someone that she cared about as much as he did for her. The thought made him happy too. As long as she didn't leave him that bloody gargoyle.

About the Author

J. Syringa is strictly a human being (contrary to what the overly large plants and equally distressing sleeping habits might indicate). Syringa lives in Canada and is a writer with a particular fondness for non-human narratives, exotic food, and natural world trivia. When they aren't networked to the hive-mind, they're writing about robots, monsters, and other unusual beings. You can find them on Twitter @robotbotanicals.

ANY
COMICS

STARVED

BY RACHEL NUSSBAUM

I don't let myself have a lot of things. Relationships, friendships, it's all too big a risk. Human contact in general is off the table—I keep even my parents at arm's length (if my arms were two thousand miles long). It's just easier that way. Easier not to let yourself get attached to things that would be dangerous if they became a habit. It's the same with all aspects of my life. I work from home. Don't exercise. Don't eat red meat. I try to avoid going outside.

Except on the full moon.

Once I realized there was a huge patch of forest close by where camping wasn't permitted, I began driving out there to shift. The concrete of my reinforced basement had been giving me night terrors, so I thought, fine—let's let the beast tire herself out.

And something just snapped. Everything I bottle up, everything I keep inside, everything I deny myself. I can split out of my human skin and scream without vocal chords, as loud as I want. I can let everything out.

I tear through the trees, shaking off shreds of human skin, the wind pelting against my fur. I'm furious, I'm ravenous, and I'm so, so free.

I slash my claws against a tree, splintering wood apart just to destroy—just to feel powerful—and I charge through the brush. I want meat. The forest knows what I am is unnatural, and the animals know to stay away.

I'm faster than they are, though.

In this body, I can smell like a shark. I bend down on all fours and gallop—past the raccoons peering down at me (too puny to be satisfying), a river flowing in the distance (meat first, water after), and ah—there it is. A herd of deer, passed by not ten minutes ago. I swivel around, following the trail their scent marked for me. I'm so hungry that I don't question the sour stench of fear clinging to the pat h.

When the deer I'm chasing suddenly start running back toward me—one buck practically bashing into me—that's when I notice.

A new scent. One I've smelled on occasion, but never this close.

Ursus americanus.

The bear was already charging through the foliage, and as it sees me, it falters to a stop. But my beast is a dumb, old girl, and she was already charging too. And she just keeps on going.

The human voice in the back of my mind finds this tragically hysterical—*Oh god, I'm going to start a fight with a bear. I'm going to get diced into ribbons by a bear and wake up with all kinds of scars and a clawed-out eye. Oh my god you stupid, fucking—*

And just as the bear surges up on its hind legs to meet me, a massive blur tackles it to the ground.

I scramble to a stop, eyes wide. The two beasts thrash across the dirt, their snarls echoing as they wrestle to the death. The scent of blood rises around us. I swallow.

A loud crack of bone sounds out and the bear sags down—its assailant's fangs found the spinal cord. Breathing deeply, the victor turns and looks at me.

Rises up on two legs.

Even as a beast, I'm shocked.

I've never met another shifter—not since the one that bit me. I've known other humans who've met them, but they were all old and told me the same thing. How rare I was. I'd given up a decade ago.

Her fur is darker than mine, her mane shorter. She's not as tall as I am, but her form is more muscular. There's no questioning what she is.

And she's staring right at me.

I break out of my trance and automatically, my hackles raise. The human bit in the back of my mind winces. The shifter tilts her head, then lowers herself down to her kill. Her eyes are still pinned on me, but her nose twitches—and finally, she breaks eye contact with me to feed.

I stand still, watching her. Even in this body, it feels painfully awkward. I'm curious and afraid and excited and angry all at once, but something about watching her eat feels far too intrusive. Awkwardly, I finally lower myself and turn to leave.

A growl echoes behind me.

I snap my head back and she's glaring at me, blood staining her snout. She slides down the carcass, lifts an elongated arm, and pats at the bear's flank.

My fur prickles. I'm not used to complex thoughts in this body. I'm not used to social situations in *any* body. I take a step back.

You shouldn't do this.

But my beast is starving, and to be fair, I *did* distract the bear for her.

I join her and tear into the bear's hide. The meat is gamey, almost pungent. Across from me, the shifter's chest puffs up and she lowers her head back down. I can barely smell her over the strong scent of the carcass, but what I do smell—it's like me, but different. Less full of anger. Maybe just a little smug?

It smells nice. Like something I just met yet something I've known for a very long time.

After we feed, the shifter and I walk to the river. I drink deep and try not to look directly at her—though I can feel her glancing at me often.

The human part of me wonders if she's met many others.

A stone hits me in the side of my leg and I growl. She's hunched by the muddy bank, motioning for me to join her. I look down to see her drawing a symbol. It takes me a moment to recognize an arrow. I look up at her and she tilts her head to the starry night, reaching her clawed hand up and touching her chest.

Her sign. Sagittarius.

My chest flares warm and my cheeks burn (can I even blush in this body? I never wondered that before). Her tongue hangs from her mouth and she whines, pointing to me.

Now I know I'm blushing.

I bring my clawed finger to the mud, but I fumble—I know I'm a Cancer, but I can't remember the sign. Goddamnit. I draw an oval and give it legs, trying to get the point across. I look over to the shifter hopefully.

She stares at the crab and her chest spasms. Her mouth parts—a series of hiccuped yips fumble out, like a hyena.

She's fucking laughing at me.

I snarl at her on reflex, but she laughs harder. Flustered and angry, I reach out and shove her, hard enough that she falls onto her side. Beads of blood prickle up from where my claws punctured her.

My ears fall flat and I jerk back. *Shit.*

The shifter shakes her head, slowly rising. Her hackles raise and she stalks over to me. I stand still, waiting for her to make her move.

She reaches up and smears a handful of mud across my snout.

I growl and sputter and she runs. I take off after her, snarling and howling. She howls back and turns to look at me with a razor-sharp grin. Something tingles under my fur—the surge of anger that propelled me to chase her fizzles out, and now, something else is pushing me after her.

And the longer I chase her and we bark at each other, the more that fury that always burns inside me feels further and further away.

After hours of chasing, slashing at trees in a contest of strength, and hunting down another herd of deer (the hunger never stops), we finally rest. Wolves howl in the distance, and I answer them back. It seems to amuse my new shifter friend, and she joins me. Her howl is deeper than mine. Stronger.

When the wolves move on, she looks over at me. Slowly, she reaches down her arm and parts the wiry fur. A thick, angry scar stains her skin. Mismatched, jagged punctures.

She's showing me her bite.

Something tight coils in my chest. Part of me feels sad—sad to see proof of her curse, sad to know she has to see it every day.

But a bigger, more human part of me feels awed. That she'd show me this mark, this deeply personal thing. I think maybe I'm the first one like us she's ever met too. And you'd think that would make me feel lonelier, but it doesn't.

This doesn't feel lonely at all.

I don't have the vocal cords to tell her this—what this means to me. So instead, I part the fur of my mane and turn.

She leans in, and I feel her breath on the back of my neck as she inspects my bite. It feels like it happened to another person now, like I was just watching from the sky as that massive beast wrapped his jaws around a young girl's neck. A bullet from a hunter saved her life a moment later, but it was a moment too late to prevent the curse from passing on.

I feel a wet lap across the back of my neck, and the past falls away. I freeze. It swipes across my scar again. My fur goes on end and my heart flutters.

Slowly, I turn to face her.

Our eyes meet, and hers drift closed. And I don't know how I even muster up the courage, but I lean in and nuzzle against her.

She lets out a deep sigh I had no idea she was holding, and her long arms circle around me tight. It takes me a while to realize how hard I'm shaking.

I didn't realize how much I missed this. How much I needed it.

I reach out and take her hand. It's funny how human, yet monstrous it is—elongated, like her arms. Fingers dotted with deadly claws. A leathery palm. Just like mine.

I'm not alone, the human and beast in me say at the same time.

Not alone.

When I wake up in the morning I *am* alone, though. I shift in the grass, back in my human body. I sit up and look around.

But she's gone.

Of course she's gone.

I think about a lot as I trek through the woods. Really, I don't know what I expected to find in the morning. A warm body still curled up to me? A smiling face framed by sunshine? My heart thuds in my chest. I forgot how much wanting something makes you ache.

This is why you're not allowed to have things, dammit. It just hurts more when you realize nothing's yours to keep.

The buzzing in my brain is so loud, it follows me almost out to where I parked my car. Barely gives me a chance to notice there's another car next to it.

I dive behind a tree, but I already hear a door slam, and a second later, the engine kicks on and the car drives off. I peer out behind the bark.

There's a torn scrap of paper under my windshield wipers. I yank it out as I dart into my car, hands practically shaking, words scrawled on the back of a ripped promotional flier.

Cancer,

Figured this was your car. So sorry I had to leave you. Got an early shift to get to. Last night was amazing! Please meet me here again next month?

~Sagittarius

That tight thing that coiled in my chest last night tugs, hard and pulsing, and doesn't let go. I pull my coat on and drive home fast, climb into bed, and pull out my phone.

And look up everything I can about the zodiac.

You shouldn't let yourself want things, that nagging, worrying human voice in my brain whispers. *This is dangerous. You know you can't have relationships.*

That was before I found someone else like me, though.

Does that matter? There are checks and balances for a reason.

What's that supposed to mean? Letting myself have one goddamn scrap is gonna open a floodgate?

Exactly.

I put in my earbuds and listen to music. The thoughts stop after that, but the nervous uncertainty stays behind.

I look over her note a lot. It makes me feel better. The week's almost over—I just need to wait a bit longer.

But one part of it...

An early shift? How the hell did she time that?

It's not surprising though, considering what I saw of her. She was...
smart. She attacked the bear when she knew it was distracted. She could
use hand gestures.

She was in control.

*She probably works a real job in the real world too, instead of locking
herself up in a cage like a rabid animal.*

I make my music louder.

I go outside for the first time in a while that isn't just a quick dart inside
the gas station for a soda with my head down.

I walk the five blocks to the library. Head up. I go straight to the
information directory. I checkout two books on anxiety and one about
zodiac signs.

On my way home, I feel elated—it was a small step, but it felt huge.
I keep my head up high now, and I pay attention to all the colorful
businesses I pass. A ballet studio. An Indian restaurant. An arts and crafts
store. It's funny how something so mundane can feel so exciting. There's
so much outside. So much to do. So much to see. To smell.

*You know what smells the best too, don't you? That tender, delicious scent
isn't coming from the restaurants.*

I falter a little. I try not to let the thought ruin this. Just walk a little
faster. I can do it.

*Who's it coming from, do you think? Those high school students passing
you by? That family coming out of the bodega?*

That woman across the street with her baby?

I break into a run and breathe through my mouth the rest of the way
home.

The books on anxiety help a little. Breathing exercises. Positive affirmations. Funnily enough, it's the stupid zodiac book that gets to me.

Cancers.

Selfish. Self-pitying. Mood swings. Manipulative.

Is that really what I am? I know the self-pity and mood swings fit. I haven't been around enough people to know if I'm selfish or manipulative.

It's pretty selfish to want something you know you shouldn't let yourself have. Risking the safety of everyone else around you for a stroll to the library. You'll risk her safety too.

I close the book. What did I expect from a bunch of read-the-stars nonsense?

Because werewolves are so much more logical.

I roll over in bed and feel the guilt rise. It's not fair. Why can't I just have this one thing?

You know why.

I dream I'm chasing down a girl. She turns and I see a face, my own face staring back at me. I look younger, and even my beast can recognize that I'm chasing down my teenage self. I'm back at the beginning.

But my beast is too hungry to care. I tackle her to the ground, her screams muffled into the grass. My jaws are around my own neck—then in the next instant, they're around an arm.

It's *her.*

Her bones snap and splinter in my maw and she screams. I feel the blood and hot marrow drip down my throat and quench my thirst as she thrashes in agony. I fall out of the nightmare before I can see her face.

I breathe heavily. Wasn't real. Didn't happen. I *never* bit anyone.

You locked yourself up before you had the chance to.

No.

Because you knew you wanted to. Because you knew how delicious people smelled walking by you on the street, the closer to the full moon it got.

That's not—

Bullshit. You couldn't even let yourself run free until you were certain there were no campers in those woods.

...

Because you knew you couldn't help yourself. You're so goddamn hungry, and you know exactly what for. The animals you hunt down will never be enough.

And what, the moment you find someone willing to put up with you for a few hours, you'll throw it all away? Throw countless lives into danger?

It doesn't work that way. You don't fix something this broken with silly self-help books. You don't starve yourself of everything for years and just let your beast off the chain like you weren't holding her back for a reason.

You'll devour everything. Destroy everything.

Cancer.

When the full moon comes, I lock myself in the basement. Let the soundproof walls absorb my screams as my skin stretches and snaps apart. Let my beast cry out in misery when she realizes where we are.

It's for our own good. For everyone's good.

Especially *her*.

I scratched at the walls until my claws bled. When I finally curl up to whimper myself to sleep, it aches. My hands, the unending hunger, the unyielding loneliness. I wrap my long arms around myself and pretend it's her.

This is why you shouldn't want things. Because it hurts this bad when you have to let them go.

I didn't *need* to let her go.

You know you did.

I drift off, the human voice in the back of my head still buzzing and berating me. I dream of her, waiting for me, staring up at the moon. Howling for me.

My ears twitch and my eyes snap open. It's real. I can hear her.

That's impossible. This room is soundproof.

I lumber to my paws and stalk over to the window. It's closed (and barred) and somehow, I can hear her.

You're imagining what you want to—

Another howl sounds out, and I just know—it's her. Out there, miles away in the forest, calling out to the moon. Asking if I'm there.

I dig my bloody claws into the concrete. I'm sorry I didn't come. I'm sorry.

You know you couldn't—

Do I know that?

Of course you couldn't. You're not like her. You're not in control. You're feral. You're—

Why couldn't I have asked her for help? Ask how she did it? Why couldn't we have figured it out together?

There's no answer. Just silence as she cries out for me.

I grind my bony knuckles into concrete. *I'm so sorry,* I want to tell her. *I was scared. I'm scared of what I am. I'm scared of what I could do. I'm scared of what will happen if I let myself have anything. Even the things I want.*

I don't have the vocal cords to say this, though.

All I can do is howl.

I don't know if she could hear me in return. She kept howling long into the night, distant and sad until she faded away with the morning.

I sit in bed, drinking scalding tea and thumbing the note she left me. Will she come back next month? Would she wait that long? I read the words again and they tug at my chest. I turn the note over in my hand, absentmindedly scanning the torn flier.

And I freeze.

I didn't notice it before (it never even occurred to me) but the cut-off bold text is a logo. I bring the note to my face—there are only a few letters, but the smaller text below advertises a local event.

This is a flier for a business—one somewhere in town.

I yank my coat over my pajamas and grab my keys as I run to the door.

It took me an hour of driving through town, holding up the little scrap of paper and comparing the logo corner to signs. After a while, I start narrowing it down. If she works morning shifts, it has to be something open early...

I can't believe it when I finally pull up to the fitness center. The loops of font that are still visible on the torn-off flier match up perfectly with the big sign on the roof.

The voices blare in my head—my human fears, my bestial rage.

I ignore every fucking one of them, and I run through the door.

The gym is loud, the sounds and scents overwhelming. The man at the counter greets me, but I pass him, eyes darting across the room.

There's a loud clatter as a pair of weights crash to the floor. I spin around, and halfway between a storage closet and the lobby, I see a woman.

It's her.

Her skin is darker than mine, her hair shorter. She's not as tall as I am, but her form is more muscular. There's no questioning who she is.

And she's staring right at me.

She brings her hand to her mouth and lets out a loud sob. I run to her, and she meets me in the middle, yanking me down into her arms.

"I was so scared I'd never find you again," she whispers.

I hold her as tight as I can.

"I'm sorry I kept you waiting," I tell her. My voice is shaking, but my words are strong. She beams, bright and beautiful.

A smiling face, framed by sunshine.

About the Author

Rachel Nussbaum is a writer and artist from the Big Island of Hawaii. Her short stories and poetry have been featured in many anthologies and collections including *Welcome To the Splatterclub III* from Blood Bound Books and Cosmic Horror Monthly. Rachel's debut novella *We Rotted In the Bitterlands* came out in 2021 from Mannison Press, and will hopefully be the first of many more longform projects for her. Rachel hopes to keep writing (and one day illustrate) her own short stories, novels, and comics.

SHINY OBJECTS

BY VALERIE B. WILLIAMS

Father whirled and peered into the darkness beyond his torch. I flattened against the side of the tunnel, willing myself to blend into the earthen walls. He paused and tilted his head, grunted, and moved on. My soft-soled boots made no sound as I crept behind, staying just beyond the circle of light. He stopped and slid the torch into a slot in the wall, then drove his pick into the roof of the tunnel.

The *thunk* confirmed my worst fear—wood. Four more whacks and he was in. Unsheathing a wickedly curved knife from his belt, he reached into the hole, grabbed something, and sawed. After some time and much effort, I heard a snap, and he pulled a large object from the hole—a partially decomposed human hand with a ruby ring on one finger and an emerald ring on another. From fingertips to wrist stub, the hand was a third as tall as Father, and he had always been on the tall side for a gnome. A wide smile split his beard as he wiggled the rings off the hand and stashed them in his pockets. He dropped the now-unadorned hand on the floor of the tunnel and hoisted himself into the hole above.

The scene in front of me was all too familiar. Father's obsession with gold and gems was getting stronger. The grave robbing started fifty years ago, when it was easier to find caskets not enclosed in steel or concrete vaults, and more common for humans to be buried wearing valuable jewelry. This cache was a jackpot.

After Father disappeared into the hole, I retraced my steps through the tunnels back to the village. I could do nothing while he was in the throes of his obsession. After many twists and turns, I exited into the village square. My twin brother, Jurgen, paced in front of the opening.

"Was he at it again?" His eyes were creased with worry.

I nodded. "He was still foraging when I left."

Jurgen touched my nose, sore from the last time I got between Father and his prize. The swelling made us less than identical.

"Horst, you must be careful. If he gets caught, we'll need to care for Mother."

"That won't be necessary because we're going to save him."

I wrapped my arm around his shoulders and we walked to our cottage. Mother would have dinner ready, even though Father wouldn't be home until after dark. All the better to hide his activities from the rest of the village.

Mother had just cleared the dishes when Father swaggered through the front door, pockets sagging and jingling. A whiff of putrefaction clung to his clothing.

"Renata, my love," he boomed, slapping her on the behind.

She squealed and darted to the other side of the table. He leered and gave chase, but she was too quick and managed to keep the table between them.

"Fritz, not in front of the boys," she said, blushing, but smiling all the same.

Jurgen and I rolled our eyes. We were 172 years old, far from boys. But to our 300-year-old mother, we would always be her boys. And we were well aware of Father's appetites. The walls of the cottage were not thick enough to muffle his almost nightly cries of delight. Or hers. It's a wonder we were the only offspring.

Father gave up the chase and dug into his pockets.

"Wait!" I hurried to close the shutters.

He pulled out two familiar rings, a necklace of emeralds, and a pair of ruby earrings, and placed them on the table.

"Jewels for my jewel," he said, sweeping his arm over the display.

"They're lovely, Fritz," Mother said. She frowned and didn't move toward the jewelry. "But I thought you said you were done with..."

"I know, I know," Father said, waving his hand. "But I happened to sniff these out, purely by accident. Couldn't very well leave them there. The prior owner wasn't using them anymore." His satisfied grin made him look decades younger than his 305 years.

He was lying, of course. He'd been tunneling toward this latest stash for two weeks. I'd seen the circled obituary of the wealthy woman. I followed him the night he went above   ground to make certain of the grave's location.

While Father was in the washroom, we gathered around the table and stared at the jewels.

"They are beautiful," Mother said, reaching for one of the rings.

I pushed her hand away. "No! You know you can't wear them. You know the penalty."

"But I didn't take them," she wailed. "Oh, why does he tempt me so?"

Jurgen put his arm around her. "We can appreciate their beauty without owning them. They must be returned."

"But no one will ever know they're missing!" she said, weeping.

She was wrong.

Our family was one of the oldest in the village, going back four generations. My great-grandfather Lothar had stowed away with his wife on a ship from Germany and settled in rural Virginia. He was escaping persecution for whom he had married—great-grandmother Gerta was not a pure-blooded gnome. A troll had raped her mother, and Gerta was the result. Though she looked like a gnome, her heritage was common knowledge and the rest of the villagers shunned her.

Trolls are longtime enemies of gnomes. They are vile, selfish, greedy, and smelly. One of their more disturbing traits is an obsession with gold and gems. A troll on the trail of treasure has been known to go without food for weeks. Gerta had the obsession, but Lothar kept it at bay by ensuring her a steady supply of jewelry. Despite being only one-eighth troll, however, our father's obsession was strong and had only increased over the years.

Jurgen and I covered for him by returning what he stole; if we could discover where it came from. Once he acquired a piece, he mostly lost interest. For him, the thrill was in the hunt. He stashed his treasures in a locked storage room where he would occasionally fondle the jewels and admire the way they caught the light. Jurgen made copies of the pieces and I replaced the originals so Father wouldn't notice.

Jurgen had done an exceptionally fast job recreating the latest booty. Two days after the theft, I set off to return the pilfered items. Father was ensconced in the pub for the evening, regaling his friends with tall tales.

"Be careful," Jurgen said. He always fretted when I went on these trips, though not enough to join me.

I followed the twisting route back to the scene of the crime, once taking a wrong turn and being forced to backtrack. Nerves must have been affecting my usually excellent memory. When I arrived at the dark hole in the roof of the tunnel, I noticed that the hand Father had discarded was partially covered by fresh soil. Strange. I placed my torch in the holder and picked up the hand, tossing it up and over the edge of the opening, then pulled myself up and through the hole. Moonlight glowed all around me. There was no trace of the casket or its contents. I stood at the bottom of an open, empty grave.

"Detective Esteves," said the medical examiner, "are you all right in there?"

Esteves leaned under the faucet, filled his mouth with water, and spat into the sink. The taste of vomit was still present, but not as bad. He fished a stick of gum from his pocket, thankful for the habit that had replaced cigarettes.

"Coming," he said and returned to the autopsy.

A woman lay in several pieces on the table. That had gotten to him. This was his first exhumation—she'd been in the ground for three weeks. Her head had been severed, her right hand was missing, and both ears had been torn from her head.

"Okay now, princess?" Malone, the lead detective, smirked. Esteves hadn't helped himself lose the rookie stench.

"Good," he mumbled. "Let's finish."

"All injuries are postmortem," Doc Simmons said. "The removal of the head appears to have been done in one motion with no stopping or sawing. Could be a large, very sharp blade or a wire of some sort." He lifted the corpse's right arm. "On the other hand..." He grinned at his own joke. "The hand was sawed off, more brute force than skill. Like the ears."

"Any chance an animal could have done this?" asked Esteves.

Malone rolled his eyes.

"Not unless it had thumbs," Doc Simmons said.

"But the hole in the casket was too small for a person," Esteves said, trying to salvage his argument. "We've got to consider all possibilities."

"Tell you what, sunshine," Malone said. "You just earned yourself the lead on the grave robbing and corpse mutilation. I'll keep after the husband. His alibi for when the wife had 'her accident' has evaporated.

Never trust a mistress." He snickered and turned his back. "Let me know when you arrest that badger."

Rookie scut work ate up the rest of Detective Esteves's afternoon. But at least the people around him were alive, assuming they'd had their coffee. Malone wouldn't give him any extra manpower unless he came up with a damn good reason. In the meantime, he requisitioned a motion detector with a camera and set it up at the cemetery on the way home.

He arrived home and Slugger met him at the door, wagging her whole body. A tan and white pit bull, they'd rescued each other two years ago. Her looks were the only thing mean about her—this dog was a moosh. He finished dinner and was sitting on the couch watching TV, Slugger's head in his lap as usual, when his cell phone buzzed. Something had tripped the motion detector. Probably an animal. Maybe Malone's badger.

Esteves touched the app on his phone and displayed live video from the detector. An object at the bottom of the grave caught his eye. A miniature person with a beard and a pointy cap. Had someone put a garden gnome in the hole as a sick joke? But then the creature tilted his head to look up. His gaze swept past the camera and the detective's vision blurred. He blinked and refocused on the screen. The gnome kicked something out of his way, then disappeared through a small hole in the grave floor.

Esteves leaned back, heart pounding. What had he just seen? He was stone-cold sober. Hadn't had a drink in forty-seven days. He figured drinking would make quitting smoking harder than it already was and hadn't really missed it. Until now. He looked at the screen again—nothing but the empty grave. After five minutes, the camera switched to energy-saving mode and went black.

Peaceful evening disturbed, the detective drove to the cemetery and parked as close as possible to the gravesite. Yellow crime scene tape flapped around the opening. Slugger walked quietly by his side. The small motion detector was perched at the foot of the deep hole, angled slightly downward. He clicked on a flashlight and found the gnome's bolt hole, about a foot across and round. From here, he couldn't see how deep it was.

"Shit, I'm gonna have to go down there," he muttered. Esteves dropped Slugger's leash. "Stay," he told the dog. She whined, licked his hand, and slowly lowered her butt to the ground.

Six feet was a long way to jump, not to mention try to climb out of. The detective retrieved a coil of rope from the trunk of the car, keeping one eye on the dog. She didn't move but wrinkled her brow at him, looking worried. He tied the rope around the nearest tree, slid the flashlight into his back pocket, and rappelled into the open grave. His light scanned the dark corners and revealed what the gnome had kicked out of the way. Propped against the side of the grave, like it was trying to climb out on its own, was the missing hand.

Esteves gagged, then swallowed, willing himself not to vomit. Pulling an evidence bag out of his pocket, he used it to pick up the hand, then turned the bag inside out to capture it. Just like cleaning up after Slugger.

"What do you mean 'it's gone?'" asked Jurgen.

"Gone. Not there. Nothing but a hole." I shook my head. "I couldn't very well leave the jewels in an empty hole, now could I? That wasn't where he found them."

"They know." Jurgen rubbed his forehead.

"Of course they don't. Humans don't believe we exist, even less so than they used to. They'll blame it on animals."

I shuddered at the thought of the last time humans discovered a gnome village. "The Harrington Massacre" was included in all our history books. The possibility of discovery was the biggest risk Father took, and the main reason the village elders were so strict about grave robbing. All gnomes enjoy shiny objects, but most know where to draw the line.

"But what if they don't blame it on animals? What if they trace the tunnel? Can we fill it in?" Jurgen shot questions at me like bullets.

I smiled. Parallel thoughts between twins are not merely a thing of lore.

We set out the next night. This was the first time Jurgen had accompanied me beyond the entrance to Father's tunnels. He imagined followers behind us at every turn, being unused to the way the tunnels echoed and bent sound. Each of us carried a backpack filled with explosives.

At the opening in the roof of the tunnel, I held up a hand. "Wait. Listen." Seconds stretched while we rotated our ears left and right.

"Nothing," we whispered the word simultaneously.

I motioned to Jurgen to stay put and hoisted myself through the hole to the floor of the gravesite. A blinding light hit my eyes and a weighted net fell on me.

"Run!" I shouted, struggling to remove my backpack, willing to die in defense of family and village, when a blow to the head plunged me into darkness.

"Looks just like a person, huh, girl?" said Esteves.

Slugger growled at the creature in her crate. She pressed her snout against the bars, and the gnome retreated to the other side. He'd lost his pointy cap and blood crusted the edge of his hairline. A thick beard reached halfway down his chest. Standing straight up in the crate, his head was still a couple of inches from the top.

Esteves sat on the edge of a chair, sipping bourbon and leaning toward the makeshift prison cell. Forty-eight days sober had been a good run, but he was quitting smoking, not drinking, and there was a damn good reason to drink looking back at him.

Capturing the little guy had been surprisingly easy; patience went a long way. When Esteves had shown Malone last night's video, he'd accused him of doctoring the recording. The detective couldn't wait to bring in the living, breathing proof tomorrow.

The gnome grimaced and rubbed his head. A bluish-purple knot stood out on his left temple. "Did you have to hit me so hard?" he asked in a deep voice, unexpected for one so small.

Esteves jumped. "You... you speak English?"

"I speak many languages." The gnome let out a whimper, followed by a couple of yips.

The detective watched in disbelief as his loyal dog stopped growling and commando-crawled toward the gnome, flipped over to expose her belly, and thumped her tail.

"Point proven. So, let's have a chat, shall we?" Esteves reached for his phone to record the interrogation. This case was going in a direction he never expected.

"Detective Paul Esteves interviewing..." He nodded toward the prisoner. "State your name."

"Horst. Horst Madder." The gnome scratched his beard and looked directly at the man for the first time. He had the most incredible sea-green eyes. Hypnotic. "Nice to meet you, Paul." Horst stuck his hand through the bars of the crate. Esteves shook the small hand. "We haven't much time," said Horst, and looked away.

Released from the gnome's gaze, the detective stared at the melting ice cubes in his drink. He was definitely buzzed, but those eyes! They were deep enough to swim in. He gave himself a mental shake.

"Oh, we've got all night."

"You don't understand. My family will come for me and they will be angry. You really don't want to meet my father when he's angry."

Esteves drained the last of the bourbon and focused on a spot just over the gnome's shoulder, careful not to meet his eyes. "I think I can handle a few more 'little people.'"

Horst winced and shook his head. "You have no idea. But if you let me go now, I'll forget this ever happened. I'll return the stolen jewels and promise there won't be any more grave robbing in your district."

If Esteves returned the jewels, he'd be a hero. Of course, he'd have to explain how he found them and come up with a theory about who had stolen them. And he couldn't tell anyone, much less Malone, that there would be no more grave robbing. If that was even true. The gnome would say anything to get out of here. No, the original plan was still the best.

"So, you admit you stole the jewels. I think I'll pass on your deal. I can get the goods back without selling my soul, *and* I'll have a perp in custody. Wait here." Like he had a choice. The detective chuckled and went to the kitchen for a refill.

On the way, he stopped in the bathroom to take a long piss, making room for the fresh drink. Ice cubes rattled from the dispenser, and he topped them with lovely, caramel-colored liquid. A thumping noise from the living room made him quicken his steps to the hallway.

The thumping noise was Slugger's tail. She lay sprawled on her side with a silly grin on her face. The door to the crate stood open and Horst was scratching her ears. Two other gnomes wearing backpacks stood behind her, one who looked just like Horst, and an older one. A trail of small, muddy boot prints led into the living room from the back door.

"My son tells me you have spoken to others about us," the old gnome said. "And that you plan to take him to jail tomorrow."

He pierced Esteves with his eyes, dark blue, like an angry ocean before a storm. The man's surroundings blurred so that all he saw were twin blue orbs.

"Yeah, that's right," said the detective, pretending swagger he didn't feel. A single gnome in a crate was one thing, but three unrestrained? He tried to tear his eyes away but couldn't. He swallowed hard.

The old gnome stepped close to Slugger and rubbed her belly with a small hand, setting off another round of ecstatic tail thumping.

"This is a nice dog. There's never been a dog who killed a gnome or wiped out his family and village." The creature flared its nostrils. "Can't say that about humans."

Esteves stood frozen. He couldn't look away from those eyes or move a muscle. What was happening? He felt like a statue.

"First, you need to write a note."

The muscles in his head and neck released. "Yes, yes, whatever you want," he said, nodding like a fucking bobblehead. The gnome released the rest of his body, and he scrabbled in the drawer for a pen, snatching up the phone-side notepad. He'd gone from statue to puppet.

"Write exactly what I say."

Esteves's mind raced as his traitorous hands wrote the confession. How would he explain this when he got out of this mess? *If* he got out of this mess?

The old gnome reached into his backpack and removed a velvet drawstring bag, the kind jewelers use. It *chinked* when he lifted it, the bottom pulled down by the weight of its contents. He took the completed note, put it on the coffee table, and tossed the bag on top.

"Now, follow the boys." He nodded at Horst and the other gnome. "Take your cell phone," he added, wagging his finger.

Horst gave the detective a pitying look. "I tried to warn you. You should have taken my offer."

The group halted in the garage, where the old gnome commanded Esteves to toss the cell phone on the floor in front of Jurgen. Esteves watched his last hope shatter with one swing of a sledgehammer.

The younger gnomes led the man into the backyard, where a large hole had appeared. Horst's brother disappeared into it.

"After you," Horst said, bowing deeply.

Esteves's body climbed in while his mind screamed in protest. Even though he wasn't locked in the gaze of a gnome, they still held him in thrall. He crouched at the bottom of the hole, then squeezed into a tunnel where the lead gnome held a torch. The others climbed in behind and he saw the glow from their torches as his body crawled down the dank, musty tunnel. His mind returned to Slugger—at least they hadn't harmed her.

Jurgen led the way, with me and Father bringing up the rear. Literally, as we had to look at the man's ass while he crawled through tunnels we easily walked through.

I almost felt sorry for Esteves. He'd begun to sob while he crawled, occasionally begging to be taken back to his house. After getting no response, he begged to be let back above ground and he would clear all this up. When we reached our destination, the detective slumped against the wall of the tunnel, tears streaming and chest heaving.

"You're almost getting your wish, Detective," Father said. "You won't be quite so deep underground."

Jurgen and I swung our picks at the roof of the tunnel, opening a larger hole than usual. We struck wood at the same time and worked until we cleared a large entry to the hollow space above.

"I hope this goes quickly, Detective. I bear you no ill will. My duty is to protect my family." I leaned on my pick and gestured toward the opening. "Climb in."

The man's eyes were wild and panicked. He shook his head from side to side even as his arms rose to hoist himself into the casket. A desiccated femur fell to the floor of the tunnel. Jurgen tossed it back in before we started to fill in the opening.

After three turns through the maze of tunnels leading back to the village, I could no longer hear his screams.

About the Author

Valerie B. Williams came to writing late in life but is making up for lost time. Her most recent publication was "The Tinker's Gift" in the *Refracted Reflections* (WordCrafter Press) anthology published in September 2022. Her short story, "Wheels Against Wings" will appear in the *Vinyl Cuts!* (Scary Dairy Press) anthology in the summer of 2023. Valerie lives near Charlottesville, Virginia, with her husband and two Golden Retrievers. When not writing, she can be found reading and drinking either wine or tea, depending on the time of day.

MORNING FIRE

BY MIKE DEADY

Leon feels an itching in his chest.

After lying paralyzed and insensate for so long, the sudden tickle surprises him and gives him a surge of hope. If he can feel again, does this mean he can now move too? He wiggles his fingers and toes. So far, so good.

He opens his eyes. Although it is pitch-dark, he can see perfectly well. He lifts his head off the ground and looks around at the abandoned silver mine the townspeople had chased him into before looking down at himself. The wooden stake is gone. Instead, there is a gaping wound in his chest crawling with insects. *Termites,* he realizes with mounting excitement. *They've consumed the stake and freed me!*

Luckily for him, the fools apparently believed the old legends that a stake would be enough to kill him. If they had taken the next step and decapitated him or burned his body, he would truly be dead.

But who is he to call *them* the fools? He's the one lying here with a hole in his chest full of bugs due to his own overconfidence and carelessness. What's more, losing so much time may have cost him his chance to get the girl back. He is filled with rage, at himself for failing, but mostly at the men who took the girl in the first place. The same men who did this to him.

He sits up. A sudden stomach cramp causes him to double over. His thirst is a living thing, gnawing at him from the inside. He must have been lying here for months as he is nothing but skin and bone. He will need a lot of blood to heal the wound in his chest and get himself back to normal. And he knows exactly where to find it.

He rises to his feet. Almost immediately, he is stymied. The entrance to the mine has been dynamited, sealing him inside. If only he could turn himself into mist and slip through the cracks in the wall of rubble, but that is another old myth. Each rock will have to be moved by hand, a daunting task in his weakened condition. But he is fueled by his rage and overpowering thirst. He picks up the first rock and tosses it aside. And then the next.

Leon steps out of the mine and into the night. A coyote howls in the distance. Another lone predator on the hunt. A kindred spirit.

He follows the mine trail until it intersects with the road into town, stopping when a pair of horsemen approach. He steps back into the shadows. When they get close enough, he recognizes them as two of the townspeople.

As they reach the intersection, Leon springs. He tackles the nearest rider off his horse, grabs the man's head with both hands, and wrenches it off. Blood spurts from the neck stump like a fountain, and Leon drinks deeply.

He drops the headless body and turns his attention to the second rider. The man appears stunned, unable to process what just happened. As Leon approaches, he smells the man's bladder empty.

The man fumbles for his weapon. Before he can pull the trigger, Leon bites through his wrist and spits out the hand, still attached to the gun. He drinks from the wrist stub while pulling the man down from the horse.

Dropping the body, he feels slightly better, but after months of starvation and the effort required to move the rockslide, he needs *much* more.

His first victim's horse has ridden off. The other one is still here, and Leon wants to ride it into town to conserve his energy. After smelling the soiled saddle, he changes his mind and strips the saddlery from the horse, gives it a swat to send it on its way, and starts walking into town, hoping the girl is still there.

He passes the town sign:

BUZZARDS' ROOST

POPULATION 101

The number currently shown is far smaller than when he first arrived. And it is already obsolete.

Two down, ninety-nine to go. He has a lot to do before the sun comes up.

The Civil War battlefields were a smorgasbord for Leon. He drank only from the mortally wounded, the dying with no chance of survival, rationalizing that these mercy killings allowed him to hang on to what was left of his humanity. By being well-fed in this manner, he would not have to harm other human beings. He had vowed never to do that.

After the war, Leon followed the army—and the bloodshed—west. As horrific as the War Between the States had been, at least it had been a relatively fair fight between two armies believing in their respective causes. The Indian Wars, however, sickened him. They were not truly wars at all, in his opinion, but attempts at total extermination.

Not wanting anything to do with that, he drifted around the West like so many others. He was attracted to darkly named towns: Deadwood, Tombstone, Canyon Diablo. He found towns with such names to be perfect for his needs. They were usually lawless places filled with the dregs of society. No one missed the killers who disappeared off the face of the earth. His moral code allowed this loophole; he considered murderers to be mad dogs, not human beings.

Leon's ramblings took him back to Arizona Territory. He quickly grew tired of the oppressive heat and the vast expanses of emptiness. He had no idea what he was searching for, but this was not it. Why would anyone want to live in this part of the country, and why had he returned?

He decided to abandon the Southwest and head to San Francisco. He could easily get lost in that wide-open city. There would be plenty of bad elements to feed on. And the cool and the fog would be a blessed relief from the heat and the dust.

He made a late afternoon ride to nearby Fort Saguaro to buy supplies for his trip. As he always did when traveling in daylight, he wore a wide-brimmed hat pulled low, a bandana, and gloves, protecting every inch of skin from the unforgiving sun.

Fort Saguaro was not so much a fort as a ragtag collection of buildings, shacks, and tents. There were several Apache from the reservation dozing in the shade. One of the women approached Leon as he dismounted.

"I have seen you here before," she said. "You are not like other White men."

At first, he took it as a compliment. Then he wondered if she had a different meaning altogether. During his ramblings around the West, he had never been bothered by Indians. He had a theory that they, being spiritual people in harmony with nature, could sense his unnaturalness and wanted to keep their distance.

"Is there something you want, ma'am?"

"You will find my sister's child."

"I will *what*?"

"She was taken. You will bring her back to me."

"Where are her parents?"

"I am raising the girl. My sister and her man are dead."

"I'm very sorry, ma'am. But why can't your own people go fetch your niece?"

She glared at him as if he were the stupidest man in the world. "We cannot leave the reservation without being pursued by your White soldiers."

"But what do you expect me to do about it?"

"I have already told you. She was stolen. You will find her and bring her back."

"Why me?"

"You have certain... powers."

So, she did know what he was. Instead of giving him away, she had come to him for help. It was unusual for an Apache to ask a White man for assistance. Leon supposed he could put off his departure to San Francisco for a few days. Perhaps doing this one good deed could balance some of the things he had done and help cleanse his soul, if he still had one.

"Who took her?"

"Ask Ferguson." She spat on the ground.

After sunset, Leon entered the cabin of Donald Ferguson, the agent for the reservation. He was already asleep, a bottle of whiskey on the floor by his cot. Leon slapped him hard. Ferguson opened his bloodshot eyes.

"Who are you? How *dare* you break into my cabin?"

"Where's the girl?"

"What girl?"

With one hand, Leon lifted Ferguson off the cot and pinned him against the wall by his throat. His feet dangled above the floor, struggling for purchase.

"I'm only going to ask one more time. *Where's the girl?*"

"The Indian girls?" Ferguson croaked.

"Girls? There's more than one?"

Leon squeezed harder. Ferguson's face turned purple. Leon abruptly released him, and he fell to the floor gasping for breath. Leon stood over him, waiting. When Ferguson could breathe again, he started talking.

He told Leon everything. That he had made an arrangement with an outlaw named Amos McCraer. That he was paid handsomely to look the other way last night when McCraer and his gang raided the reservation and took several of the choicest Indian maidens away. That McCraer planned to sell the girls off into slavery and prostitution. That the gang was headed to its lair at Buzzards' Roost.

Leon was revolted. How did a polecat like Ferguson ever get posted here? He was as foul a creature as Leon had ever encountered. The reservation would be far better off with a new agent.

He was tempted to drink Ferguson dry. But if he left a drained body behind, he would risk being found out for what he was. And if he took the body away, Apache from the reservation could be blamed for Ferguson's murder and disappearance.

Leon had a better idea.

He bent down and bit Ferguson on the neck, not to drink but to put him in thrall. Ferguson's eyes widened. He stood and walked across the room like a marionette. He picked up a coil of rope, formed one end into a noose, and placed it over his head. His hands were trembling as he climbed on the chair, threw the other end over a ceiling beam, and tied it off. Tears streamed down his face. He kicked the chair away.

Leon wasted no time taking off in pursuit of McCraer and his gang. They had nearly a full day's lead on him, but he knew their destination. He hoped he could catch them on the trail before getting there. Surprising and overpowering a dozen raiders in the open would be preferable to facing a hundred or more in a town they knew well. And every hour that passed increased the chances of something happening to the girl. *Girls,* he corrected himself. He could not rescue the one and leave the others behind.

To relieve his own horse, he took Ferguson's and put it under his control. He alternated rides to keep them both fresh. When they smelled water, he let them go to it. When he needed to feed, he lit a bright campfire as bait and waited to see what he reeled in. If a bandit seeing an easy target approached with gun drawn, he quickly became Leon's dinner.

On the fourth day, he came upon signs that the raiders had stopped and met up with another band of riders. This second group had then headed south toward the Mexican border. It could have been simply a chance meeting between two sets of riders. Or it could have been a planned meeting where some, or all, of the Apache girls were sold off. Leon had assumed the sale would take place at Buzzards' Roost and that he would get there in time to stop it.

Should he head south into unfamiliar territory, or keep pursuing the raiders? The wrong decision would waste valuable time and could have dire consequences for the girls. He continued chasing the raiders.

Leon arrived at the outskirts of Buzzards' Roost. He had missed catching up to the gang by less than an hour. Now they had all the advantages. They knew the town and he did not. More importantly, it was still a couple hours until sunset.

He knew he should wait until dark when he would regain his nocturnal powers, but he felt that time was of the essence. He decided to head into town. It should be safe enough. Even in the daylight, when he was as weak as a normal man, he could only be killed or permanently harmed in specific ways. And they would have to know what he was to use those methods.

As he approached the town, he noticed a trail on the left and saw that it led to an abandoned silver mine. He left Ferguson's horse there. Up ahead, he could see a bullet-riddled sign:

BUZZARDS' ROOST

POPULATION 130

From what he had learned of the town, its only inhabitants were vicious gangs of bandits and their women, some of whom were even more cutthroat than the men. Killers all, they lived in an uneasy peace frequently interrupted by deadly disputes over women or cards. The town was reputed to be even more violent than Canyon Diablo.

The population had been several thousand back when the mine was a going concern. It was the same story all over the West. Former boomtowns would go bust once the local mine was played out. People would move on in droves, leaving behind a near ghost town filled with the worst of humanity. The number on the sign had been painted over various times as the population decreased.

He rode past the sign and into town. Even without his night senses, he could feel eyes upon him as he traveled down Main Street. Many of the buildings were deserted and falling apart, but a large two-story building was in good shape. Whatever the original name of the place had been, it was now painted over in big, red letters and read:

McCRAER'S EMPORIUM

SALOON - GAMBLING - GIRLS - ROOMS

McCraer must be the town's head buzzard, Leon thought. He got off his horse and left it untied by a water trough. It would not go anywhere without him.

He pushed open the door to the saloon. Conversation stopped and everyone turned to stare at him. He walked to the bar and ordered a whiskey. He did not drink, but he wanted to look like he fit in.

The bartender scowled. "Who the hell are you?"

"Just passing through. That a crime here?"

"Son, *nothing's* a crime here. You should get out of town while you still can."

A scruffy redhead standing next to Leon snorted.

Leon looked at him. The redhead was with a group of sweaty, dusty, tired-looking men who were guzzling beer and whiskey. Almost certainly members of the raiding party.

"Oh, give him a whiskey, Gus," the redhead said.

Gus slid a shot glass to Leon. "One drink, and then get out."

Leon raised the glass to his lips, pretending to take a sip.

"Where you from, stranger?" the redhead asked. "Where you headed?"

"Oh, I've just been rambling around since the war."

The redhead narrowed his eyes. "You ain't old enough to've been in the war."

"I'm older than I look."

The redhead still looked doubtful, so Leon told him some of the places he had visited. He was walking a fine line, stalling as he waited for sunset, while also trying to locate the girls as quickly as possible.

The redhead looked impressed. "You were in Tombstone? Did you know Wyatt Earp? Bat Masterson?"

"Sure. Turns out I have a lot in common with Bat." Leon took another pretend sip. Enough beating around the bush. "There's another reason I'm here. I heard you have Indian girls for sale."

Conversation ceased again. The redhead and Gus exchanged looks. Gus sauntered to the end of the bar and spoke to a man who then ran upstairs.

"I don't know where you heard that, stranger. We got perfectly good White whores who can show you a good time."

And then try to cut my throat and take my money, Leon thought. "You don't understand. I want to *purchase* the Indian girls. I can pay whatever you want."

"Is that right?" The redhead glanced upwards. Leon followed his gaze and saw another redhead, an older man with a graying beard, standing on the second-floor landing overlooking the bar and gaming area. He nodded down at the younger redhead, who pulled out his gun and jammed it in Leon's ribs. "Why don't you come with me, stranger?"

The redhead and his companions prodded Leon up the stairs, down the hallway, and into a room at the end of the corridor. The older man was waiting for them.

"I'm Amos McCraer. What are you doing in my town?"

"Like I told your lackey here—"

The younger redhead slammed his gun against the side of Leon's head.

McCraer snickered. "You should be nicer to my son."

"Like I told your *son*, I heard there were some Indian girls for sale here. I want to buy them."

"*All* of them? You starting up your own sporting house?"

"That's my business."

"Even if I had these Indian girls you speak of, it would cost you a pretty penny to buy them all."

"I've got the money."

"Do you. In that case, why don't you hand it over."

"I'm not stupid enough to have it on me. Show me what I'm paying for, and I'll show you where the money is."

"Well, as it turns out, I already sold the girls," McCraer said. "Except for one of them. I was kinda thinking of keeping her for myself. But I'll tell you what, you give me all the money you were going to pay for all the girls, and you can have her."

Leon knew McCraer had no intention of letting him or the girl go once he had the money. Not that McCraer could do anything about it once darkness fell in about another half hour. Leon just had to play along until then and find out where the girl was. He would rescue her even if she was not the one he had come for.

He pretended to think the offer over. "That's a lot of money for one girl. Before I decide, show me the merchandise. If she's worth it, we have a deal."

"Why not." McCraer turned to his son. "Junior, go get the girl."

Junior left the room. He returned with another man, a Comanche. They dragged an Apache girl between them. She was stunningly beautiful, despite being dusty and bedraggled from the week-long ride across the Territory.

"Well, there she is," McCraer said. "Do we have a deal?"

"What is your name?" Leon asked her.

She looked at him for the first time. Her eyes widened. The Comanche, noticing her reaction, looked curiously at Leon.

"I'm getting impatient," McCraer said. "Who the hell cares what her name is? Do we have a deal or not?"

"I'm paying a lot of money here. I want to know her name. What's the big deal?"

McCraer rolled his eyes. "Fine. Tell the man your name."

"I am called Morning Fire."

Leon could not believe his luck. It was the right girl. "She'll do," he said to McCraer. "We have a deal."

"Where's the money?"

"Hidden right outside town. I'll go get it."

"We'll *all* go get it."

Leon and the girl were herded down the stairs and through the saloon. Outside, McCraer and several of his men mounted up. They were loaded onto the back of a buckboard with Junior, who kept his gun trained on them. The girl sat as far away from both Leon and Junior as she could get, as if unsure which of them was the lesser of two evils.

Leon directed them to the mine trail where he had left Ferguson's horse. Everyone from the saloon followed to see what was going on, trailed by the rest of the townspeople. It did not matter. Once the sun set in fifteen minutes, he would be able to overpower them all if necessary.

Junior stepped off the buckboard. "Where's the money?"

"It's in the saddlebag on the horse."

There was no money, of course. At least, not enough to buy one girl, let alone several. But his ploy had eaten up time and gotten McCraer and the townspeople out in the open. Now if the sun would only set...

Junior walked away toward the horse. Leon was momentarily alone with the girl.

"Stay away from me," she said. "I know what you are."

"You have nothing to fear from me. Your aunt sent me to find you."

The girl looked doubtful. "My aunt? Sent *you*?"

"Yes. She was very persuasive."

The girl's expression softened.

"I promised her I would bring you home," Leon continued.

"That *place* is not my home, merely where my people are."

"You speak very good English. Just like your aunt."

"They forced us to learn it at the Agency." She spat on the floor of the buckboard.

Just like your aunt, Leon thought.

She inclined her head toward McCraer and his men. "I fear *you* may need rescuing yourself."

The Comanche was pointing urgently at the setting sun. He whispered something to McCraer who looked sharply at Leon.

Junior had reached Ferguson's horse. As he grabbed for the saddlebag, the horse rose on its hind legs. Junior fell backward. The horse stomped a hoof down on his knee and reared up for another strike.

"Shoot it! Shoot it!" Junior screamed.

A panicked voice cried, "There's another one!"

Leon's own horse had followed him and the others from town and was now stampeding through the crowd. It pulled up next to the buckboard. Leon hoisted the girl onto the horse and jumped on. Just as he thought they might make it, the horse was shot out from under them.

He grabbed the girl by the hand. They ran for the mine, McCraer and his men in pursuit. Leon kicked through the rotten boards sealing off the mine entrance and pulled the girl inside. He only had to evade the gang for a few brief moments until the sun was fully set.

Leon and the girl ran for a crosscut tunnel, but they were not fast enough. Leon was tackled, turned onto his back, and spread-eagled. McCraer's men pinned his arms and legs and ripped open his shirt, exposing his chest. He struggled vainly to free himself.

"Hurry up, the sun's almost down," McCraer said.

The Comanche bent down, holding a jagged piece of timber. He placed the point against Leon's chest with one hand and lifted a rock with the other.

Leon took a last look around. The townspeople were cramming into the mine to witness his ignominious demise. Junior was being supported by two members of the gang. Two others were dragging the Apache girl away. She looked back at him.

"I'm sorry," Leon said.

The Comanche pounded the stake in.

By the time Leon arrives at McCraer's Emporium, he has already hunted down a good number of the town's denizens and fed. He feels much better. His chest itches, not from termites now, but from the wound starting to knit together. He has regained most of his lost body mass and strength. Knowing the remainder of the townspeople will be inside, he pushes open the door.

All heads turn to gape at him as he enters the saloon. He can see himself reflected in the bar mirror, covered head to foot in blood. He stands still for a moment, surveying the crowd as if lining up a billiards shot. Then he moves.

He scythes through the crowd, opening up throats with his nails. Only a few of the gunmen react quickly enough to draw their weapons and open fire, but Leon is so fast that they only manage to strike fellow outlaws. He takes them down easily.

Gus is the last man standing. He brings up a shotgun from behind the bar. Before he can pull the trigger, Leon wrenches it from his hands, lifts him up, and hurls him headfirst into the bar mirror. He picks up the dazed bartender, opens his throat, and drinks as Gus's life gurgles out.

Leon hears a groan and turns around. The saloon is littered with bodies, overturned tables and chairs, broken bottles and glasses. The floor is a soup of spilled blood, whiskey, and beer. One of the gunmen is still alive, barely, crawling through the mess toward the saloon door. Leon lifts up the dying outlaw and lets the blood pour into his mouth. He tosses the body aside and feels eyes upon him. He looks up.

Attracted by the gunfire, a group of half-naked outlaws and whores is standing on the second-floor landing. Leon sees Junior McCraer bull his way through the crowd, look down, and turn pale. Leon starts up the stairs slowly, savoring his fear.

"Hold him off!" Junior commands. He turns and limps down the corridor toward his father's room.

Leon barely feels the bullets that strike him. As he gets to the top of the stairs, the gunmen and their women panic and try to run, but the hallway serves the purpose of a cattle chute. Leon makes quick work of them. He checks the rooms to make sure he has not missed anyone. Only then does he approach McCraer's room.

He bursts through the door.

Standing next to the bed, Amos McCraer is restraining the Apache girl. His left hand covers her mouth, pulling her head back to expose her throat. He holds a knife against it with his right hand.

"I don't know what it is with you and this girl," McCraer says, "but if you come near me or my boy, I'll cut her throat."

Leon stops to assess the situation. Junior is standing next to his father, no longer looking fearful, but smug. *Something is not right,* Leon thinks.

He sees the girl's eyes flick sideways. He is already ducking when he feels a slight displacement of air caused by a machete slicing where his neck just was.

Leon was so focused on the McCraers and the girl when he entered the room that he failed to notice the Comanche hiding behind the wardrobe. With virtually no warning, McCraer devised a trap and lured Leon into the perfect killing position. Once again, he has underestimated McCraer. If not for the girl's warning, his head would now be bouncing across the floor.

Leon takes the machete from the off-balance Comanche and knocks him to the floor.

"Let's see how *you* like it," Leon says.

He plunges the machete into the Comanche's heart.

Leon turns his attention back to McCraer, who looks dumbfounded at the turn of events. His mouth is hanging open and the knife has drifted a couple inches away from the girl's throat. It is all Leon needs. He closes the distance in the blink of an eye, disarms McCraer, and hurls the knife out the door. Before McCraer can react, Leon leans in and bites him on the neck, not to drink but to control. McCraer becomes still.

Junior tries to run. He limps out of the room. Stepping over a body in the hallway, he slips on the blood-soaked floor, much to Leon's amusement. He gets up, hobbles toward the stairway, and looks back. Leon is right behind him. He picks up Junior and lifts him over his head.

"Looks like your knee is bothering you," Leon says. "Let me help you down the stairs."

With Junior dispatched, Leon returns to McCraer's room. The girl has pulled the bloody machete from the Comanche's chest and is advancing on McCraer. Leon stops her.

"Why have you let him live?" she asks Leon. "Why have you not drained his blood? Torn him limb from limb as he deserves?"

"I have a better idea."

The girl is sleeping in one of the abandoned houses off Main Street. She refused to sleep in any of the rooms at the Emporium, and Leon cannot blame her. He can only imagine what she has endured in those rooms over the last few months due to his botched initial rescue attempt.

While she sleeps, Leon loads a buckboard with as many bodies as it will carry. It takes several trips to transport every carcass to the outskirts of town. He dumps them near the town sign on top of his first two victims. It is an impressive pile, although it dwarfs in comparison to the stacks of dead buffalo he has seen in his travels.

Leon turns his attention to Amos McCraer, who has been standing motionless while Leon worked. McCraer takes off all his clothes, climbs up the mound of bodies, and spread-eagles himself on the summit. He will not move again, but Leon will allow him to see, smell, hear, feel. And sc ream.

Leon rides back into town one last time. He washes off the blood and finds clean clothes. He goes into the livery stable intending to get horses for himself and the girl but stops short as he sees something much more interesting: a stagecoach, painted black and outfitted with black curtains. He has heard of many stagecoaches being robbed. He has never heard of the stagecoach itself being stolen.

The vehicle will work out perfectly. It will protect him from the sun during the day. He puts eight of the best horses under his control and releases the rest. He hitches up the four that will pull the first leg of the journey. The others will follow without needing to be tethered to the back of the coach.

He sees the sun is about to rise. He has managed to get all the heavy work done before losing his nocturnal strength. Shading his eyes against the direct sun, he watches the horizon light up. *Was this the inspiration for the Apache girl's name?*

He locates food and water for the girl, grain for the horses, saddles in case they abandon the stagecoach for any reason, and other supplies they may need, and loads everything onto the coach. He drives down Main Street.

The girl is waiting for him outside the Emporium. Leon steps off the stagecoach. He enters the building and goes behind the bar, broken glass crunching under his boots, and splashes several bottles of whiskey around. As he leaves, he *very* carefully drops a match. He is always wary when it comes to fire.

The Emporium starts burning. Leon hopes it will spread and burn the whole damn town right off the map. The girl nods her approval and climbs into the stagecoach. Leon follows her inside. The coach takes off.

"But there is no driver!" the girl says.

"The horses know where to go. We'll make one quick stop outside town. Then we'll head home."

"No."

"No? No, what?"

"We will not head home. You will take us to Mexico to find the other girls first."

"I will *what*?"

"And you will be more careful this time. You are a very poor rescuer. How you have managed to survive this long on your own is a mystery to me. From now on, you will follow my directions."

Leon glares at her. She glares right back.

"Damn it, girl. You're as bossy and pigheaded as your aunt."

His comment seems to please her. He will never understand women.

"Speaking of pigs," she says, "you never told me what you did with McCraer."

Leon and the girl get out of the stagecoach. The pile of corpses is simmering in the morning heat. He looks up. Turkey vultures are already circling, riding the thermals, attracted by the succulent aroma of death below. He knows McCraer can see them too.

Leon looks at the girl. She is watching the scene intently.

He looks up again. The buzzards are closer. He watches the hypnotic rhythm of the vultures as they swirl around and drop closer and closer with each pass. Finally, one lands and takes a tentative peck at one of the carcasses. The rest of them descend, landing all around McCraer in a feeding frenzy. His dangling, soft tissue is the first to go.

The girl lets out a loud whoop.

McCraer's tongue is next as he opens his mouth to scream. Then his eyes. He is still alive until his liver is torn out.

The girl smiles. She gives Leon a nod that she is ready to go and climbs back into the stagecoach.

Leon takes one last look behind him and is gratified to see the fire has engulfed the entire town. Before joining the girl in the stage and riding away, he takes off a glove, careful to keep his exposed hand shaded from the sun. He scares a buzzard away from one of the bodies and dips a finger into the gore, drawing a red line through the number on the town sign and replacing it with a new one:

BUZZARDS' ROOST

POPULATION 0

About the Author

Mike Deady's work has appeared in Wicked Sick, That Is So Wrong, Bag of Bones: 206 Word Stories, and Totally Tubular Terrors. He is a member of the New England Horror Writers and a lifelong resident of Massachusetts. After retiring from a forty-two-year career in engineering, he started writing horror fiction at the urging of his brother, Bram Stoker Award-winning author Tom Deady.

ANY
COMICS

DE CASIBUS

BY J. ROCKY COLAVITO

There's always someone, or something, that wants to knock a king off his throne. It's part of the job description when you wear the crown. I've faced so many wannabes that it's become routine. Someone or something decides that they want to take their shot at me, and they rise from the depths of the ocean, fly trillions of miles through space, or crawl out of the bowels of the earth to knock me off the top of the mountain. Some have been bigger, some have been faster, some have greater powers. But I'm still standing, looking down at their headless, broken bodies. I have a trophy room where I keep the heads, necks cauterized by my unholy fire to keep them from bleeding all over the place. I look at them and laugh, occasionally talking smack to them when I'm bored.

Don't get me wrong, the battles haven't been easy; I have the scars to prove it. My powers of regeneration have become overtaxed as my many adversaries take their shots more frequently, sometimes teaming up against me. Cowards, the lot of them. Too chickenshit to face me alone. I'm not as strong as I once was; what gets me through these days, when I'm not raiding nuclear plants or munching on atomic-powered crafts for sustenance, is the fact that I'm smarter than your average kaiju. I know all the tricks, and I've seen everything that an opponent can throw at me. Sometimes these idiots turn tail and run before I can finish them off. They'll come back again with a new strategy, or with cybernetic parts grafted on. One time, some humans decided it would be fun to try to use some of my genetic material as a template for a robot version for me to face. It did a job on me; it had a host of weapons systems that it deployed all at once to take me down, but I played possum, let it get close to me, and then I tore its head and arms clean off and beat it into scrap metal. Then I took one of the arms and golfed the head into the ocean.

Not meaning to brag here, but I've got a pretty good win streak going and there's no end in sight. Matter of fact, I may have run out of opponents. These goofs who wanted to take over my planet threw a whole menagerie of creatures at me one right after another, and I killed 'em all, taking down several world cities in the process. The puny humans tried to take me out with these old-school robots; there's gratitude for ya. I let the operators exit and then smashed the robots to scrap metal. There wasn't enough left of those automated tin cans to use as toothpicks; believe me, I tried.

You may wonder, why do I bother protecting the humans from other menaces if that's the thanks I get. Strange as it sounds, we kinda feed off each other. No, not like you're probably thinking. I don't eat humans; they taste like shit. Give me a whale or a school of tuna any day. If you have a megalodon or giant octopus lying around, I'll make short work of it. Humans don't give me any pleasure, other than nourishing the side of me that craves veneration. They do call me king after all. That counts for something. And they need a safety net; they tend to get ahead of themselves and not know their limits. Many's the time I've had to clean up one of their messes, whether it's mutated pollution or something that got out of control because of some idiot's unchecked experiment. I keep them safe so they can do these sorts of things, which you'd think sets boundaries on what they attempt.

Which, of course, the humans forget the minute they get interested in the next big what if.

So, here I wait, just itching to answer the bell again, but not given the pleasure. I could go out on another raid, or look up one of the other monsters that's still prowling around and see if they want to go city smashing. But that kind of fun sounds boring; same shit, different day if you know what I mean. I just ate a few weeks ago, and the batteries are still fully charged. I listlessly spew out some fireworks, starting a forest fire on the side of the high mountain where I lounge. I like fire; I like the way it dances and creates different colors. Sometimes I'll go roll around in it; the heat soothes me and does a good job of sealing the various cuts and scratches I get in my scraps with others.

But not today; nothing interests me. Truth of the matter, I'm bored.

Bet you find that whack. A monster overwhelmed by ennui. What the actual fuck?

Look, if you've seen and done it all, you'd be bored too. Just because I'm four hundred feet tall and can breathe atomic fire doesn't mean that I can't suffer from been there, done that, and stained the T-shirt.

I need action; the sooner the better.

From the top of the mountain, I can see the ocean. It's a short walk for me, and there's usually something that's new and different somewhere in the darkest depths. Some idiot humans crossed a shark with a squid and subjected it to a nuclear bath. The thing was bigger than I am by the time I caught up with it, and it nearly choked me out with the tentacles, one of which took out an eye (which has since grown back—don't forget that I can regenerate). I vanquished it like everything else, and it was actually pretty good eating. I like calamari.

The possibility of more calamari makes the decision for me. I slowly plod down from the mountaintop and make for the sea. I'm not as careful as I usually am, and I trample a few houses and knock over some skyscrapers as I near the cliffs that signal the boundary between the land and the water. There's a storm brewing on the horizon; it stretches as far as I can see in both directions. I let out one of my patented roars and cannonball myself off the cliff. The splash I make causes a small tidal wave that washes several thousand feet inland. I take in the storm again, and then dive toward the depths, arms and legs pulling in unison, tail offering some added thrust.

I cruise the deep deliberately, on the lookout for a giant squid, a megalodon, a plesiosaur, just about anything that could give me a challenge and a meal. But there's nothing. Not a single, blessed thing. I swim by something the humans set up for deep exploration, an ugly structure that looks like a mutated mushroom. It's completely dark, which is out of the ordinary. There's always some kind of activity there, and on those occasions when I pass looking for deep-sea food it goes crazy, locking down, descending into a dome on the seafloor, and creating camouflage. It's as if it's been vacated. I file this for future reference as I swim by toward the trench and dive even deeper.

The trench is lit as it usually is by the vents that raise the water temperature to manageable. There's a weird, orange glow that reveals all kinds of rock formations twisted into art forms by the intense pressure. But there's not a single form of life to be seen. At some point I'd expect to run into something, but nothing swims out to confront me for trespassing.

Too fucking weird, I think as I reverse course and swim back for the surface, taking my time, trying to find something to eat or fight. The normal schools of small fish that I leave alone because they really aren't worth eating are absent. Dolphins, humpback whales, sport fish—not a single, solitary marine creature crosses my path.

It's then that I notice the sun that lights the surface of the ocean isn't there, either. I stop my ascent and ponder this. I float, and then decide to try something that will tell me if I'm disoriented. I spin myself so that I am facing the direction that I've come from and let loose a blast of fire. It will tell me which direction is up, kinda like spitting to figure out which way you're buried if you're caught in an avalanche.

The beam goes down until it winks out in the darkness, but I can feel the reverberation when it strikes something. Where I sent the beam is down. So, I set a course for the surface again, pushing myself a little harder because I'm curious why there's no sunlight. I haven't been down here that long.

When I break the surface, I see why it's dark. Everything is enveloped in this thick mist.

I can barely make out the cliffs in the distance. I head for them. The mist doesn't seem corrosive in any way. I have no issue with breathing or seeing. But there's nothing to hear. No seabirds, no waves against the shore. No shouting from the port at my return. It's a ghost town.

I stomp my way into the port, knocking over a crane and throwing some shipping containers. I let out one of my loudest roars. The only sounds are those that I made.

Lucy, you got some 'splainin to do crosses my mind as I tromp through the outskirts of the port and into the city. This is where things get very strange.

Cars are piled up at intersections, the tops of some buildings have been sheared off, and there's rubble burying smaller buildings. Webbing that seems to pulse is all over the place, covering some of the still-standing skyscrapers.

Aha, I think; this is the work of some of those giant insects that I used to call friends until they tried to kill my son.

I inhale and then release a fire blast at one of the buildings covered in webbing.

It bounces right back at me and slams down both of my throats. I fall backwards, coughing.

That's for sure something new. Stuff usually goes up like flash paper. I struggle to sit up, and then stand.

I rise just in time for something to land on my head and slam something sharp that drips caustic into my left eye. I immediately make a grab for whatever it is and disengage it after a struggle.

It's like nothing I've ever seen, and believe me, I've seen a lot.

It's a bit bigger than one of my hands, and it looks like a cross between a dragonfly and a scorpion. It won't stay still, and the stinger hits my hand as I try to throttle it. It makes a high-pitched trilling sound until I finally manage to crush its head. I throw the body aside and let out a bellow. My eye is damaged, my hand is numb, and I think I hear more of them coming.

I hate being right in situations like this.

I'm enveloped by a swarm of the things that latch onto me and start stinging. I must protect my remaining eye, so I'm spitting fire breath and slamming into buildings trying to crush as many as I can. Somehow, they manage to lift me off the ground and carry me for a few feet, right into the shell of the tallest building in the city. The collision starts pancaking it, right on top of me and the gadflies. Things go dark and I'm left with the survivors who continue to pump me full of that caustic. I call on my reserves and start smashing my way out of the rubble, losing strength as I work. When I do, I turn my breath on myself, incinerating the few that are still clinging to me, and cauterizing some of the open wounds they've left. It's painful, but no worse than what they were doing to me.

I really should cut my losses and regroup in the ocean, but I'm beyond pissed with this situation and am determined to show them who's boss. As they used to say in old flicks that sometimes double billed with movies about me, "There ain't room enough in this town for the both of us." So, despite my sapped strength and loss of vision, I decide to look for answers.

I get another one right away. Something long, thorned, and sinuous strikes out of nowhere and wraps itself around my neck. Others grab my arms, and one wraps around my leg. I feel the thorns starting to vibrate, like a saw blade. I can smell my own blood as they do their work.

I instinctively grab the tentacles that have my arms and yank. Whatever they're attached to emerges from the mist.

It's about three-quarters my size and looks like one of those things that's supposed to bow to me. All the extrusions are centered in its mouth; the rest of it looks feline but covered with scales. It throws out more tentacles, which I manage to bat away or duck. The one around my neck is getting ever tighter, and if I don't find a way out of this quickly, my head is gonna be in someone's trophy case. The pressure won't let me use fire breath, so I rely on old-fashioned brute strength. I grab one of the tentacles encircling my arms and yank. It's a brief tug-of-war, but I win. The thing squalls as I manage to free my other arm and set to work on the one around my neck. This one is thicker, and trying to maintain my balance with one around my lower leg is not easy. I decide to let it pull my leg out from under me. I fall backwards into the pile I'd just escaped, and the tentacle around my neck snaps.

I let loose with some fire breath, hitting the whatsit square in that mass of writhing tentacles. It explodes, covering me with multicolored gore. I lick some off my face; it's not half bad.

I let out a loud bellow; it's smack talk in kaiju. I rhetorically inquire, "Is that the best you've got?"

My answer comes in the form of loud footfalls that shake the ground I stand on. A huge shadow washes over me. I can hear and feel heavy breathing. For the first time in my life, I don't want to look something in the face.

But a king doesn't go down a coward, so I turn around. It's worse than I thought.

It towers over me on hundreds of legs the size of tree trunks. Its eight red eyes regard me with amusement as its mandible-bordered mouth clicks hungrily. Its sides shake as it starts to laugh.

I should run, but I refuse to abdicate. This thing is gonna have to take my crown by force.

It reaches out two of its legs for me. I set one of them on fire and move out of the way of the other one. The thing draws back the burned limb and looks at it, puzzled. I see the burned part turn to dust and crumble.

If I can hurt it, I can kill it.

It roars, drowning out my war cry. It moves toward me with surprising speed. The collision slams me backwards, but I somehow manage to take hold and pull the thing with me,

which is stupid, because it lands on top of me and slams my lungs empty. Its mandibles fasten around the side of my head. The pressure is intense, and I feel them rip the left side of my face clean off.

I let out a roar of pain and hammer away at the gigantic thing on top of me. By rocking side to side, I manage to throw it off-balance and use its momentum to reverse the situation. I can see my blood drip onto the thing. It sticks out a couple of tongues to lap up the drips. I manage to twist my head to the side as it spits.

I'm glad I did; the gooey mass hits part of a still-standing building and immediately starts smoking. What is left of the building melts.

I narrow my one good eye and blow a blast of fire breath into the thing's face. It squeals, and struggles.

I hurt it; I can kill it.

I go for what might be its throat. My bite yields foul-tasting fluids that burn, but I hold on. With a twist and a yank, I pull out part of its throat. Its head hangs oddly. It wraps its remaining legs around me and starts to squeeze. I thrash, blow fire, bite, but there are just so many and they're getting close to rendering me immobile. It takes the last of my strength to free one of my arms, which I ram into the hole that I made in its throat.

It starts thrashing again; I think I may be stopping its breathing. The legs tighten and I can feel my bones starting to crack. It tries spitting at me again and this time the mass hits me in the shoulder. I watch my skin dissolve and the caustic begins to work on the bones, but I keep my arm jammed in the thing's windpipe; even though I am fading fast, my adversary is fading faster.

It gives up the ghost first. I'm stuck in its embrace, but I managed to eke out this win.

But I know it's my last because I've lost so much blood and have been pumped full of so much poison that my own functions are failing. The bones in my shoulder where it spit on me dissolve, and the arm falls away. I manage one last roar and I sink down on top of my last foe, secure in the final thought I have before the curtain falls.

I went out on top.

About the Author

J. Rocky Colavito is a sunsetting academic who is impatiently watching the minutes tick off until the "last bell." He is the creator of Buck Neighkyd, former porn star turned occult detective, and has published in a variety of genres, collections, and magazines.

VESPER'S GARDEN

BY VILLE MERILÄINEN

At dusk, when cranes left the lake and rain stopped whipping reeds, we carried a fallen child to the shore. The small bundle rested on my arm, head against my chest, weighing almost nothing; the soul was gone now, and with its loss, the body of my son had shrivelled to the size of an infant.

I wept not for his passing, for he was with his mother, sleeping safely in an everlasting night. My grief bloomed from letting him go to waste. His arms were strong, anointed with the blood of my enemies. His mind was sharper than a young boy's had a right to be. Had he lived a few wheels more, I've no doubt he would have learned to speak spells faster than his half-sister.

He had fought and killed four huntsmen, drunk his prize from the bellies, and eaten their flesh. We had watched, awed by his skill, how sluggish the weak man seemed before him.

It became clear only after he had fed that the huntsmen had ingested poison.

We stopped at the water's edge. Isa Oberon and Asa Irium stepped past me, setting afloat the wicker basket they'd made. Half-siblings to one another, my daughter and older son had grown from children to adults this past spring. There were no mates left for either, so they stayed with me. Though borne to different mothers, they looked strikingly similar, with straight, black manes shorn at the waist and hard, sharp faces set with eyes of amber and blue. Tall too; their bodies reached to my chest, and though their frames were still willowy, their skin had begun to turn hard with bark, their antlers showing the thickness of maturity.

I laid my younger son in the basket while Asa Irium lit the torch. They shared a mother and so her family's name, but I had yet to give the boy one. A nameless scion deserved no marker, but fire cared nothing for his lack of a legacy.

I gave Asa the honour of lighting the basket. His face was dry, though mournful—but if he broke, the gesture meant I would not look down on him, on either of them.

Isa Oberon fell on the sand, keening as the basket sank. Asa Irium faced me, as if still seeking permission. We all knew the torch passed to him for Isa's sake, but I couldn't spurn him when I could scarcely keep from joining her. He folded his arms, bowed his head, and gave into grief.

Isa wailed long after the smoke had cleared, long after Asa Irium and I had left to rest. She loved fiercely, cared for us deeper than I could begin to care for them. I had watched her tear the weak man in half after he'd wounded her younger half-brother, when the boy's fur was still wet with infancy and he was fearful of battle. It pained me to think she might never have children of her own.

Isa Oberon returned at dawn. I had slept through her lamentations, but Asa's eyes were bleary. She sat between us, still shaking, and spat in the remains of our fire. Asa offered her a bearskin for warmth. She snatched it and wrapped it around her shoulders.

"He told me," she began, pausing to calm her voice, "that he wished to be called Dyrn."

I chewed on the name and nodded. "I would have respected the wish."

"Then that is whom we remember," Asa said. "Dyrn Irium. Shall I carve the wood?"

"Your brother's name and deeds live and die with us. The world need not remember them."

This earned a sniffle from Isa, though she would accept it, given time. She tucked her knees and crossed her arms over them, her face growing dark even as the sun touched it over mountains.

"We kill their young," she said, a growl from the depths of her hurt soul. "Every last one. I will bathe in the flood of their veins and drown the weak man in it."

"How?" Asa Irium said. "The children sleep in the shelter of his walls."

"And he will awaken to their screams when I tear down those walls and crush their skulls beneath my hooves."

"The wood-dwellers speak spells you cannot repel, horrid words Mother Moon forbade us to speak."

"I piss on Her laws! The sole permission I need is father's. My tongue will boil theirs before they can bring a word to mind."

Asa sighed when I stayed quiet. "There's no wisdom in anger," he said. "I do not claim to yearn for vengeance as much as you—but I *do* yearn for it. Now is not the time. We will return when the orchid wheel grinds winter to spring and—"

"Now is not the time?"

He cringed when the eye of her storm fell on him. She pointed a finger towards the lake. "There lie the bones of the closest thing I will have to a son, Asa Irium. No, to call him anything but my son would be injustice—there, in cold, autumn water sleeps the boy I loved and reared after your mother gave her life birthing him. I will not be silenced when I speak of revenge. You will listen, and if you disagree, say nothing." She faced me with a scowl. "Though I trust *your* silence speaks not of reluctance."

"It does not," I admitted. "But I would hear what you have to say before offering my piece."

"We owe Dyrn our lives," she went on. "It was no coincidence the weak men were four. They were cowards, but not for numbing themselves in the face of death—they drank the poison to make themselves into traps. Had he not demanded to prove himself and slain them alone that night, we would have eaten one each."

"This is true."

"We are in debt to him. It cannot be paid with kindness, so it must be paid in blood. Dyrn was vindictive—I do not stain his memory saying this, for we all know it's true. Do you ask me to not respect who he was, Father, by giving the weak man a season to celebrate the death of your child?"

I considered her words, how she stoked the heat rising in my thoughts. What greater shame is there than a life-debt to someone you were meant to protect, and then hesitate in repaying it? Had I taken the bane in their stead, my body would dry and wither where it fell, waiting for burial only after the woods burned before the wrath of my children.

I stood. "Lead us, Isa Oberon. We kill their young."

Asa stared long into his half-sister's eyes, then nodded and stood. "We kill their young."

Isa smiled. She had two smiles: one for those she loved, reminding me of her mother with its warmth, and one often seen during slaughter, when she no longer fought for survival but bared her fangs to bring carnage. This was the latter.

"I will carve his name on their walls, claw it on their bodies," she said. "Dyrn Irium *will* have a marker, and it is calamity."

The weak man's parish sat in a clearing where he had felled pines that were old when his seed was new. A wall of wooden poles protected the settlement from all sides, but tonight I would allow Isa Oberon her transgression. She would kill enemies who knew not that she was there so that we could step in undetected. It dishonoured her more than her victims, but she would not care, and so I wouldn't either.

A perpetual groan ran through Isa's teeth, forced out by the effort it took to force her bark-skin's growth into claws. She had spent the day lengthening them. Her slender fingers had turned into tools of death, sharp and thin and hard but sensitive, letting her feel the warmth of an open throat when she'd fulfil her promise. Asa Irium and I carried swords, stone weapons as likely to smash the weak man's child into a pulp as to cleave off its head. Isa's way was more personal, yes, but unnecessarily painful.

Yet, she bore the pain with a smile.

By the time we saw the weak man's lanterns beyond the trees, her claws reached past her knees. Two guards kept watch outside the gate, one leaning against the raised poles, one sitting on a rock with his head resting on a fist, lantern on the ground beside him. We stayed out of the light, watching them yawn and prattle idly.

I felt Isa's eyes on me, but did not turn to her. I blessed her sin with a nod.

Her tongue wove a mortal harmony, the verse of Mother Moon's nightingales the weak man had stolen to use against us. I knew not where she had learned to speak it, nor wanted to, but what I had expected to be clamour in my ears was the softest tone I'd ever heard. She spoke of spite and vitriol in a soothing voice, notes drawn from somewhere deeper than the hatred strong in her words.

The weak men gazed towards us, a languid trance clouding their eyes. They listened without realising what was happening to them, as enthralled by the song of Isa Oberon as her half-brother and I were.

But, her song was not meant for us. When the weak man clutched his throat, Asa Irium choked back tears of bliss. When the weak man's organs were crushed by bones crumbling inward, I felt a fracture circle my heart from knowing I would never hear this song again. When the weak man's skin seared with the blood burning in his veins, Isa let a content sigh of perfect euphoria escape as her coda.

The bodies had become as sacks, squishing under our hooves when we walked over them.

The settlement was dark, but we needed no light to see. The weak man feared the night, and rightfully so, for it had belonged to us since time immemorial. He slept through it, praying to a sun he thought strong and begging it to guard him through the empty hours. Such a fool—he should have been begging us.

We singled out those whose scents were fresh and without the pungency of omnipresent fear. "Two in the house before us," Isa said lowly.

"One far to the right," Asa said, sniffing the air with a raised nose.

"Two far closer," I returned, ears pricked at a sound from the barn.

We stalked towards the source of muffled giggling and breathy whispers. The weak man had no cows left after we had discovered the pastures, but he had brought his woman here instead. This man was young, as was she, no longer children but not yet far removed. They were wrapped around each other and spoke softly between kisses, unconcerned by the shadows watching them. The barn door was too small for me to fit through, but not so for Isa. There was nothing left of the weak man and his woman but ribbons of flesh flung to the rafters when she ducked out of the barn.

We wheeled as one towards the creak of an opening door and padding footsteps, accompanied by the strengthening of the scent Asa had identified. The weak man's child appeared briefly past the houses, lantern bobbing as she dashed for a hole in the wall. With puffing breaths, she pushed the logs apart just enough to squirm through. We followed her into the woods.

The child ran, but limited sight and short legs made her easy to chase. We stalked the pine-needle path silently, but her feet rustled in the growth, excitement wafting as a cloud after her. She slowed when the sound of flowing water drew nearer and stopped at the bank of a brook, set her lantern atop the rock there, and sat against it. From her satchel she took out sweet-smelling pastries the weak man liked, a slice of cured pork, and a book. She ate, the book open on crossed legs. All the while, her excitement grew; all the while, we watched unnoticed. Once she was done with her last meal, Isa Oberon moved in for the kill.

The child gasped before Isa reached her sights. "Who's there?" she demanded. Notes of fright seeped into her scent, but the odour was still strangely thin. When Isa came into view, the girl's mouth hung open as she regarded her taker.

Then, she uttered words I'd never have expected from a mouth so small. "My," she breathed. "You're beautiful."

"I am," Isa replied, head cocked. The weak man's speech came stiff from her tongue; maybe surprise spurred her to answer with it. Her back was turned to us, but I imagined her surprise mirrored ours. "It is often hidden from the weak man."

The child gained her feet, crying out when she noticed Isa's stained claws. She continued to surprise us—by running to Isa, not away from her. "You're hurt!" she said, taking her hand and examining it. "Oh, no. It's just dirty."

She took a step back and looked up. I don't recall ever having seen Isa more bewildered than when she circled the tiny creature and asked, "Do you not fear me?"

"I should, shouldn't I?" said the child, following Isa with an awed gaze. "But you're... enchanting. Like an elk made of wood walking upright. You're a moondeer, are you not?"

"I am."

The weak man's child hesitantly reached up to Isa's thigh, where her skin was still soft. "May I?"

Isa gave a grunt the girl took as affirmation. She ran her fingers through the fur, traced where Isa's skin turned into bark. "I thought moondeer were made *entirely* out of wood."

"I am young."

"My mother tells me not to come to the forest at night, because you'll take me away and eat me. But, you taught us to speak spells, did you not?"

"My forefathers did."

"Then we must have been friends, once," the child said. "I don't see why we couldn't be again. What's your name?"

Isa remained still, staring her down. "Isa Oberon."

"Pleased to meet you, Isa. I'm Irene." She reached out an open hand, fidgeted with a glimpse at Isa's claws, and cleared her throat. Her eyes fell back on the book—then, her air brightening, she showed it to Isa. "Would you like me to read you a story? It's my favourite."

Isa said nothing.

"I won't tell anyone you were here. I'd get in trouble too."

Isa bowed her head. "What is it called?"

"*Vesper's Garden*. Do you know it?"

"I know no stories."

The child beamed, returned to her place by the rock, and patted the ground. "Please, sit. I'm sure you'll love it."

Isa Oberon gave us a look of perplexity. The child's heartbeat was steady, quickening only for a second when Isa obliged and sat next to her. The child flashed her a smile before leafing through the book and starting to read.

Once upon a time, when Father Sun was a man and the sky was always dark with Mother Moon's night, all the stars still lived on Earth. One of them, a girl called Vesper, lived alone in a beautiful garden where no other star was welcome. It had belonged to her family, but they were all gone now. Vesper had stayed to ensure the garden would be pure when they returned.

Vesper often watched the other stars from her loft atop the tallest tree in the garden. They never tried to break in, but sometimes called for her through the gates, asking if everything was all right and if she wanted company. Vesper hated the other stars, hated their kind smiles hiding venomous intent. She never answered, only watched, and as more stars joined Mother Moon in the sky, soon there was no one left to call for h er.

As Mother Moon's night stretched on and on, stars filled the sea beyond her, but Father Sun still wandered the land somewhere far away. When Vesper had grown from a girl to a woman, she realised no star had passed the garden for a long time. Carefully, she approached the gate and peered past the rails, listening for distant chatter, spying for stars hiding in ambush. The city around her was quiet and empty, houses taken over by vines and seeds that had grown out of her home. The longer she watched, the safer she felt, until she realised all of the city was now a part of the garden.

For the first time, Vesper stepped outside. She passed through plazas where stars had gathered to mingle, under arches where lovers had kissed, and walked to Father Sun's temple in the heart of the city. Everything was covered in flowers and vines and roots, moss and weeds and trees. It all belonged to her, she decided, for her garden had conquered it.

But, when Vesper entered the temple, she found she was not alone. Huddled inside were small stars, children, who weren't yet old enough to go to the sky. She looked at them with fear; they looked at her with hope. One gained his feet and approached Vesper, saying, "Miss, would you help us? We've nothing to eat and nowhere to seek shelter but here. It is so cold we'll surely die before long."

Vesper drew away from the approaching boy. "You are trespassers in my realm," she proclaimed. "You are not welcome here. Leave at once."

"Miss," said another child. "We have always been here."

But Vesper only turned her back and said, "There is no place for you in my garden."

She returned to her home and sealed the gate. The little stars came to the gate now and again to cry for her mercy, but she ignored them, content on keeping all the fruits and vegetables for herself. As misfortune would have it, for the children that is, nothing edible grew outside her walls but bitter and venomous berries. The children's lustre waned as the night stretched on, until one of them perished.

Even then, Vesper's heart was hard. Big or small, she hated other stars.

Eventually, her pile of fruit began to rot. There was simply far too much for her to eat alone. She brought the spoiled fruit to the gates, piling them there within an arm's reach from outside when the children were away. When the pile grew smaller and the children sick, they asked why she'd been so cruel. Vesper laughed and said, "I left them there so they wouldn't stink, not for you to eat."

More little stars dimmed away, but Vesper did not yield. Soon, the boy who had first approached her came alone to her gate. "Miss, why are you so wicked to us?" he asked, as he often did. As often Vesper only ignored him, but now thought to amuse herself.

"Because you would be as cruel to me," Vesper sneered, "if I was out there and you were in here."

"We would not," said the boy. "If you came to us asking for help now, we would abandon you, because we've seen there is no love in your heart. If you had come to us as we did to you, we would have taken you in as one of our own."

"Liar," said Vesper. "The stars outside the garden were cruel to my mother."

"She was cruel to mine."

"They were cruel to my father."

"He was cruel to mine."

"So why should I not be cruel to you?"

"Because," said the boy, "I've shown you no cruelty."

"Your family has."

"I am not my family. Nor are you."

Vesper regarded the boy with contempt. Neither spoke for a long time, until the boy said, "We did not like your family, that is true. But were not all stars kind to you, even when you watched and mocked us from your tree? Did they not wonder if you were lonely?"

"Yes," she admitted, "but only because they wanted to steal my garden from me."

The boy shook his head. "They wanted to steal you from the garden before its seed of hate bloomed in you."

Vesper turned her back on him and returned to her tree. From there, she watched the small stars dim away, and when they were all gone, wondered and waited when would she be called to Mother Moon with all the others. But, she never was; when Father Sun finished his journey, gave up his disguise as a little boy, and joined his wife in the heavens, Vesper still sat in her tree, looking up to the sky and waiting for Mother Moon's call.

The weak man's child closed the book and faced the pensive Isa. "Did you like it?"

"Yes," Isa Oberon replied, drawing a beaming smile from the girl.

"I knew you would. It is my very favourite, even though it's sad."

Isa cocked her head with a puzzled look. "Sad? Why? Vesper was strong. She did not give in to the weak star's plea."

"Well, yes, but because of that she was left all alone."

"It is better to be alone than weak."

The child shook her head, frowning at Isa. "She wouldn't have been weak for helping others."

"They deserved death for disdain towards her family."

"I don't think so at all. If I did, I should hate you for no other reason but for being who you are. Do you hate me for being small and soft-skinned? For being human?"

"Yes."

Fear returned to stay, weak in the child's voice but strong in her scent. "I have never hurt you, nor do I want to."

"You are the weak man's child," said Isa, with a hand on her knee to push herself up, "and the weak man is a pestilence. You say you see no reason why we could not be friends, but I see plenty. The orchid wheel has ground seasons bathed in bad blood between us for so long, its petals are stained red."

At last, horror was pungent in the child's breath and sweat when Isa reached her full height, laying a shadow between the girl and the lantern. "Have you come to kill me?"

"I have."

Her voice fell quiet. "Why?"

"It is my right. Retribution for my son."

"What happened to him?"

Isa's face was hidden from the child, but the pain that flashed on it tore at my heartstrings. "He was taken from me."

The child gasped. "Taken? Did my people do it?"

"They did."

I heard the child swallow hard before she carefully took Isa's hand. "I am truly sorry. I cannot begin to imagine how it feels."

I wanted to see Isa cleave the child in half, but she only stood, hunched over the tiny creature, letting her stroke the part of the deadly nails she dared to touch.

"If you were to kill me," said the child, "my mother would hurt as you do."

"As is just."

"Is it? Would you not rather be spared of sorrow?"

I liked neither Isa's expression nor the uncertainty in her tone. "I would, but it is not possible."

"If I had the power to change the past, I would in a heartbeat, but I do not." She let go of Isa and looked up. "You, however, have the power to show mercy."

"Why would I care for the weak man's grief?"

The child went quiet. I made to move in; this palaver had gone on for too long, and Isa's hesitation troubled me. Before I had taken a step, Asa Irium grabbed my wrist. I spun to find him looking austere.

"This is her quarry," he whispered. "Let them speak until she decides it is over."

"Release me, Asa Irium."

"Not until you lower your sword."

I gave a rumbling exhale that made the child turn. She squinted, then turned to Isa and said, "Being kind doesn't make one weak. Vesper did not learn this, but I hope you might."

Isa stared long at the small creature before saying, "Do you now fear me, child?"

"Terribly. I wish I hadn't come out tonight. I wish I'd stayed in my bed, with my mother in the other room, waiting for my sister to come back inside. But," she went on, after pausing when shivers took her voice, "I came here instead, and met you. Now I can only hope you find it in you to show compassion."

"You showed my son no compassion. You slew him with poison, as a coward would."

"I have never met your son, Isa."

"Your brother has."

"I do not have a brother."

A brooding disquietude overcame Isa, as though the shadows over her had deepened. "Child," she said, in an oddly weary voice. "If the girl, Vesper, had given the little stars something to eat, she would have had less for herself. Would this not have made her weak?"

The child shook her head. "She had too much. If she had given some away, she would have lost nothing and helped someone else."

"I bear too much pain. Should I not share some with your kin?"

The child pondered quietly upon the question, her devious mind working to mislead Isa. "It isn't the same. If you spread your loss, you will not reduce it—you will redouble it. I've read so many stories of revenge, and they all end in nothing but sorrow."

"Then, what would *you* have me do?"

Now I started, as did Asa Irium. In a flash, Isa had been reduced from the constitution of stone to near weeping, the sorrow she carried as clear as spring water on her face.

"This is the only way I know how to ease the ache in my soul," she continued, lowering herself to one knee. "If you're so wise, weak man's child, what cure can you offer for a wounded heart?"

With a hum, the child took a step closer to rub Isa's hand. "Time. Time heals everything and hurts no one else. Grieve for your son until the wounds scar over."

With bated breath, I waited for Isa's answer. When she said, "Father, come forth," I glanced at Asa Irium and raised the sword to my shoulder. We emerged from the shade and the child spun towards us, flushing with a relapse of such terror I thought she might faint.

Isa stepped to the child's side and gently placed a hand on her shoulder. "We are done here. She will go home tonight."

"Dyrn is not yet avenged."

Isa Oberon bowed her head. "He is. His killers are dead, and so is—" She glanced down at the child, swallowing the confession. "The debt is paid. That is enough."

My children faced me; I fixed my gaze on the child. As I held it, she turned slowly, rotating her body but not her head, until her eyes were locked with mine while she hugged Isa's leg. Again, when I advanced, Asa Irium stopped me.

"It's over," he said. "She called for blood and we accepted. She leads us to battle and away from it."

"Not enough has been spilled," I snarled and shook myself free, only to find Isa's claws raised at me.

"That is not for you to decide," she said.

My chest heaved as I glowered at her. She did not wilt beneath my stare, nor did Asa. The child had the decency to show me the respect I deserved—but, even with my wrath inflamed, I saw my children were no less right. "If you consider your oath fulfilled, Isa Oberon, it is so," I rumbled.

She lowered her hand back on the girl's shoulder, careful—infuriatingly careful—not to cut her. "Then it is so."

"Are you sure?"

The child had done something to Isa. I had heard no spells spoken, but somehow, she had grasped my daughter's mind and twisted it. Yet, even as Isa repeated, "It is so," I heard no lie leave her lips—only words I didn't want to hear.

Reluctantly, I nodded. As we strode away, the child asked, "Will you come back tomorrow, Isa?"

Isa stopped and inhaled deeply. "Does your sister smell like you?"

"Uh," uttered the child. "I suppose she must."

"Tomorrow you will not want me here."

Isa followed us into the woods, leaving the child's "Why?" lingering after us.

We returned to the grassland, my heart afire and hungry, but difficult as it was, I chose to respect Isa's decision.

We killed a bear on the way, cooked and ate in silence. Isa left us after we had picked the bones clean and did not return for the rest of the night. At dawn, I crested the hill at the edge of the grassland to find her sitting on the lake's shore, gazing towards the mountains beyond it.

She returned with dusk, lured by the scent of cooking rabbit. She'd broken off her claws and left the flesh of her slender fingers without bark, exposed. She did not join the conversation between Asa Irium and me, but once the discourse came to a lull, said, "When the lake freezes, I will cross it."

I nodded slowly. "We will cross—"

"No, Father. *I* will cross it. To find a mate."

I waited until she continued.

"The strong man still hunts beyond the mountains. I am sure of it. I want to find him and bear his daughter." She hesitated, glancing at Asa Irium and me. "I want to raise her to be as kind as the weak man's child—this child. Irene."

"Has sorrow driven you mad?" I said, hiding no scorn from my laughter. "A kind heart gets you killed."

"Dyrn was the most warlike of us and the orchid wheel spun twelve times before his blossoms wilted. I will fill my daughter's heart with kindness, and if it sees her dead, I will hunt and slaughter and eat those who slew her. I will do so until one survives."

"What in Mother Moon's name do you hope to achieve?"

"Nothing. I will achieve nothing, nor will my child. But, perhaps her scion will, one day. When the weak man wants to hurt her, she will not strike back. She will only ask 'Why?' until he cannot answer."

"Did the story touch you so deeply?" I drawled after the worst of the disappointment passed.

"The child did," Isa said lowly. "I have thought long about her and decided she was right. She had no part in the death of Dyrn Irium. I trust she truly does not hate us." She averted her eyes before going on. "In taking revenge, we have given her reason to. I can only hope her heart is more forgiving than mine. Not for our sake—we deserve her hatred. She does not deserve to suffer it."

"In sparing her, you invite her to hunt us."

"In sparing her, she hopes the child remembers the night when she sat with a creature who came with anger, and left without," Asa said quietly. His gaze flicked away when ours briefly met.

With a growl rumbling in my throat, I stood to face the mountains. "Will you go with her, Asa Irium?"

"I am sworn never to leave her side, Father. If we do find the strong man, I will challenge him and take his daughter as my bride."

"Will you raise your sons and daughters to carry kind hearts like your half-sister's?"

"The daughters of my women will be as fierce as Isa Oberon when our hunt began. My sons will make Dyrn look as peaceful as Isa when it ended."

"Your words mock her, but your voice does not."

I turned to find his head hanging. "Her feelings run deeper than ours, always have. I do not understand them, and so I do not agree with her reason for leaving. But, I know better than to try to change her mind, and choose to trust her decision."

"Will you bring your bride back to me?"

"This land has no love for children, Father. You are always welcome wherever I make my home, but I will not return here."

Watching my last seed silhouetted against a fading sun, I thought their antlers might have grown a little thicker. None of the wounds chipped in my sides by blade or pellet had ever hurt as much as watching my beautiful daughter standing proudly with her decision as I effaced her name from my mind.

"Asa Irium," I said, beckoning him over. I laid my hands on his cheeks. "You are a good son. When the snows come and the lake freezes, I will send you away. Find a good mate and give her everything. Give her love, give her children, give her sisters. Give her all that and more."

"I shall, Father."

He stepped away. I turned to my daughter, but could not speak yet. She held her breath for the whole of my silence. The captured inhale left with a shudder when I beckoned her over and said, "Oberon."

She stood before me, untouched. "You are no longer my child. You will not use the name I've given you. You only have your mother's, for death has denied her the right to forsake you. When the snows come and the lake freezes, I will banish you."

"Yes, Fa—" She bit back the word, closed her eyes, and numbed her tongue with my name. "Yes, Aras Menaras."

Though my affection for Isa Oberon became strained, snows came sooner than I'd have cared for. Yes, I, too, was weak—I made sure never to speak her name aloud, but cherished it in my most private thoughts. Perhaps I had been too quick to place all the blame for her soft heart on her mother.

When my children stood at the shore, dressed in animal skins and bearing what little I had to spare them—Asa more than Isa, though I well knew they would share all I'd given—I built two pyres where their journey began and their childhood with me ended. I let Asa light his, but held Isa's torch until she prompted, "Throw it down, Aras Menaras. I will light it again."

I held it forth, palm facing down, but did not drop it. I held it until she cocked her head, cautiously approached, and grabbed it. When she did, I said, "Through shame, I love you no less. I think you're a fool—and *will* think of you, fondly. Light your pyre, Isa Oberon. Find yourself a mate and give him a host of daughters, ones as proud as you. Hunt all who would hurt them and teach them to protect their own." I bowed my head to spare her some dishonour. Her mouth had fallen open, eyes grown so wet I doubted she could see anything but an underwater flicker. "And, if it makes you happy, teach them kindness. Tell them of the weak man's child who did not hate us as we hated her."

I reared my head to find her eyes closed, the wells within them emptied on her cheeks. When her lids rose to unveil their amber and blue, she smiled in the beloved way I'd thought lost since Dyrn's death. "I shall, Father."

After dark had swallowed my children and their pyres had gone out, I sat on the frozen shore, watching the stars and reminiscing the night we sought to avenge Dyrn Irium. I knew the story well, for one very close to it was my mother's favourite. Asa and Isa hadn't known theirs long enough to hear any, and I found stories foolish—but as I watched the stars appearing alongside Mother Moon, I returned to my childhood, sitting at my mother's breast while she wove the tale. She had called the story "Daughter of the Moon." The daughter, Vesper, was a goddess who mothered all men, weak and strong. There were no rotten fruits in this story, but Vesper's jealousy for her sisters in the sky beside their mother manifested in a song of spite so beautiful and deadly, she became a kinslayer. Vesper's cruelty cursed her children to wander the earth, without hope of ascending to their celestial home when their souls dimmed to join the night.

My mother had understood the story as I did, as Isa claimed to have: it is better to stand strong alone than weak together. The weak man's child saw something else in it. I now suspected Isa did too.

I lay down in the snow to count the stars, a bearskin wrapped up as my pillow. One night, maybe, when I've reached the last and know them all, a distant child of mine will inherit the too-sweet heart of Isa Oberon.

And maybe, somewhere out there, Vesper still waits in the tree in her garden, watching the sky when a new star is born.

About the Author

Ville Meriläinen is a Finnish author of fantasy and horror fiction.

QUARRY

by Liam Hogan

To the best of my knowledge I have always been here. Lurking in the deepest, darkest depths of the flooded quarry, my myriad tentacles are the only part that ever moves, drifting through still, cold waters like delicate, long-stemmed grasses. Like hair, like spider silk, bowing this way and that as though in a gentle wind, alert to anything that breaks the surface. But my knowledge—of grasses, of wind, and even of quarries—came relatively recently, with the humans. Before them, I knew no words and had only stolen flashes of more primitive urges: the hunger for food, the fear of predators, the rough, *insistent* imperative of sex. Along with wistful remembrances of movement—soaring through the air, or scrambling up a tree, or lying stealthily in wait (just as I wait, deep underwater). Punctuated, and terminated, by the fall—so often the fall!—that delivered these small mammals and birds and reptiles to the grasp of my ready tendrils, homing in on their brief, thrashing struggles, pulling them down, down, down...

Humans have *so* much more going on. And now, it seems, so do I. In devouring the tender meat that hides inside my victim's skulls, I also devour their language, their memories, even their dreams and desires. T he *fresher* the brain, the headier the meal; the more vibrant and lurid the thoughts, the more their dreams become mine.

Which doesn't make for restful slumber, as I squat in my underwater hollow, momentarily replete, processing my food. They are full of contradictions, these second-hand visions, these murky snatches of life lived above and beyond the water's edge. It is tricky to separate fact from fiction, what they have experienced from what they *wanted* to experience, from what they now never will. For my dreaming their dreams means they dream no more, and that their fate, as a succulent morsel for something utterly strange and alien to them, is probably the very last thing they would *ever* have imagined.

But feed I must, especially as my hunger is for more than mere nourishment. Each meal complements all that has come before. Each adds to my absorbed experiences, my collected recollections, my museum of memories. If I am what I eat, then I contain multitudes and am far from reaching my capacity.

Because as yet, none of the mortals I had consumed had the answers I desired the most. I longed to know more about what *I* am and how I came to be. None of them gave clue to the mystery that resides in the dark, in the Stygian gloom. None shed light on my own existence.

The first was a young lad, each scoop from his skull rich with recent memories of fallen fences and faded warning signs, the temptations of bushes thick with untapped blackberries, the excitement of trespass, the possibilities of discovery and adventure leading him to scramble along a treacherous rock ledge. Beneath lingered the notes of endless school holidays, of late summer boredom, of a hot, dusty walk from an over-crowded terraced house, of older sisters (flashes of their flesh, simultaneously held tight and shoved violently away, contradictions indeed!) and a remote mother, a chain of sketchy male friends eager for the lad (the only other man about the house) to spend time "in the great outd oors".

As my serrated palps scoured the insides of the lad's brain cavity—so much, contained within such a small space!—for the very last scraps (grainy black and white images from a too-close screen, eldritch horrors from outer space, strident, discordant music, an actress's fake screams, exquisite complex layers of make-believe fear...) I knew only that *this* creature had not known enough, had hardly known anything, that his scant years of experience and his peculiarly narrow worldview only o-ffered glimpses of what *might* be available to me. I sucked thought-fully on his other organs, organs I could not name for nor could he, disappointed they offered nothing more than a smorgasbord of rotting flavours (even though that alone had once been more than enough to excite me). As I waited for the action of time alone to grant me access to the liquefied marrow of his bones, I slowly digested what little I had learned from him.

It was a long, frustrating wait until my next sentient meal. Though I did not go hungry in between, not when, in the dead of an autumnal night, sharp rain dancing off the surface of the lake and swamping my senses, a bulky body, long dead and weighed down by a chunk of con-crete, was delivered to me as though an offering. But the brain contained within the tough wrapping of inedible plastic was a mindless blank. I ate dispiritedly, as bored as the lad had been. More so, for this meal lasted longer than that skinny kid had. And from it, I got nothing, nothing but faint echoes of violence and fear. They were, alas, *empty* calories.

I toyed with his bones awhile, draped them in the plastic shroud that flared in currents I created for that purpose. But I couldn't see how to put them together properly, and the smallest kept slipping through my grasp. So I abandoned them all to the ghostly creatures that feast on my slim leftovers, and fell into my usual somnolent state. My tendrils are an underwater web, spanning almost the entire quarry pool, so that I know if anything larger than an insect enters my languid waters.

The depth at which the bulk of me resides is such that only my outer extremities, tasting the surface, are aware of the seasons that pass above me. It was those tentacles that told me when the surface froze over, a rare event; leastwise, I could not remember it so, and nor could those minds, animal or human, that I had consumed. I despaired. So imprisoned, there would be no meals at all, and I would go hungry, for both food and stimulation.

I was wrong.

I felt the vibrations in the tendrils that remained frozen, bonded to the surface. Like a bone being dragged across stone, someone—a small group of someones—was up there, on the other side of the ice, slipping and sliding and shouting with something that might have been joy.

Until it turned, in an instant, to *fear*. The ice wasn't frozen enough for such daring winter activities. I felt and heard the creaking, the eerie pings ringing like a bell as cracks raced across the perfect frozen layer. And then the sharpest of retorts.

Perfect no more. Something, *someone*, fell through the shattered ice and despite frantic struggles, was unable to haul themselves out. It was the work of a moment to wrap their struggling limbs in mine, to drag them down, even as the rest of the vibrations scattered and the ice fell ominously quiet.

This one was a girl, fourteen, the last remnants of puppy fat that she would never grow out of but that I would feast upon. Not, though, until after I had sucked out her plaintive teenage dreams, the forever thwarted happily ever after endings, and relived her final waking nightmare with its ripe spike of desperate, primal fear.

I was still mulling this over, still feasting, when there was more commotion above, more shattering of ice. A whole host of people seeking the girl who had fallen through. But they could not have her. She was *mine*, and I would not let her go, not until there was nothing left to glean from her shivered bones.

There was a much longer gap, after that. An agony of seasons. This perplexed and frustrated me, for I wanted—*needed*—more. Two youths and a dead man had merely whetted my appetite, and only let me guess at what must be happening above. New fences, new warning signs? It seemed, when I selected one from a group, the survivors raised the alarm, and in the aftermath of a fruitless search, the quarry was once again off-limits and out-of-bounds.

Should I only take those who entered my waters alone? Could I be that selective, avoiding the temptations presented? And would temptation ever present itself again?

But it seemed no matter the warnings, the dark history, or the physical obstacles, my body of water would always be attractive, to some. A year after the ice, a thin line descended into long-undisturbed waters, crowned by a metal hook, a wriggling worm pinioned on the barbed point. Such lures did not interest me, but what was at the *other* end of the line did.

It was easy to tempt him into the water. To play with that lure, to tug and twist, pulling hard, but not so hard that the plastic should snap. To let go for a moment, before reeling him in, even as he tried to reel *me* in.

He was a fool, that fisherman. There are no fish in my lake. I have long ago eaten them all. And his thoughts, his dreams, were dulled by the empty bottles he left on the shore, his mind tainted by cheap booze along with the rest of his fatty flesh. Perhaps the young are a better meal, after all.

When first I fed, a feast such as he would have sustained me for a long time. Long enough to ignore any clamour of vibrations that might greet his disappearance, ignore the search parties, waiting patiently until the next solitary soul broke the surface of the lake, long after unsubstantiated rumours of hidden danger had died down and the always tranquil waters proved tempting once again.

When the fisherman's eyeball tried to float towards the surface, I was almost disappointed that there wasn't something *else* to excite the tendrils that throng about my body. The sightless orb didn't get far. As my serried teeth pierced it, I half expected a flash of vision, the last thing he saw while alive, but it was merely a tasty bite, offering no insight. A pity because, like his corpse that I held tight as it decayed and developed flavour, I cannot see. My sight is as stolen as my knowledge of what happens above the water, in the exotic domain of air, and of man.

I wonder what colour the eye was? So rarely do people's memories and dreams depict themselves. Nor do I know what I look like. I know my basic *shape*, as sketched by my questing tendrils. But none of my victims have paid much attention to what was dragging them down, too fixated on fighting the swirling waters that swallow them up.

With the return of summer, a gaggle of older teenagers, a half dozen boys and a couple of girls, arrived on my shore. The boys were naked, *skinny dipping*, the giggling girls in their pants and bras. There was an almighty splash as one jumped from a rocky promontory (and the quarry is surrounded on all but one side by such rocky promontories). A hasty retreat of the girls to lie instead on sun-drenched rocks, when my delicate tendrils unnerved them, cries of "there's something in the water! It *touched* me!" The boys professing innocence, saying it must be a fallen leaf, or merely a fish. All this gleaned from the vibrations of the lake surface.

I meant to leave them unmolested. They might have gone home, told others of this fabulous swimming hole. I might then have had my pick of those who chose to brave the frigid waters alone. But one was already in difficulties, the cold of the deep quarry lake, even in summer, too great a shock to his system, his youthful limbs uncoordinated and weak, his head sinking beneath the water, not enough air in his gasping lungs for even one final desperate plea for help. It was perhaps a mercy, my taking of him, even if I did it for entirely selfish reasons.

And once again, shortly after, the surface *seethed* with activity. I knew enough by then to know that I shouldn't... but I did it anyway. I took a rubbery-skinned man who invaded my depths, with hard, metal cylinders on his back and a frog mask over his face. He panicked, as I ensnared his legs, puzzling over how to open up this intriguing morsel. He fought and thrashed, when usually my dragged-underwater prey were quiet and still. He tore *savagely* at my tendrils, causing me not inconsiderable pain. But I did not relent. I wrapped him tighter still, tendrils prying at his ears, his nostrils, his many weak points, my palps tugging at the mask until, with an explosion of bubbles, my way was clear to enter his skull as I had all my meals, via the tender eyes.

And there I discovered the *freshest* of thoughts, the delights of a warm, almost still-active brain. His name—I knew his name!—is, or was, Constable Harry Barns, a specialist police frogman, an underwater search unit diver, trained to find and recover drowned and bloated bodies. His memories were full of the terrible things he had seen in his career, and I knew then what I was, to him: a *monster*.

I knew too that his disappearance would lead to more such invaders. I knew fear, for the first time. Knew I would have to *fight* to defend my home.

I sent back to the surface his shredded, gore-slicked goggles, a warning and promise to those who might dare follow. But it was the tentacles he tore off in his struggles that brought me my next meal. Another diver, and—since my clear warning had been ignored—I felt only determination as I dragged her down, delicately removing her regulator, stopping the sudden, shocked *O!* with my tentacles, leaving her eyes intact as I explored the roof of her mouth and the back of her throat, finding access there so that she might watch until the very last moment, and so that I might shortly after see what she saw, think what she thought.

She was a scientist. Doctor Meredith Anwar. And oh, how very *bright* her mind was! Full of wonder, of interesting ideas and rare knowledge, of Cephalopoda and Medusozoa, clues at last to what I might be!

But she also foretold my doom. With the mounting deaths, with samples of my uncategorisable tendrils, the quarry is going to be sterilised. I have sealed my own fate.

She brought other thoughts, a faint glimmer of hope. Prominent among her concerns was how I propagate. The word, and the concept, is novel. I am aware of the thoughts of the young men and women who entered my waters as a dare, to impress potential mates. Aware of the animal urges of lesser beasts, aware that there really isn't as much difference as these pubescent youths believe. But I had not thought any of it applied to *me*. Alone as I am, no such coupling is possible. I did not dismay, for the desire of others was not reflected in mine; it was like watching something on a flickering screen, bizarre and otherly, but most definitely not for me.

The Doctor knew of other ways. Ways that did not require the coupling of male and female (for which was I? It was impossible to say). Ways that didn't even require a mate.

From deep within her grey matter came words like *parthenogenesis*. And I knew, with instinctive certainty, how to attain it.

But what help would it be? My offspring would populate the same, despoiled waters, the same, dynamited lake floor. It would be no more hospitable for them than it was for me.

Dispersal, then, was key. I could never leave this place. My tendrils have no great strength, my pulpy body can never escape the comforting hug of deep water, no more than a fish could ride a bicycle. But my much smaller offspring *might*.

The quarry isn't a perfectly closed system. Life drops into its depths from above, and sometimes, the sheltered surface is broken not by another meal, but by an outpouring. On the side not guarded by cliffs there is a channel, following a disused railway line. It carries the overflow, when rain swells the lake. It leads I knew not where, but Doctor Meredith Anwar did, so now I do. The channel flows into a stream, threading a landscape of lower, lesser diggings, and on to a river, and then to the sea.

I pray for heavy rain, and my prayer is answered. As each newborn polyp floats to the surface, guided on its way by my tendrils, it also carries away a piece of my consciousness, the memories and dreams I have stolen. It is the strangest feeling. But my children, my clones, will have benefits I did not. They will be careful, as they slowly grow, not needing to feed perhaps more than once a year. And a single death in any one waterhole will hardly register, I hope.

As the last polyp makes its way to safety, the rains have stopped rattling the surface and the forces of my destruction gather on the shore. My children will know that humans are the direst threat, as well as the greatest reward. I hope they act accordingly. I hope they take their time, before they take their revenge.

As for what remains of me, it is nothing. I am so much less than I was, but still enough, so that when they finish with their depth charges and poisons and the pool is once again silent and still, with fences re-erected and signs fresh and new, their vindictive curiosity will be satisfied.

This is my fate. Even though I wonder if some infinitesimal part of me might survive, to begin anew, many years from now.

And if not... then I have passed all I can to the next generation. So eat well and wisely, my hungry, hungry children, and dream a stolen dream for me.

About the Author

Liam Hogan is an award-winning short story writer, with stories in Best of British Science Fiction and in Best of British Fantasy (NewCon Press). He's been published by Analog, Daily Science Fiction, and Flame Tree Press. He helps host the live literary event Liars' League, volunteers at the creative writing charity Ministry of Stories, and lives and avoids work in London. More details at http://happyendingnotguaranteed.blogspot.co.uk

THANK YOU

We would like to express our deepest gratitude to our staff editors, **Susan Russell, Rachael Swanson,** and **Kasey Kubica,** for their tireless efforts in reviewing submissions, proofreading, and overall helping us stay on track throughout the creation of this anthology. Their dedication to this project and attention to detail have been invaluable.

We also want to thank **Dany Rivera** for her beautiful story art, which has added a new layer of meaning to the stories we've collected. Her talent and creativity have truly enhanced this project. You can find her at danycomicsarts.com

We are also grateful to our volunteer submission readers, **Suhas Sridhar, rklep13,** and **Blake Pingleton,** who generously shared their time and expertise to help us sort through the many submissions we received. Their feedback and insights were crucial in helping us identify the most compelling stories for this anthology.

A special thank you to our Anthology Contributors: **Jennifer Povey, Bert S.G, T.M Morgan, Zachary Rosenberg, Alex Wolfgang, David Rider, Liam Hogan, J. Syringa, Rachel Nussbaum, CM Toolson, Valerie B. Williams, Mike Deady, J. Rocky Colavito, Rachel Ashcraft, Christie Hansen, Ville Meriläinen**

Finally, we want to extend our appreciation to all the authors who submitted to this anthology. We recognize the time, effort, and passion that goes into writing and submitting work for consideration, and we were grateful for the opportunity to read and appreciate each submission.

Thank you to everyone who has contributed to this project in any way.

We could not have done it without you!

If you liked any of our stories, take a moment to stop by our Amazon page and leave a review!

Coming Soon

From beneath the water's surface to high above the clouds, a collection of **Uncanny & Unearthly Tales** is ready to introduce you to eerie, twisted, and exceptional characters coming from all corners of the universe. Be drawn deeper into the supernatural anthology where nothing is as it seems, and even the most innocuous objects and people are so much more than they appear.

Check out our other anthologies!

Paramnesia

The Devil Who Loves Me

More Than a Monster